LOST IN AN INSTANT

I heard Michael grab his keys before opening the garage door. I leaned my head back, closed my eyes, and smiled. Michael was, and has been since I've known him, therapy for me. He was a man I loved like no other man. Hearing the fire crackle interrupted my thoughts. I stood up with the intention of closing the fireplace screen but was thrown against the wall beside me.

All I could hear was an explosion and glass breaking and I felt the air being sucked out of the room. My ears felt like they, too, had exploded. It took a few moments to realize what exactly had happened.

It was only when I crawled to the large hole in the wall where the windows used to be that I saw that Michael's car was engulfed in flames.

The past had finally caught up with me. . . .

The Body Mafia

STACY DITTRICH

LEISURE BOOKS NEW YORK CITY

A LEISURE BOOK®

March 2010

Published by

Dorchester Publishing Co., Inc.
200 Madison Avenue
New York, NY 10016

ISBN 10: 0-8439-6289-5
ISBN 13: 978-0-8439-6289-5
E-ISBN: 978-1-4285-0823-1

The name "Leisure Books" and the stylized "L" with design are trademarks of Dorchester Publishing Co., Inc.

Printed in the United States of America.

10 9 8 7 6 5 4 3 2 1

Visit us online at www.dorchesterpub.com.

To my loving family, Rich, Brooke, and Jordyn

The Body
Mafia

PROLOGUE

"Two hundred fifty thousand U.S. dollars, my friend . . . as promised," the man said as he handed the American the large yellow envelope.

The American slowly opened the envelope, pulling out the crisp, clean bills, flipping through half of the stack like a deck of playing cards. He was making a conscious effort to keep the bills hidden from view.

An intimidating man, the American, thought the Filipino as he eyed him up and down. Standing well over six feet tall, and wearing a shiny black suit that most likely cost him thousands of dollars and polished black shoes, the American never spoke during their meetings. After the quarterly packages were delivered to the hospital by those who worked for him, the American would meet the Filipino to collect his money in the crowded marketplace. Then, with no more than a nod and the slightest glimpse of a smile, the American would be on his way. The noise of blaring motor scooters, cars, and street merchants would make it difficult to engage in a lengthy conversation even if the Filipino insisted. But today things would be different. Today the American would have to speak. The Filipino's boss wanted a definitive answer from the American and his employers.

Satisfied he had accurately counted the money, the American turned to walk away.

"Sir, one moment, sir . . ." the Filipino began in his broken English.

The American turned and faced him with a look of unconcealed curiosity. Remaining silent, the American nodded for the Filipino to continue, his expression changing to disdain.

The Filipino was nervous. He knew who the man was and where he had come from. He'd heard the stories from his boss. This man, his employers, and their colleagues were among the FBI's highest priorities, but even they couldn't touch them. His mouth dry, the Filipino did his best to swallow before speaking.

"Sir, he want more and he want them quickly. He say he double money if packages come sooner. Here's list." The Filipino handed the man the small piece of paper and noticed his hand was trembling. "He want answer from you before you get on plane."

The American looked intently at the list before focusing back on the Filipino. The man's eyes narrowed to mere slits before the tiniest hint of a smirk formed at the corners of his mouth. The Filipino, worried the American would see his heart beating through his shirt or the sweat that had formed above his brow, did his best to smile. He was terrified while waiting for the man's answer, which came sooner than expected.

"Tell him . . . we'd be happy to."

CHAPTER ONE

"Are you ready for this one, CeeCee?"

My good friend and fellow detective, Jeff Cooper, stuck his head into the doorway of my office. Coop wore his trademark grin, and his blue eyes were sparkling. Married to the boss, Captain Naomi Cooper, Coop was our division comedian. We were all detectives in the Major Crimes Division of the Richland Metropolitan Police Department in Mansfield, Ohio. I, Sergeant CeeCee Gallagher, was working diligently on a rape case when Coop interrupted.

"If it's the one about the retarded guy in the pool, you already told it to me yesterday," I said, referring to Coop's endless jokes.

"No, it's not a joke." He walked into my office and sat down in one of the chairs facing my desk.

"Spit it out. I'm busy on the Taylor rape case."

"You might as well put it aside. You and I are headed down to Bunker Hill Road. A lady was driving south toward State Route 97 and a buzzard dropped a hand on her car."

I stopped shuffling papers and looked at him. "A what?"

"A hand."

I quickly caught on. "Coop, I don't have time for this . . ."

"I told you, CeeCee, it's not a joke. The lady was driving and said she saw a couple of buzzards on the road chewing on something. She thought maybe it was a dead possum. When she got close enough, it scared the birds off the road, and one of them kept the chew toy in his little claws when they flew up. Or are they called talons?" His hands rose up, mimicking claws. "Apparently, the damn thing couldn't hold it very well, because he dropped it right on this woman's windshield, and yes, it was a human hand. Needless to say, she freaked out and wound up smashing into a tree."

"Is she okay?" I asked, knowing I'd have done the same thing.

"Yup, physically, but you can imagine how you'd feel if you just left a shitty day at work and then had a hand dropped on your car."

"Since you haven't mentioned it, I'm assuming the mystery of where the hand came from is still going on?" I couldn't imagine a living person who recently had their hand cut off would leave it lying around for the damn buzzards.

"The uniforms are walking the woods right now, looking for either a body or other parts. We've already called the hospitals to see if someone came in missing a lefty. Maybe from an industrial accident, or a car mechanic—who knows? But none of them have." He ran his fingers through his thick dark hair.

The "uniforms" Coop referred to were the uniformed patrolmen who drove marked cruisers and worked out on the road. In the southern part of Richland County, the woods around the area where this had occurred were very dense. I was sure there had to be at least fifteen to twenty uniforms down there. I started shoving files into my briefcase while Coop stood and waited impatiently, tapping a pen on my desk.

"You should ask your dad about the time someone found an entire arm in the middle of the road. I guess some motorcycle guy was drunk off his ass and wrecked. Tore his arm clean off. He got back on the bike and drove away like that."

"I don't need to ask. Uncle Max probably took a picture of it, and I've probably seen it already." I grabbed my keys, ready to leave.

My father, Mitch Gallagher, and his brothers Max and Mike were old-timers with the department—all lieutenants. Each supervised a different shift of road patrol; my father was in charge of the night shift. I wasn't joking about the picture, either. My uncles, thanks to their morbid sense of humor, had albums full of homicide pictures and body parts that they passed around to my cousins and me during family functions. Needless to say, growing up surrounded by cops made for a less-than-normal childhood. My father's other brother, Matt, was shot on duty in the late 1970s and had to retire early. He lives in North Carolina.

"Yeah, I'm sure you have. God knows I've seen Max's album plenty . . . Don't remember an arm in the road, though. Of course, he probably has ten to fifteen different albums of that shit."

I laughed and shook my head as I walked out of my office behind Coop. We were going to ride to the scene in Coop's car, and after I had gotten into the passenger seat, I looked at my watch.

"Damn," I muttered.

"What?" Coop started the car and began pulling out of the parking lot.

"I need to call Michael and tell him I'm going to be late." I pulled my cell phone out of my briefcase.

My husband, Michael Hagerman, was a supervising agent with the FBI in Cleveland. We had met several years ago when we worked together on a case. We didn't have any children together, but my two daughters from my previous marriage, six-year-old Isabelle and thirteen-year-old Selina, would be getting home from school soon. Michael needed to be there to get them off the bus. My ex-husband, Eric Schroeder, a uniformed officer with Richland Metro, and I share custody of the girls. Michael's seven-year-old son, Sean, stays with us every other weekend. It took several rings before Michael answered his phone. I explained the circumstances.

"I'm still up here in Cleveland, Cee. There's no way I'll get home in time."

"All right, I guess I'll have to call Eric and see if he or Jordan can do it. How come you're still up there?"

"I'm up to my ass in this case I've been working. I don't know when I'll be home." He sighed into the phone. "I wouldn't wait up if I were you."

I imagined Michael rubbing his temple with his free hand, which he sometimes did when he was stressed. The thought of not seeing him tonight upset me. I loved him more than I could ever explain, and even regular workdays seemed too long until we saw each other. I imagined his handsome face, which put most famous actors to shame. His thick brown hair, bright green eyes, and dark complexion made even the most masculine of men take a second look. Not to mention his tall, muscular body. I myself was no slouch. I modeled in New York right out of high school and still maintained my tall, athletic body and long, blonde hair. My large chest and green eyes still turned quite a few heads, but I had just as much insecurity as anybody else. To be with a man like Michael upped my daily self-maintenance to an entirely new level. He says I'm nuts, and I say, "Not all of us were born perfect, buddy."

After I finished talking to Michael, I called Eric's house and spoke to his wife, Jordan, who like everyone else is a uniformed officer with the department. On her days off, she had no problem picking the girls up and keeping them at her house until I got home. Crisis solved.

"What's Michael working on?" Coop asked as he drove toward Bunker Hill Road.

"I haven't a clue. Normally he talks about his cases, but not this one. It's some Secret Squirrel, hush-hush investigation. If he doesn't discuss it, I don't bother to ask."

"Oh."

It was another twenty minutes before we pulled into the scene of the crashed car and cutoff hand. By then, most everyone had finished up with their duties and was getting ready to leave. I saw our crime-laboratory van parked by the wrecked car and thought that would be as good a place to start as any. One of the laboratory technicians was loading evidence bags into the back. It was Bob English.

"Whatcha got for me, Bob?" I peered inside the van.

"Hey, CeeCee. Not a lot, but what I do have is freakin' weird. Here, look at this." He pulled out a plastic, Tupperware-looking box and opened the blue lid, exposing the hand.

"Oh my God!" I turned my head away and, for entertainment purposes, made a loud, gagging sound.

The hand looked like a Halloween prop—except for the smell. Most of the flesh had been chewed away by the buzzards and probably other animals. Some flesh was still attached, but the protruding metacarpals were very evident. It was large enough that I took a wild guess and assumed the hand was from a male. The pinky finger was the only digit in decent shape.

"Are you going to be able to print the pinky, Bob?" I held the box up and looked underneath to see if I could see through the plastic.

"I should be able to."

"If you get anything back on it, let me know ASAP. Where's the female that was driving the car?"

"A uniformed sergeant took her home. She was upset as hell, as you can imagine."

"I needed to talk to her!" I started to get angry.

"Relax, CeeCee," Coop interrupted. "I talked to her on the phone, which is how I knew what happened. I told her when she settles down, we'll be over to talk to her more extensively."

"How do we know she isn't some whack-job that cut off her husband's hand and drove around with it? Maybe he's in pieces somewhere else."

"We don't, and the uniforms found nothing, but if you want to start walking the woods looking for her husband's severed penis, be my guest," he quipped.

"I do believe I'll pass on that offer."

Once Coop and I had gotten all the necessary information and taken our own photographs, there was little else for us to do until the fingerprint came back from the lab. Or until someone showed up wanting their hand back.

We got the results on the fingerprint back the next day. The pinky print belonged to forty-two-year-old Daniel Huber, address unknown. When Coop and I tracked down family members, we learned that none of them had spoken to Daniel in years. After Daniel had battled a drug addiction that included stealing from his parents, the family gave up on him and he became homeless. And now handless.

It was while Coop and I were sitting in his office pondering our next course of action that our captain, Naomi Cooper, came in. A beautiful woman by most standards, Naomi had transformed her severe businesswoman look over the years. Now, with her dark blonde hair falling loosely on her shoulders, and exchanging dark suits for the khaki pants and light blue blouse, she made Coop's eyes light up. Naomi was a very close friend of mine, but that hadn't always been the case. When we'd both started in major crimes, it was like oil and water: the darkest sides of our personalities continuously clashed. After several close calls on the job (meaning near death), Naomi and I learned to work together and became friends in the process.

"Hey, sweetheart, come over here and give daddy some sugar." Coop puckered out his lips.

Naomi blushed and smiled. "Later at home, knucklehead . . ."

"Thank you, Naomi," I interrupted. "If I had to look at his lips for one more second, I believe I might have fainted."

She giggled. "Actually, I just popped in to see what

the deal is on the hand. If it amounts to anything, I'll assign your open cases to the other detectives."

I explained to Naomi where we were in the case. She agreed that unless we found the rest of Daniel Huber, there wasn't much more we could do.

This was a short-lived theory, because exactly two days later, the rest of Daniel Huber turned up. It was two o'clock in the morning when Coop called. Michael was still awake, working in his home office, and answered the phone. It took more than several shakes from him to rouse me from the coma I was in. I was only half-awake when he handed me the phone.

"Yeah, it's Gallagher," I whispered, my voice hoarse and scratchy.

"CeeCee, it's Coop. Sorry to call so late, but we found the rest of Daniel Huber."

"I'm assuming, since you're calling me this late, that he's no longer among the living?"

"You assume right. He's got another piece of him missing, too."

"His other hand?" Still lying down, I looked over at the alarm clock on my nightstand.

"Nope . . . We think it's his liver."

I sat straight up, now wide-awake. "His liver!"

"Right. Just meet me behind the E&B Market on Fourth Street. That's where he was found about half an hour ago by the garbagemen. I'll fill you in on the details when you get there."

He hung up. I got out of bed and dressed while Michael sat on the bed and watched silently. It was unusual for him to not ask me a million questions when I got called out like this.

"I guess they found the rest of the guy that lost his

hand," Michael said. I had given him details of the
case earlier.

"It looks like they also took his liver out. Can you
believe that?"

"I heard." He stared at the floor.

"Michael? What's the matter with you?" I stopped
putting my shoe on and looked at him.

He looked at me with a halfhearted smile. "Nothing. I'm just tired is all."

"Then instead of staying up all night like you have
been, why don't you try and get a good night's sleep?"

"Can't." He stood up. "I've got too much work
to do."

He walked over and kissed my cheek before heading back downstairs to his office. I merely shook my
head. Michael was highly intelligent. He was one of
those people whose mind never shuts down, not for
a minute. When he was really involved with something, it was hard for him to focus his attention
elsewhere. I've learned to live with it, but I had yet
to see him as involved as he was now. I didn't bother
to say good-bye when I left; he probably wouldn't
have heard me anyway.

The E&B Market was on the north side of the city, in
the worst neighborhood. The Hot Zone, or THZ, we
called it. It was where the Detroit and Chicago drug
dealers fought their battles. It was also where we
wouldn't be able to find one cooperative witness. In
that particular area of town, no one dared to be caught
speaking to the police. The ramifications of doing so
had in the past proved fatal. Coop had beaten me
there and was talking to one of the garbagemen when
I arrived.

The entire area behind the market had been cordoned off with yellow crime-scene tape, with the county coroner and the crime lab inside the perimeter. The crime lab had erected mobile lights to illuminate the scene. I could see several lab techs hard at work. Some were taking photographs, another was on his hands and knees, and one was carrying evidence bags to the van. One uniformed officer stood just inside the tape. He would be keeping the crimescene log, documenting every person that went in and out of the crime scene.

Standing on the outside of the tape was a group of uniformed officers, mainly rookies, hoping to get a quick glimpse of blood and gore. There was always a group like this at every homicide scene. We kindly referred to the group as the "pigpen." One rarely saw senior officers in the pigpen. They had seen enough murders and dead bodies in their careers, so they began driving in the opposite direction as soon as a homicide call was put out. I felt their pain.

As each year of my career passed, with each homicide, I consistently found myself saying, "This is it, this is the last one. After this I'm transferring to the traffic division." But I kept plugging away in Major Crimes. Once, after I had investigated a serial child murderer, I went so far as to fill out a transfer form and give it to Naomi. She wadded it up right in front of me, threw it in the garbage, and told me to get back to work.

Walking into the crime scene, I gave the officer in charge of the log my name and rank. The body was a good twenty-five feet away from the entrance. The closer I got, the more I felt my stomach flip. I don't care how many homicides a cop has gone to; if he's human, he'll always react.

Daniel Huber was lying on his back, his face appearing to look directly up at the sky. His eyes were open, and he was completely naked. What drew my attention was the part of his body that was opened up—his right side. Of course, there was also the stump at the end of his left arm where his hand used to be. Whoever had filleted him almost cut him in half. I immediately noticed the lack of blood—not a drop. A cut like his would have bled out a sizeable amount, but the ground was dry. I waited until Coop was finished talking to the garbage man before I waved him over.

"Certainly not the prettiest I've seen." I nodded at the body. "Explain to me how, out of that mess, you could tell his liver was missing."

"One of the first uniforms on the scene was a female who had completed her first year of nursing school before she decided to go to the police academy, Carla Reynolds. Have you heard of her?"

I shook my head.

"Anyway, she told me her opinion when they called. The coroner confirmed it. He doesn't know if anything else is missing, but he said definitely the liver."

"Witnesses?" I looked around at citizens that had gathered in the alley outside of the tape.

"Please. Here in THZ? You know better than that. I've got uniforms knocking on doors trying to get statements, but the majority of people won't even open them." The lines in his face deepened. "Basically, the garbage truck pulled up behind the building, and there was the body. They didn't pass anyone or see any cars. This is going to be one of those 'most difficult' cases, I think."

"I think you're right, Coop."

The next several hours were spent knocking on doors, taking statements, talking to the officers who were first on the scene—including Carla Reynolds—and taking photographs for our own file. Once the autopsy was performed on Daniel Huber, we would know more. Unfortunately, that would take several days, if not a week. The crime lab didn't recover much: cigarette butts next to the body that could've come from anyone and several of the full garbage bags, to name the most important.

Daniel Huber, according to the coroner, had been dead for at least four days. An important bit of information the coroner told me was that whoever removed the liver had pretty decent medical experience—they had to, or they'd have risked damaging the organ. The downside is that we were dealing with a secondary crime scene, merely a "body dump," the site of the actual murder still unknown. Hence the lack of blood.

Once I finished at the crime scene, I went home and slept for a couple of hours. Michael was already gone, and the girls stayed at Eric's, since they were supposed to go there today anyway. I had a slight theory about Daniel Huber's murder when I got to the office the next morning, and relayed it to Coop.

"Do you think it's possible that someone has a family member dying and is desperate for an organ donor? So desperate that he or she would take one from a homeless person?"

"I guess it's possible," Coop said, mulling my theory over. "But that doesn't explain the hand. It's not like a left hand is a hot commodity on the donor list."

"I know, but I think we should still try and obtain a list of local people on the waiting list for organs. There can't be *that* many, and we'll have to check out their family members. The coroner said the killer absolutely had to have medical experience. This would narrow down the list considerably."

"You could be right." He thought for a moment. "How 'bout this? You type up all of the statements and get the file in order, and I'll start making phone calls to get ahold of the list."

"Works for me." I knew Coop hated paperwork.

It took me two hours to get the file in order. I went home afterward, deciding I had done enough for the day. Not to mention, I missed Michael horribly. As luck would have it, he was home. Predictably, he was in his office working his "mystery case." I stood in the doorway for several seconds before he even noticed me. He looked up from his file with surprise.

"Oh! Hi, honey." He got up from his desk and started my way. "I'm sorry, I didn't even know you were there." He kissed my cheek.

"I can see that." I gave him a tight squeeze. "Still working the secret case, are you?"

"Yeah. Cee, honey, I know I've been distracted, and I'm sorry. Hopefully, this will all be over soon."

"I hope so, too. Why don't you join me for a glass of wine while I watch the news? I'll make dinner in a little bit. You could use the break. Please?" I stuck out my bottom lip like a small child.

He grinned broadly. "Okay, you suckered me into it, even though you know how much I hate the news."

Michael brought in two glasses of wine just as I

was getting comfortable on the couch, and turned on the television. The newscaster was repeating a news clip that made Michael stop dead in his tracks.

"Cleveland businessman Niccolo Filaci was brutally murdered in his South Euclid home just over an hour ago. Details are sketchy, as police are still on the scene. Co-owner of several construction companies in the area, Mr. Filaci has long been suspected of having ties to the Mafia. An anonymous source at the FBI would not confirm or deny the allegations . . ."

I looked at Michael and saw his face had gone completely white. He set the glasses of wine down on the coffee table just before his office phone started ringing loudly. I wanted some answers.

"Michael, you need to tell me what is going on," I demanded, standing.

"Let me get my phone." He waved me off and headed back toward his office.

I followed him but stopped as he closed the door in my face. Pressing my ear against it, I tried to listen to his conversation to no avail; it was completely muffled. I was starting to worry. His reaction to the newscast answered at least one of my questions. When he finally opened the door, I confirmed what I already knew.

"You're investigating the Mafia, aren't you?"

He leaned against the doorframe, crossing his arms, and quietly answered, "Yes, I am."

"Please, Michael, tell me, what's going on? I saw your face during the broadcast. I'm worried. Who is Niccolo Filaci?"

He reached out and gently stroked a piece of my hair. "I'm sorry, Cee, but I can't."

"What do you mean, you can't?" I was floored.

"Michael! We've never kept secrets from each other. You *have* to tell me what's going on!"

He took me by the hand and led me to the small love seat that sat beside the window in his office. After we both sat down, he pulled me to his chest and embraced me.

"Look, I know something like this is difficult for you. God knows you flip out if you're not in on everything, but please, trust me, Cee. It's nothing to worry about. When the time is right I'll talk to you about it."

I was a little angry and pulled away. "What? Don't you trust me? I mean, my God, you act like I'm gonna go post what you tell me on the department bulletin board!"

"That's not it . . . You just don't understand. Please, trust *me*. Have I ever lied to you?"

"No."

"All right then . . . Let's go have that glass of wine."

"It's done."

The large man with thinning gray hair sat behind his impressive cherry desk, leaning back in his chair and folding his hands. The news that his employee had just delivered was well received. Niccolo had gotten what he deserved. How dare a Filaci try to cut in on his money!

"Did he suffer?" the man behind the desk asked.

"Greatly, sir."

"Did you give him the message?"

"Word for word."

The man behind the desk clapped his hands together and let out a loud whoop. He would reward this particular employee with a large bonus. Now that his cash flow was greater than ever, he could afford to. He further suppressed his excitement as his employee took a seat in a chair by the wall. He is certainly an intimidating fellow, *the man behind the desk thought of his employee. He could only imagine the fear that had run through Niccolo Filaci's body at the last moment—the moment when he knew he was going to die.*

"Well done, Frank. Well done. There will be a large bonus for you at the end of the week. Now, on to further business." The man behind the desk sat up straight in his chair. "You said earlier you told the Filipinos we were okay with the new order?"

The man in the chair against the wall nodded.

"Good. Now, what about the agent? He's bringing entirely too much heat."

The man in the chair smiled. "Don't worry. I'm working on it."

CHAPTER TWO

I was thinking about Michael's reaction to the news again the next morning at work. The night before, while trying to sleep, I kept trying to pinpoint what it was about Michael's expression that concerned me. Now, sitting here, I realized it was fear, an emotion I'd rarely seen my husband display. My concern growing at an alarming rate, I tried to call him several times, but only reached his voice mail.

"Some lady called this morning. I guess she saw Daniel Huber at the welfare clothing store about five or six days ago." Coop had walked into my office and taken a seat, a fact I was oblivious to, but welcomed nonetheless.

"So?"

"Sooo, that would be the only, and last, confirmed sighting. That would put the coroner's estimated time of death right on the nose . . . or liver." He chuckled at his own gag.

"Cute. How are you coming on the organ recipient list?" I reached over and grabbed my mug of hot coffee.

"So far there are only five. Hey, you have any more java?"

I nodded toward the small, newly purchased coffeepot I kept on a table by my desk. "I thought there would be more than that. I keep hearing how people are dying before they can get an organ donor. It sounds like there are thousands."

"That very well may be, but here in good ol' Mansfield, Ohio, it appears there are only five. I'm still waiting to hear from the kidney-dialysis center, so it may go up a bit." He slowly poured the coffee into a spare mug I had, being careful not to spill it. "Cream and sugar?"

"In the drawer. Now all we have to do is find out if any of those people are in the medical field or have relatives who are. This is going to be a lot of work, Coop. We're going to have to interview the doctors and nurses to find out if there's any family members that have been highly agitated over not getting an organ donor. We also have to interview Daniel Huber's family. They may know who his drug connections were. This could also be a case where he pissed one of them off, and it's a simple torture murder."

Coop shook his head. "Forget it. We already contacted his local family. They don't want anything to do with him, and they have nothing to say to us. As a matter of fact, they're refusing to claim the body." He sat back down.

"Can they do that?"

"Yup. We can't even donate the poor guy to the colleges, since he's missing parts."

How very sad, I thought. *No wonder the guy was so messed up. I'm sure Daniel Huber's drug problems somehow stemmed from the coldhearted family he grew up in.*

It was apparent, with all the interviews we would have to do, that this case was going to be lengthy. While Coop sat and slurped his coffee, another thought came to mind.

"You're married to the boss. Why don't you get her to assign two other detectives for the recipient-list part? If they could go out and interview the families, doctors, nurses, and whoever, that would free us up to get to the meat of the case."

He mulled over my proposal. "That could work. I just overheard Sinclair tell Naomi he was on the low side of cases. He and that new detective, uh, I keep forgetting his name . . ."

"Justin Brown."

"Right, he and Justin Brown could do it. It'd give the new kid some experience in interviewing." Coop stood up. "I'll be back in a flash. Keep the coffee hot while I go run this by the old lady."

Coop was going to have a tough time convincing Naomi to go along. The other detectives had already picked up our extra cases on top of their own so we could work on this. But he'd have a better chance than I would. Sleeping with the boss every night clearly had its upside.

While waiting for Coop, I started to brew another pot of coffee. I had just poured the water when my desk phone rang. I grabbed it, hoping it was Michael.

"Sergeant Gallagher."

"Sergeant? This is Steven Snyder, Director of the Quinn-Herstin Funeral Home over on Marion Avenue. We're the large white and brick house that—"

"I'm familiar with it, Mr. Snyder. What can I do for you?" I sighed with disappointment.

"I just spoke with the coroner, and he told me to call you. He said you were the final say—"

"The final say on what?" Interrupting again, I couldn't imagine what he wanted. Plus, I was starting to get irritated.

"Well, on the Huber body, on when it can be released, and if we can have it."

I was slightly taken aback. "You want Daniel Huber's body? Why?"

At first I thought he was going to tell me they were donating their services, since no one had claimed Daniel's body. But then I wondered . . . If that was true, how did *he* know that? Before I could answer, Coop appeared in my doorway. Waving him in, I pointed at the phone and made a face. He shrugged his shoulders as if to say "What?" Motioning for him to sit down, I replied to Steven Snyder.

"Mr. Snyder, as I'm sure you well know, only family members of the deceased have the right to the body and its arrangements."

"So you've finally found a relative who is willing to claim him then?"

"Mr. Snyder, I'm very busy this morning and I'm not in the mood for games. I certainly don't mean any disrespect, but I think it's time you got directly to your point." Curiosity had now overwhelmed me.

"I'm truly sorry, Sergeant, of course. You see, Quinn-Herstin supplies a tissue-donor corporation, LifeTech Industries, with space. We rent to them for a substantial fee per month. Part of our contract is to acquire, if we can, tissue donations to the company. We do that through local homeless people that are unclaimed. Once the donor is acquired, the company takes the necessary tissue for transferal, and Quinn-Herstin then provides a proper burial for the donor, including the casket and plot." He laughed slightly. "I know it sounds like an awful thing, Sergeant, but really, if we didn't take them, they'd wind up cremated and thrown in a field somewhere. It really is quite tasteful."

"It certainly doesn't sound quite ethical, if not illegal!" I was shocked and thoroughly repulsed. I had no idea this kind of company did business in our city.

"It's quite ethical, Sergeant, and very legal. Let me put it this way. Next time you go to Akron Children's Hospital, walk down to the burn unit and look at the small children who are missing over half of their skin. When the doctors do skin grafts on them, where do you think the skin comes from? Let's say you have a close family member who is in dire need of a heart valve. Where would they get it? Sergeant, this type of corporation saves lives, and I am certainly not ashamed to be a part of it," he said defiantly.

"It sounds just great, Mr. Snyder," I said with an extensive amount of sarcasm. "My biggest question is how you knew that Daniel Huber was homeless and that no one claimed the body."

"We have our name registered with the local homeless shelters, county welfare department, and so on. We read the obituaries every day, of course. We're funeral directors—why wouldn't we? When we see an obituary where it reads the deceased lived at 'address unknown,' we start checking into it further. When I called the coroner, he confirmed the body had not been claimed, but said you were the only one with the authority to release it. That is the point of my call, Sergeant."

For the first time in my life, I was almost speechless. It took me a few seconds to come up with an answer.

"Mr. Snyder, the autopsy on the body is not completed, which I'm sure the coroner informed you. Secondly, I will not allow you, or anyone, to claim the body for medical purposes until I confirm that business is legitimate and legal. I'm assuming LifeTech Industries maintains a license with the state Department of Health?"

"Of course."

"Is your funeral home a type of subpost, or whatever you call it? I'm sure it is not their main location."

"No, ma'am, it's not. They contract with homes throughout the state. Their main facilities are in Cleveland."

"That's fine, Mr. Snyder. I'll leave it like this: I'll do some checking into LifeTech—and *you*—as well as making more attempts to contact any living relatives of Daniel Huber. I will only sign his body over to LifeTech after that is all completed, after I've determined that there are no living relatives, that the body is officially unclaimed, *and* I have a court document signed by a common-pleas-court judge ordering me to do so."

"Sergeant, I have *never* had to go through court proceedings to claim a body. Most people are more than happy to—"

"There's always a first time, Mr. Snyder. Tell me, who does the actual tissue removal for LifeTech in this area? Local doctors?"

He was silent for a brief moment. "Sergeant, I'm sorry, I've just had someone walk into my office. I'll be in touch."

He promptly hung up, giving me the impression that he didn't want to answer any questions about the doctors. Coop, who had miraculously stayed silent through the entire conversation, was ready to explode.

"For Christ's sake, what was *that* all about?" he barked.

"*That* was probably one of the nastiest things I've ever heard of." I shivered. "Eew."

Then I filled Coop in on the details.

"You've got to be shitting me? You mean they take pieces and parts of dead people and ship them all over the country?"

"Yup."

"Ugh. That *is* nasty. Nooo thanks. I'm keeping all my shit when I'm dead. My luck, they'd hack off my dick and send it to some poor soul whose wife caught him fucking around and whacked his off before feeding it to the family dog." He unconsciously, I think, placed his hands over his groin.

"Don't worry, Coop. From what Naomi says, I don't think they make needles small enough to sew on what you have. Superglue, maybe."

His face turned red. "Is that right? Well I'll show you a needle small . . ." He stood up and started to unbutton his pants, just as Naomi appeared at the door.

Laughing uncontrollably, I yelled to her, waving my hands. "Naomi! Please! Tell him not to unleash Godzilla!"

"What the hell is going on?" She looked horrified.

Before Coop could lash into her, I intervened. "Coop . . . settle down, big boy, I was joking. Trust me, Naomi said you're no less than Tarzan himself."

Naomi caught on and began laughing, too. Coop, realizing for the millionth time in his life that he had been the butt of another joke, calmed down and reclaimed his seat. We filled Naomi in on LifeTech Industries. Her reaction was more forgiving than ours.

"I know you guys think the concept is gross and all, but places like that really do help people. I had an uncle who received a dental implant from a corporation like LifeTech."

"It *is* gross," I said. "I just don't know how I could cope, waking up each day knowing I had a dead guy's bicuspid in my mouth."

"Would you rather be toothless?" she asked.

"I guess you're right." I looked at Coop and raised my eyebrows. "Well? How'd we fare on getting the other detectives?"

"You can have 'em. Coop said he'd watch five straight days of sports channels if I didn't agree." She glared at him. He smiled.

"Fabulous. Coop, if you want to pass the list along to get them started, I'm going over to Quinn-Herstin. I'd like to speak to Steven Snyder personally."

I grabbed my briefcase and keys and tried Michael again before heading to the funeral home. He still wasn't answering his phone. More than dismayed, I called the office. I knew he was never actually in the office, but I presumed I could at least get an answer from his secretary on his whereabouts. All she would tell me is that he was working "in the field" today, as if I didn't already know that.

"He's close, Sal."

"How close?" the man behind the desk, Sal, asked.

"Close enough that we may have a problem."

This angered Sal. He didn't need or want another snag. Things had been going too well. The money was flowing, and he wouldn't stand for a goddamn agent fucking it all up. He turned his chair away from his number-one man and faced the wall.

"I thought you said there was nothing that could lead him to us?"

"I didn't think so, but according to Tommy, he saw him pokin' around the warehouse this morning, asking a lot of the right questions."

"Do you think it's a leak?"

"No, boss, I don't think so. He's smart, but I don't think he can put something together that isn't there. Unless he makes shit up—but I think he's too clean for that. The problem is we need to keep a constant eye on him, and that distracts us from other things. Yeah, he's close, but if you ask me if he'll come all the way, I'll have to say no. But it's still a problem."

Sal turned around and faced the man again. "You're goddamn right it's a problem! As for the agent being clean, think again! If you look back into his past, you'll see not everything is clean. And you're forgetting who he's married to! If that bitch starts poking around, we're gonna have more than a 'problem'!"

The man nodded and stayed silent. He knew better than to infuriate the boss even more than he already had. Sometimes the boss took out his frustrations on the person standing right in front him, the bearer of the bad news. He needed to shine some light, so to speak, in the boss's eyes.

"There's no reason for her to poke around. She's local. She's not even suspicious, so there's no worry there, Sal. As for the agent, like I said before, don't worry, I'll take care of it."

Sal glared at him. "You just make sure someone's keeping an eye on her, regardless."

There wasn't a funeral going on when I pulled into Quinn-Herstin, something I had worried about. This would hopefully give me Steven Snyder's undivided attention. He wasn't hard to find. When I walked in, I immediately noticed a small, thin runt of man with thinning hair and glasses. He was setting flowers on a stand, looking just like he had sounded on the phone.

"Steven Snyder?"

The man looked up from his flowers and turned around, his small mouth forming an artificial welcoming smile. I saw it as aggravation that he had been interrupted.

"Yes?"

"Sergeant Gallagher, Richland Metro." His smile faded completely. "We just spoke on the phone a while ago." I held out my badge and identification.

He stood silent, and I noticed his eyes flickered to the direction of a wooden door on the far side of the room. Purposefully trying to wash away his trepidation, his smile reappeared as he walked toward me, hand extended.

"Sergeant Gallagher! How are you? I must say I wasn't expecting you so soon after our conversation."

I briefly shook his hand. "I had an interview down the road and thought I would stop by and see you in person."

Deliberately locking my eyes on the wooden door, I hoped to stir him a little. It worked. His smile faded again. Stepping in front of my view, he held his arm out and pointed in the opposite direction.

"Why don't we go into my office? We'll have more privacy there."

I looked around at the empty room. "It doesn't

look like business is booming, Mr. Snyder. Does it get any more private than this?"

"I really need to be by my phone. I'm expecting an important call."

I relented and followed him to his office, where I sat on a quite ugly maroon and gold couch that faced his desk.

"Now, Sergeant, I have an appointment in a few minutes, but until then, what can I do for you?"

I got right to the point. "I'd like the names of the persons employed by LifeTech that work out of this funeral home."

A scowl washed over his face, and his eyes looked behind me at the door of his office. It was so obvious, I turned to see if someone was standing there. No one was.

I was annoyed. "Mr. Snyder, is there something you want to say? Is there someone else here?"

"No, no, Sergeant, I'm sorry, I just thought I heard the front door open, and looked to see if it was my appointment. Now tell me again what you need?"

"The names of employees."

"That's right. Now let's see . . ." He started looking at the gray file cabinets that lined the wall to my right. "I'm not sure which file those are in. Why don't you leave me a card, and I'll call you with the names. It could take a while."

"I'll wait." I was not about to let him evade me again.

"I see." He paused and chewed on his thumbnail before grabbing a pad of paper and a pen.

He began writing. "Here are the names of the two doctors that perform the tissue removals. If you want other names, I cannot give those to you today. It will take phone calls and time, which I do not have right now, unless *you* have a court order, Sergeant." He handed me the paper.

I looked at the names on the paper. "Dr. Donovan Esposito and Dr. Neal Schmidt? I've never heard of either one of these men before."

"I can assure you they exist, each with a flourishing practice in Cleveland. They're subcontracted by LifeTech to perform the tissue removals in this area. All of the doctors contracted by the company are out of Cleveland and assigned certain districts. When a procedure needs to be done, they fly by private plane so they can get here quickly."

"That makes no sense at all. Why wouldn't they use local doctors?"

"Because not all are qualified to perform such procedures, and they want the best. LifeTech opens subposts, as you call them, in areas with a high homeless population. Cleveland, Columbus, and Cincinnati are givens, but also in the smaller cities: Mansfield, Youngstown, Akron, and Lima. You get it?"

"I got it." Not that I really did.

"Now, Sergeant, if you'll excuse me." He stood up. "I really need to attend to some things. I'll be in touch with the rest of the list."

"I probably shouldn't hold my breath, should I?" I smiled.

Returning the smile, he led me to the front door. I had to admit, everything about LifeTech sounded solid, but it was Steven Snyder himself who bothered me. He was hiding something, but I didn't know if I should chalk it up to the genuine weirdness of a funeral director or to something else. Folding up the piece of paper with the doctors' names and putting it in my purse, I jumped a little when my cell phone blared to life.

"Hi, honey, it's me." Michael's soothing voice came through the phone.

"Michael! I've been trying to get ahold of you all day, for crying out loud. How come you haven't called me?" A sense of relief washed over me.

"Honey, I've been busy, but guess who's on his way home right now?"

"You are!" I looked at my watch. "I didn't realize how late it was. So, you're finally going to be home before dark, huh? I guess I should make it worth my while and beat you there."

"You could make it worth *my* while and be naked by the time I get home."

"Sounds good to me."

I stopped and grabbed Chinese takeout on my way home. It had been a while since Michael and I had time together, and I didn't want to spend it cooking—not that I cooked much anyway. I wasn't naked when Michael got home, but planned to be so later. My plans turned into fantasy when, immediately after dinner, Michael's office phone started ringing. Once again, he stayed behind a closed door. Cleaning up our dishes, I found myself slamming plates into the dishwasher out of sheer frustration. After several minutes of the clanking dishes, Michael came into the kitchen.

"What the hell is going on?"

"Nothing, babe, I'm just cleaning up after dinner." I literally dumped a handful of silverware right onto the rack before slamming the dishwasher door and turning it on.

"You have to put the silverware in the trays or they'll fly all over the place." He walked over to the dishwasher, turned it off, and opened it.

When he was finished, he came up behind me and stood while I opened a bottle of wine, which I fully intended to finish before the night was over. Feeling his hand on my shoulder, I quickly shrugged it off.

"All right, I know you're mad . . . I'm sorry." His pleas falling on deaf ears, he continued. "For Christ's sake, CeeCee, you know how our jobs are! I can't just ignore things, just like you can't."

I turned around and grabbed my briefcase, pulling out the Daniel Huber murder file.

"You may not be able to ignore things, but I can." I let the file drop onto the floor. "I can ignore this for six whole hours to spend time with my husband. Unlike you, obviously, I've learned that life is too short to be consumed by this fucking job!" I was on the verge of tears.

He sighed and took my hand. "Come with me."

He led me into his office and made me watch as he unplugged his desk phone. He then turned off his cell phone and went even further by turning off the fax machine.

"There, now." He leaned against his desk. "What about your promise of being naked when I came home? Still looks like you got your clothes on to me."

Smiling before lunging into him, I let him carry me upstairs to make love like we hadn't done in weeks. Satisfied and no longer angry, I fell into a peaceful sleep, Michael right next to me. I thought it had all been a figment of my imagination when I awoke several hours later to find Michael back in his office.

"You just couldn't keep away for one—" I stopped and saw that Michael was looking at my Daniel Huber murder file.

Looking guilty, he quickly set the file down on his desk as if I hadn't seen it. "What are you doing up?"

"What are *you* doing looking at my murder case?" I raised an eyebrow.

He avoided my eyes. "Nothing, I just needed a break from mine and thought I'd poke around in yours. I saw where you put Coop on obtaining a waiting list for donors. Good move."

"Thanks." I went in and sat on the small love seat that was against the farthest wall. "I thought there would be more than that. From what I've heard, there are a lot of people waiting for organs."

"You wouldn't believe how many, or the lengths people will go to get them," Michael said matter-of-factly.

"You sound as if you know this for a fact."

"Just stuff I've heard," he said nervously, before changing the subject. "I'm sorry to be working again, Cee, but I thought of something when I was trying to go to sleep. I needed to look at the case file for a minute. C'mon, let's get back to bed." He stood up and walked around his desk.

I didn't move. "Getting anywhere on the Niccolo Filaci murder?"

He looked at me with surprise. "What makes you think I'm investigating that?"

"Because I'm not a moron, and I know you. Your reaction to the news the other night said it all."

"I can't tell you that, honey. We already discussed this."

"Fine, but you can tell me something else. I

thought the Cleveland and Youngstown Mafias were wiped out in the Mafia wars of the seventies."

"That's not entirely true. When the boss of the Cleveland Mafia died in the late seventies, he didn't name a successor. That leads to a great power struggle within families. By the early nineties, there was no known boss and no known members. This was actually a myth, since one of the successors who no one, especially the FBI, was aware of, built the family back up. By the year 2000, they were going strong again."

"And Youngstown?"

"Youngstown has always been hot. Don't you remember when they tried to kill the county prosecutor just a few years ago?"

I nodded. "I remember even more that the county sheriff who took kickbacks from them got indicted, was found not guilty, and went on to be a lovely state senator."

"Larry Beneditto."

"That's the one."

"He's actually a made member of one of the families. Everyone was too scared to touch him. He controlled parts of the NFL for a while, until someone bigger than him took over."

"Who's that?"

Michael smiled. "Oh, I forgot his name."

"You're so full of shit. What's his name?"

"C'mon, it's late and we both need to get some sleep. Don't bother asking me anything again, because I'm not telling." He grinned and mimicked zipping his lips.

Sleep was forever a fantasy in my world. I had only gotten two more hours of it when my phone rang. It was Naomi, informing me there had been another murder similar to Daniel Huber's. Michael had been in such a deep sleep, he hadn't heard the phone, so before leaving, I put a note on our bathroom counter telling him where I'd be.

This current victim, John Kruse, age twenty-five, had been found just inside the fence at the Mansfield Airport. The fence went for miles around the landing fields, some parts of it in dense areas. Finding a body there was nothing new. People seemed to think that no one ever walked the fence of the airport, and if they dumped a body there, it would be months, if not years, before it was found.

I remember when I worked uniform, we would frequently put bets on who would be the first officer to find a body inside the airport fence in the spring. Most of the body-dumping there occurred in winter months, when the snow was so deep no one would think to look. However, with this particular murder, the body had been thrown over a section of the fence that lined a moderately driven roadway. Anyone would see it. Again, whoever was responsible had made no attempt to hide it.

Naomi and Coop were already on the scene when I arrived, Naomi the first to wave me over.

"It looks the same as Daniel Huber. We've possibly got a serial killer on our hands," she said.

"No, he's not a serial killer. He's a *multiple murderer*," I corrected her.

"Sorry, I forgot."

People automatically assume that if one person commits more than one murder, they are deemed a "serial killer." This is incorrect. Only if law enforcement can prove that the murders are driven by sexual motivation does the term apply. Bundy, Gacy, and Dahmer committed their crimes out of their own sexual urges, making each one of them a serial killer. If you take the sexual aspect out of the crime, the term *multiple murderer* or *mass murderer* applies. To my knowledge, there was no indication of sexual trauma or gratification in the Daniel Huber murder, just as I suspected there would be none here. This reasoning also applies to child molesters. Most people call pedophiles child molesters. Again, not true. Only when a pedophile physically acts out his urges on a child does he become a child molester. Although rare, there are a few pedophiles in the world who will never be a child molester.

Naomi led me to the body, which looked eerily similar to Daniel Huber's, except John Kruse had both hands. His right side cut almost in half, he was naked and lying on his back without an ounce of blood in sight.

"Liver again?" I bent over the body, straining to see inside the wound.

"Not just the liver. According to the coroner, from what he could see, he's missing his liver *and* a kidney."

"Both!" I looked at Coop, who had joined us, and anticipating my next question, he answered it.

"No. There's no one on the waiting list for both, if that's what you wanted to know."

"Well, I guess that shoots my angered-relative-of-a-person-in-need-of-an-organ theory right in the ass." I sighed. "I suppose he was homeless, too?"

"It looks that way," answered Naomi. "The shelter actually called us yesterday inquiring about filing a missing-persons report. I guess he was a frequent visitor who at least checked in daily for food and stuff. They hadn't seen him for several days, which they thought unusual."

"Fuck." I looked at Coop. "Now what?"

"Funny you ask. I was watching TV earlier tonight, and there was a show that had some type of black-market organ-removal ring. I didn't know such a thing existed. I'd say it's something we might want to look into."

"You're right, Coop." I had an epiphany. "And I know just where to start."

CHAPTER THREE

It was time I contacted the doctors associated with the Quinn-Herstin Funeral Home. To Naomi and Coop's surprise, I told them I would be in touch, before starting toward my car. Coop, resorting to a slow jog, caught up to me.

"CeeCee! What do you think you're doing? We've got a homicide scene to work."

"I'm well aware of that, and I'm investigating it. Just not here." I opened my car door and got in. "You and Naomi can take care of things just fine. Trust me—this is something that needs to be done."

He stood quietly and shook his head as I drove away. While heading toward the department, I called our records division and requested them to find any information, including phone numbers, on Dr. Donovan Esposito and Dr. Neal Schmidt. The clerk said she would call me in my office shortly. I anticipated at least a forty-five minute wait. My office phone was ringing when I arrived on station a few minutes later. The clerk had found the requested information in less than fifteen minutes—a new world's record.

My watch showed four thirty A.M. It would be quite rude to call these doctors at this hour of the morning. *Hell with it!* I thought, before picking up the phone and dialing Donovan Esposito's number. It rang several times before a groggy-sounding woman answered. After informing her who was calling, I requested Dr. Esposito.

"Lady, do you know what time it is?" She sounded more awake.

"It's Sergeant, and yes, I can tell time."

"Miracles never cease," she whispered flippantly. "My husband is sound asleep, and unless you have a good reason for calling, you'll have to contact him tomorrow during office hours."

"I'll let you decide if this is a good enough reason. I have two dead bodies that each had a major organ removed—while they were still alive, no doubt. I was just made aware of your husband's tissue-donor side job today and feel he may have the answers to some quite important questions. To sum it up, your husband is the closest thing to a witness, or a suspect, that I have. Now, I can certainly subpoena all of his medical records and possibly serve a search warrant on his office if that's the route he chooses," I said wryly.

"Oh, please, spare me the drama," she snipped. "Hold on."

The sounds of Mrs. Esposito attempting to rouse her husband came loudly through the phone. After a few grunts and groans, I could clearly hear her relaying our conversation to him.

She ended it with ". . . she threatened to serve a search warrant on your office. She's a real bitch."

The feeling's mutual, lady, I thought. After a few coughs and obscenities, Donovan Esposito picked up the phone.

"This is Dr. Esposito. What do you want?" He was pissed.

"Dr. Esposito, this is Sergeant Gallagher . . ." I began, in my most enchanting voice.

After informing him of the homicides, I made a futile attempt to contradict his wife's interpretation of our conversation.

"Doctor, I couldn't help but overhear your wife telling you I threatened a search warrant. Perhaps she misunderstood. I was merely telling her about standard procedures in a homicide investigation, and how I would very much like to avoid something like that. If you can only imagine the amount of paperwork involved, it's horrible. That said, I was wondering if I could meet with you sometime this morning so we could talk." I was disgustingly charismatic.

"Well, I suppose I could give you half an hour during lunchtime." His voice softened considerably. "But you'd have to meet me here, in Cleveland. I can't possibly take the time to drive down there today. I have a full schedule."

Mission accomplished. We arranged to meet at his office at noon. I went even further and asked if it was possible that Dr. Schmidt could join us. He didn't think it would be a problem but couldn't guarantee anything.

Since my trip to Cleveland was several hours away, I utilized the remaining time to catch a few hours of sleep. Naomi was still out on the homicide scene, so leaving a message on her voice mail informing her of my impending interview would have to suffice. Michael was already awake and ready to leave when I got home, a quick opportunity to suggest a lunch date later.

"I can't, Cee. I'm busy all day and probably won't even eat lunch."

"I just thought, since I would be up there, it would be nice to see you, is all." I sighed. "I feel like we hardly see each other anymore."

"I'm sorry, baby." He put his strong, muscular arms around me. "I promise again, this will all be over soon. In fact, I think a trip to Aruba might be just around the corner." He pulled away smiling.

"You promise?" The thought of Aruba sent me into immediate euphoria.

"Yes, I promise."

After kissing my forehead and squeezing me one last time, Michael was out the door. It took a while for me to fall back asleep, and it was only for an hour. Later, standing at my bedroom window, I thought about questions to ask Dr. Esposito. They would have to be direct, as it had become quite clear the doctor would see through any type of sugarcoating. It was also clear that he certainly wouldn't tolerate being jerked around. After watching a jogger stop in front of my house and tie his shoe, I started to get myself cleaned up and ready to go.

The drive took less than an hour. Esposito's office was on the south side, near Strongsville. Pulling into the parking lot of his building, I wasn't the least bit surprised to see the architectural-award-winning edifice looming before me. Twelve stories high, it had an old Spanish-style design, with light pink ceramic tiles and a deep peach stucco exterior—a building more suited for South Beach, Miami, than Strongsville, Ohio. It looked odd among the other, standard glass-and-brick buildings.

The physicians list inside the lobby told me one thing: only the crème de la crème of Cleveland physicians had their offices here. They were the plastic surgeons, the neurosurgeons, the oncologists, and the cardiologists. Looking at the list reminded me that I hadn't even determined what type of doctor Esposito was. I couldn't imagine any doctor this high on the food chain would need a side job with a tissue-donor company.

Scanning the doctors' names on each floor, I found DR. DONOVAN ESPOSITO, MD, PLASTIC SURGERY, in suite 6-A. After a brief elevator ride, I stopped in the ladies' room on the sixth floor to make sure everything was in order, appearance-wise. I had to be at the top of my game. My previous experience interviewing doctors had educated me to the fact that although they vary in their expertise, a great number of them are arrogant.

Some border on blatant narcissism, especially if they are called onto the carpet. They don't believe laws apply to them. They expect to be admired for their godlike talents. How dare anyone question a man who had just performed an eight-hour, life-saving surgery on a five-year-old car-accident victim? Even if he did just break his wife's nose the day before. Most are the same, and I didn't expect Donovan Esposito to be any different.

No surprise, the waiting area of his office was professionally—and tastefully—decorated. Contemporary paintings on the walls were paired with a modern vase full of fresh roses that adorned each corner table. The three taupe leather couches looked so inviting, they would have made any patient want to run and dive on them. At the far end of the room was the receptionist's window. Behind it (again, no surprise) sat a twentysomething blonde who appeared to have been nipped and tucked to death. Her chest was so large on her small frame, it looked uncomfortable, and as I got closer, the earlier notion that she was in her twenties faded. This woman was clearly in her forties and had made multiple attempts to maintain her youth. Her face had taken on the shiny, plastic, cat look that most people associated with too much tweaking. I stood and listened while she was on the phone, instantly recognizing her voice.

"Mrs. Esposito, I presume?" I asked as she put the phone on its cradle.

"Yes. Do you have an appointment?" Her smile seemed permanently fixed on her face.

"Yes, I do. I'm Sergeant CeeCee Gallagher with the Richland Metropolitan Police Department. I'm here for my noon appointment with Dr. Esposito." I smiled back.

Her smile faded. "Oh, yes . . . I'm not quite sure he has enough time blocked off for the amount of Botox injections that you'll need."

"If you could let him know I'm here, that would be fine." I turned, still smiling, to walk away but couldn't resist a retort to her comment. I faced her again. "I'm sorry, Mrs. Esposito, but if you don't mind me asking, does that hurt?"

"Does what hurt?" She looked confused.

"Your face, when you talk, smile, blink, and breathe? I couldn't help but ask . . . It just looks excruciatingly painful." I walked away and grabbed a magazine before sitting on the large, comfy couch.

Her face turned ten different shades of red before

she stood up and walked out of the reception area, going to her husband, no doubt. He was standing in front of me in less than five minutes.

"Sergeant, if you would like a statement from me, I expect from you a little professionalism when you're in my office." He glared.

Even seated on the couch, I could still determine he was only a few inches taller than I was. Donovan Esposito might have been attractive, if not for the sizeable nose that took up the majority of his face. Being a plastic surgeon, one might think he would've liked to take care of it. However, he probably thought it was sexy.

In his late forties, he had a ruddy complexion that set off his dark brown, hard, and unfriendly eyes. His professionally groomed hair was significantly gelled. His blue designer shirt, tie, and black slacks bore not a hint of a wrinkle. Shining prominently from his left wrist was a two-tone platinum and gold Baume & Mercier Swiss watch with small diamonds surrounding the dial, worth, at a minimum, ten thousand dollars. Donovan Esposito was a walking bank.

"I extend my apologies to you and your wife, Doctor. I was merely responding to the rude comments made by your wife regarding my need for extensive Botox injections." I stood up.

Dr. Esposito glared toward the reception window where his wife stood. Receiving the silent message, she looked down at the desk in shame before walking away.

"I guess I'll have to apologize for Mrs. Esposito as well, Sergeant. We certainly don't need to start this off on the wrong foot, do we?" He stood back and looked me up and down. "Well, you certainly are attractive, aren't you? I see no need for Botox! And I have to say, whoever did your breast augmentation did a fabulous job. Someone local?"

My face burned. "No one you know."

He had succeeded in degrading me, a strategic step in his attempts to dominate the interview. It took a conscious effort on my part to gather my wits as he led me into his office. Now it was game time.

"Please, have a seat, Sergeant. I have just a few minutes before my next patient is due." He sat behind his impressive oak desk while motioning for me to sit in one of the leather chairs in front of it.

I sat down. "Doctor, as I explained to you on the phone earlier, I'm investigating two homicides in the Mansfield area. Each of the victims had major organs removed surgically, and I believe you can assist me in filling in some gaps."

"Whatever I can do to help, Sergeant." He leaned back in his chair, smiling and clasping his hands together.

I grabbed my pen, notebook, and file out of my briefcase, covertly pushing the record button of the tape recorder that sat inside.

"Doctor, this is protocol, so bear with me. Are you speaking to me voluntarily? Have you been coerced, threatened, or intimidated into giving me this statement? Do you understand that you are free to cease this conversation at any time?" I hated having to say this. It merely reminded someone that they could tell me to get the hell out of here.

"Yes, I understand all of that."

"Great. Now, if you would, please explain to me your position at LifeTech Industries and the Quinn-Herstin Funeral Home."

"I'd be happy to, but first, Sergeant, can you explain to me again why you need to know all of this? I was a little tired this morning when I spoke with you on the phone. What does this have to do with your murders?" His position and facial expression remained unchanged.

"I was unaware a corporation such as LifeTech operated out of my city. So it was a little odd to receive a phone call from Steven Snyder requesting one of the homicide victims for tissue donation. Especially since the victim was missing his liver."

He leaned forward. "Sergeant, you seem to be coming very close to insinuating that I am a suspect in this case."

"Not at all, Doctor. If you can just explain the inner workings of LifeTech and your duties there, I'll be on my way."

His eyes narrowed. "Fine, but any more hints at suspicion and I will phone my attorney."

I nodded in agreement.

"Now," he began, "I will try and explain this in laymen's terms, without all of the medical terminology, so you can understand it." This was another attempt to belittle me. "LifeTech Industries is a corporation that was formed in 1999 by a group of prominent physicians from all over the country. It had become increasingly frustrating for us, as doctors, to see the countless number of patients suffering from a variety of physical impairments. Even though the donors needed were only for tissue, there was still a significant wait for these patients. LifeTech formed and set up offices throughout the state to have immediate access to bodies that are left unclaimed. You see, if they didn't have the offices spread out, a dead homeless man in Cincinnati would go unnoticed. He would be buried in a potter's field, or cremated and thrown somewhere, when all the while, his skin or bones could have been used by someone in dire need. This way, each LifeTech office is notified by numerous agencies when a body is left unclaimed. We have contracts with city homeless shelters, Salvation Army housing, state prisons, and county human services all over Ohio."

He cleared his throat and continued. "I don't have the numbers right this second, Sergeant, but I can assure you, LifeTech has dramatically alleviated the wait for patients in need and has also aided the less fortunate, who don't have the resources to obtain their needed tissue."

"And you do only tissue? What about organs? If these people are being given to you, why not take their heart and other organs?"

He laughed, wittingly insulting me. "Oh, Sergeant! Come on! You can't be *that* ignorant concerning organ transplantation, can you? Do you realize there are over ninety thousand people waiting for an organ transplant? And only roughly twenty thousand transplants are performed each year. Every day, sixteen to seventeen people die waiting for an organ. Every day! Don't you think if we could just pull a heart from a homeless man who's been dead for three days, that the numbers I cited would be obsolete? Need a liver? Go on down to the county morgue! There's a construction worker that fell off a high-rise last week—take his!" he mocked.

I bit my tongue. "Why don't you enlighten me, Doctor, since I'm so ignorant, on how harvesting organs works?"

He looked at his watch. "Our time is coming to an end, so I'll make this brief and use an example. Essentially, if you have an organ donor that was just involved in a fatal car crash and is flatlining in the emergency room, the staff will keep him on life support. They'll take his eyes out right there, if that's the organ needed, throw 'em in a nice little cooler, and hand them over to LifeFlight, who flies them to where they need to go. With organs, time is the key. Once the body dies, the organs die and very quickly become unsuitable for transplant. Tissue—things like skin, bones, and heart valves—is different. There's a wider window of opportunity with tissue. You have more time. It's pretty simple, but you get the gist."

"It sounds like a very lucrative business," I said flatly.

"Let me put it this way: a man once put his kidney up for auction on the Internet, and the bid was up to five million dollars before it was shut down by the Web site." He stood up.

"One more question, Doctor. How long have you been employed by LifeTech, and what is the last procedure you performed in Mansfield?"

"I have been employed by them for five years, and the last procedure I performed was back in March. It was a dental removal from an inmate who hanged himself in his cell. He was thirty-five."

"Was he at Mansfield or Richland Correctional?"

"Mansfield—maximum security. I believe his name was Richert Saldivar."

He walked to the door and opened it. "I'm sorry, Sergeant, but that's all the time I have for today."

"Did you speak with Dr. Schmidt?"

"Yes, I did, and he has a full schedule today and

couldn't meet with you. I'm sure if you contact his office you can make an appointment. And before you ask, Dr. Schmidt hasn't performed a tissue removal in Mansfield for well over a year."

I thanked Dr. Esposito, ignored his wife as I walked out, and sat in my car, thoroughly troubled by the interview. He had controlled it, undeniably. He had told me exactly what *he* wanted me to know and nothing else. The county coroner confirmed the suicide of the inmate in March when I phoned him, so basically, I had zero on Dr. Esposito. Throwing my cell phone on the passenger seat, I was shocked to see him walk out of the front of the office building and get into a sleek, black sports car parked near the front. Apparently, he didn't have an appointment after all. Without thinking, I slowly turned my car around and began to follow him.

"Do you have everything ready to go?"

"It's set for Friday. After that, it should be smooth sailing, Sal."

"Good. What about her?"

"Only what I told you today. She's nothing to worry about, especially after Friday. Also, the quarterly shipment is in."

"Make your plane reservations, first class. You deserve it."

The man smiled—even though he had to go to the Philippines. He hated the Philippines, especially that dirty, retarded messenger boy. What did they call him? Tao-Kek? Something like that. It didn't matter. One of these days, Tao-whatever-the-fuck would die. He would take pleasure in snapping the little fucker's neck. The man couldn't believe how the boy smiled at him when he gave him the list, as if they were old chums. Never again. He would make it look like an accident, and no one would think any differently or, quite frankly, give a shit. Certainly, the boy's boss wouldn't care. He could find another boy in the street within five minutes.

He had to be in the Philippines within twenty-four hours to ensure the quality of the shipment—his third trip in less than two weeks. With the new, larger order, the man was getting tired of traveling. Nonetheless, he needed to get back to the states quickly. There was the other matter that needed to be taken care of.

Dr. Esposito gave me no reason to be skeptical. Everything he'd said was factual, and his only downfall was a pompous attitude. In spite of this, my suspicion began to grow. Driving onto the interstate, he was unmistakably headed toward the city. Fifteen minutes later, we were pulling into the Warehouse District, a thriving area downtown made up of nightclubs, restaurants, offices, and storage facilities.

He pulled into a three-story parking lot that was adjacent to a large warehouse. I furiously looked everywhere for some sort of business name or corporation, but found none. The only thing to do was jot down the name of the restaurant across the street; this would at least give me a landmark. Cleveland Police could tell me later what they had listed for the warehouse. I waited at the side of the building for an hour before submitting to my hunger pangs and taking a front window seat at the restaurant.

It was another hour and a half before I realized I needed to go. Dr. Esposito, it seemed, did not intend to leave any time soon. On my way home, Cleveland Police informed me they had the warehouse listed under

"LifeTech Industries Storage Facility." There was no reason for LifeTech to maintain a storage warehouse that was so large. I mean, really, how much room could pieces of skin take up?

Arriving in Mansfield, I stopped at the office to see if I could catch Coop or Naomi before they left for the day. Naomi was in the parking lot, ready to leave. Rolling my window down, I pulled up next to her and told her about my interview.

"I know you thought he was an asshole, CeeCee, but he sounds pretty solid."

"Sounds like it, huh? I don't care. Something's not right with him, and something's not right with that warehouse." I started chewing on my lip. "I think I'll call one of my contacts at Cleveland PD tomorrow and see if one of them will sit on it for a while."

"Unless you have something more concrete, I don't know if they will or not. Listen, I gotta get going. Coop and I are going down to my parents' for dinner." She tapped the side of my car and walked away.

I was thinking about whom to contact in Cleveland when my attention was drawn to the vending-machine supply truck that had just pulled in the lot. There was something ominously familiar about the driver that I couldn't put my finger on. He looked normal, whistling loudly as he unloaded the truck. When he went inside the building, I silently berated myself for being paranoid and headed home.

It was getting late, so it wasn't a surprise to see Michael's car parked in front of the house. I realized I hadn't talked to him all day. He had dinner waiting for me, with two lit candles on the table.

"Wow! What's the occasion?" I tossed my coat and keys on a nearby stool.

"You and me together, and alone." He smiled, but for an instant I saw something flicker in his eyes.

"That sounds wonderful! I know what's for dessert." I pulled him close to me by grabbing his belt buckle. "But what's for dinner?"

"Your favorite: basil and shrimp pesto, Caesar salad, French bread, and tiramisu for dessert . . . *one* of the desserts! I also managed to get my hands on the best bottle of Pinot Noir in town." He pulled me into a tight embrace, one that lingered just enough to make me suspicious.

"All right, mister." I pulled away. "You better tell me what's going on! Let me guess. You mistakenly drank a glass of water laced with LSD, and since you were out of your rational mind, you cheated on me with one of the Cleveland Browns cheerleaders," I quipped, although I was a little scared of the answer.

He tilted his head back, laughing. "Oh, how your mind works. Baby, you put all of those girls to shame. Even the strongest LSD wouldn't make me be unfaithful to you. C'mon, let's eat."

We managed to get through dinner before we wound up in the bedroom. Frankly, I wasn't sure I'd get through the salad. The girls were back with us tomorrow, so we needed to utilize our time together. Lying in bed, our bodies intertwined, I remembered how fortunate I was.

"Why I deserve any of this, I'll never understand," I said softly.

"What do you mean by that?" Michael propped himself up on an elbow.

"You. The girls. Sean. All of this." I waved my hands around. "I look back at things I've done in the past and keep wondering when they're going to catch up with me."

"Cee." Michael turned my face toward his. "I've been thinking. When Selina and Isabelle come back, why don't you take them to Florida for a couple of weeks? I estimate, by the time you get back, I'll have this case wrapped up and things will be normal again. Most important, I think you need the break."

"As wonderful as it sounds, I'm in the middle of two homicides." I groaned.

Michael sat up. "So what? You have fifteen detectives under you who are more than capable of handling it! Why do you have to be in the middle of every goddamn case? Don't you think that there are more important things in life? Like me and the kids?" He was angry.

I was stunned. "Do you want to tell me where the hell *that* came from?" I sat up, too. "Because right now, I feel like I was attacked without warning."

He put his face in his hands. "I don't know. I'm sorry. I just wish sometimes that you could put your job aside for a while. I think that taking the girls down to Siesta Key would be a wonderful way for you to unwind and spend some time with them. You could take Sean, too."

"Honey, they're all in school." I was confused. "Maybe you should tell me what this is really about. What happened to Aruba?"

He sighed and took a while before answering. "It's probably guilt. I feel guilty because I haven't been spending enough time with you guys lately, and I guess, if I knew you were down there having fun, it would ease my conscience a little."

I locked my narrowed eyes on his. "I'm sorry, but since when do *you* feel guilty about work? Since when do you think I put my job above my family?" I was angry now, and incredulous.

"I don't. Just forget I said anything." He did his best to put on a smile.

"No, I won't forget it. You brought it up—now I want a better explanation! This *guilt* bullshit isn't going to cut it. If I didn't know any better, I might think you wanted the kids and me away from here for a more suitable reason, like our safety. Is there something I need to know, Michael?"

"No, Cee, there's not. I was telling you the truth." He embraced me again. "God, I just love you so much! Do you know that?" He pulled away and looked at me with such intensity that it sent a barrage of chills through my body.

"Yes, Michael. I do," I whispered, and felt both mystified and frightened.

"Just don't ever forget that."

After we made love for the second time, we decided to venture back to the kitchen to clean up the remnants of our romantic dinner. While I was rinsing off plates, Naomi called.

"I thought you might want to know this. John Kruse was last seen at the unemployment office by one of the clerks."

"And?"

"Not much. He was in line, and she saw him walking out the door behind some guy. She could only see the back of him and said he had on a black coat. Not a highly trained observer, the clerk."

"Obviously. But that doesn't really mean anything. She doesn't know if he was with the guy, right? He could've just got tired of waiting for ten hours and left, probably right behind another customer." I smiled as I watched Michael load the dishwasher.

"True, true. She's coming in tomorrow for a formal, probably three-word statement, but I thought you'd want to know just the same."

"Of course. Thanks for the info."

It was another fifteen minutes before Michael and I were finished with the dinner dishes. Michael was a wonderful cook, but a messy one. We went into the living room where he put a couple of logs into the fireplace. I stood and looked out the window for a minute before relaxing on the sofa.

"How come you parked on the street?" I had noticed his car again.

He looked perplexed. "Oh," he finally remembered, "when I got home, the delivery guy was here and blocked the goddamn driveway. I meant to just park there for minute while I signed for the package." He prodded the logs with a poker, trying to get the fire going.

"What was the package?"

"Toner for the fax. I'm going to run out and pull the car into the garage before some idiot rips out my stereo."

"It's not like we live in crime central, hon. I think it'll be all right for one night." I didn't want him to leave me for a second.

"My short absence shall make your heart grow fonder." He kissed me gently. "Keep the sofa warm."

I heard him grab his keys before opening the garage door. I leaned my head back, closed my eyes, and smiled. Michael was, and had been since I'd known him, therapy for me. He was a man I loved like no other man. Hearing the fire crackle interrupted my thoughts. I stood up with the intention of closing the fireplace screen but was thrown against the wall beside me.

All I could hear was an explosion and glass breaking, and I felt the air being sucked out of the room. My ears felt like they, too, had exploded. It took a few moments to realize what exactly had happened.

It was only when I crawled to the large hole in the wall, where the windows used to be, that I saw that Michael's car was engulfed in flames.

The past had finally caught up with me.

CHAPTER FOUR

I didn't realize that I was screaming, or that I might be on fire, until someone pulled me out the front door by my arms. Several of my neighbors had heard the explosion. Everything happened so fast. My screams drowned out all of the voices around me asking if I was okay. Feeling no pain, at least no *physical* pain, I pushed the numerous arms away and flipped over onto my stomach to crawl on my hands and knees toward Michael's fiery car.

Please, God! Let him be okay! my head screamed. At least I think it was my head, but the words may have escaped my lips nonetheless; it didn't matter. My head felt foggy, like things weren't real. As the heat of the flames began to burn my face the closer I got, it became all too real. The arms grabbed me again to prevent me from going any farther, and there was no pushing them away this time.

"CeeCee, no! It's too hot!" It was my neighbor, Dave McDonald. "Listen to me! Are the kids in the house? CeeCee, please!"

I shook my head back and forth while listening to the sounds of the wailing sirens, growing closer.

"At—at Eric's!" The only words I could manage.

My eyes were locked on the fiery remnants of the car, looking for anything that would indicate Michael got out in time. I scanned the yard around me, hoping the force of the blast had thrown him far enough away, but I saw nothing. Maybe he was somewhere looking for me. Maybe he thought I was hurt, too. With Dave's burly arms still locked around me, I began screaming his name.

"Michael! Michaaael!"

My voice, hoarse by now, sounded so foreign to me I didn't even recognize it as my own.

"Michaaaael!"

Hearing no response, I began screaming again and felt Dave's arms tighten up their grip. Time was nonexistent. Things seemed to catapult into fast-forward, and when I looked back at the car, the firemen were putting out the last of the flames, steam rising from the burned-out and blackened shell.

Feeling the arms around me relax, I pushed them away and attempted to stand up. My legs shook and wobbled but were sturdy enough to get me to the car. When I saw one of the firemen look into the opening of the driver's side, I knew I should stop. He looked at the coworker standing next to him and began to shake his head in disbelief. Then they all looked at me. Their faces said it all: *You don't want to see this.* There were other people around, but I saw none of them. I heard nothing but silence.

Everyone watched as I made it to the passenger side of the car. The smell of gasoline and burning plastic would have been overwhelming to anyone else, but I was oblivious to it. Focusing on the pool of black, bubbling plastic, formerly the bumper, that lay on the ground, I tried to will myself not to look inside the car, but it was no use. With my body shaking and my breaths short and quick, I leaned toward the hole in the passenger side, just enough so that I had a clear view of the blackened, charred remains of the body that sat in the driver's seat. My tongue felt thick, and the bile began to rise in my throat. The sight was too much for my mind to absorb at that moment. It was almost as if my brain kept deflecting the image in an attempt to make it disappear, my mind screaming, *I don't want it! Take it away!*

Unfortunately, the image won. As it sank in and was absorbed, the foreign voice rose again with its horrific screams. It was soon after that I found myself mercifully succumbing to darkness.

I don't know how long I was out—maybe twenty minutes, maybe an hour. When I opened my eyes, I was in my bedroom, and an emergency medical technician was zipping up his bag on the floor next to my bed. My father, the sheriff, and two men in suits stood around me. I bolted upright, my heart racing, and grief ripped through me like a torrential downpour.

"Michael! Where's Michael?" I knew, but I wanted someone to tell me it had been a dream.

"Cee, baby . . ." My father, his voice quiet and hesitating, sat next to me on the bed and took my hand. The frown lines on his face made him look like he'd aged ten years.

"Oh God! Nooo!" My chest heaved forward and the reality of my irrevocable loss kicked in.

My father held me tightly to his chest while I screamed, cried, gagged, and hyperventilated. I kept praying over and over that I was having a nightmare. I remembered when I was young, I'd had nightmares that were so real, no one could ever convince me that

I had been asleep. I was silently begging someone to tell me that was the case now.

But no one did, and I didn't wake up with Michael next to me. Michael was dead, and the thought of never seeing him again was too much to bear. For one of the first times in my life, I didn't think I would be able to survive the blow. Of all the unfortunate and deadly situations I had found myself in, ones where I knew that no matter what, I would go on, this topped them all. Only when I heard my father soothingly whisper the names of my two daughters did I begin to get it together.

"Cee, honey, I know this is hard, but you have Selina and Isabelle to think about. You have to be strong for them. They need you," he said softly, while still holding me tight.

Sitting still and trying to take deep breaths in between sobs, I visualized their faces, and Sean's. Sean, who was the spitting image of his father and the light of his life, would be forever devastated. Even Selina and Isabelle had grown to love their stepfather in a way that would take them both to the brink. My father was right. Those three children needed me more than ever right now, and I had to be strong for them. But at that moment, they weren't here, and I would allow myself to grieve.

I hadn't noticed when Naomi and Coop walked in, or when Naomi went and got a cold washcloth, until she gently placed it on my face. Looking up, I saw her own eyes were red and puffy, tears streaming down her cheeks. We were all such close friends, the four of us. We had been through so much together. I knew this was hard for them as well. She knelt down beside the bed.

"CeeCee, I'm so sorry," she whispered between sniffles.

I could only nod and wipe my face with the soothing cloth. My head was pounding from the mother of all migraines, and my eyes were so swollen I could barely see. I continued taking deep breaths as my father left the room, while everyone else stood in silence, the pity in their eyes bearing down on me. When my father came back, it dawned on me he was in uniform. He must've heard the call go out over the police scanner and rushed right over. He handed me a small glass with brown liquid in it.

"What is it?" I asked groggily.

"Straight whiskey. Drink it—it'll help you calm down."

I'd once had a very bad experience with whiskey, and even as I smelled it, the nausea in my stomach churned like an out-of-control washing machine. However, after a couple small sips, my body began to relax, if ever so slightly. Laying my head back on my pillow and looking up at the ceiling for a moment, I realized the two unfamiliar men in suits were still in the room, their faces somber.

"Who are you?" My voice was almost inaudible.

The tall, elderly man in the dark navy blue suit stepped forward. He looked to be in his late sixties and had thinning gray hair and glasses. His face was as somber as everyone else's, but I noticed he had kind eyes.

"Mrs. Hagerman. I'm Supervising Agent Alan Keane, with the FBI." He spoke slowly. "I am—was—Michael's supervisor from Washington, DC."

My body subconsciously flinched when he called me Mrs. Hagerman, and it almost convulsed when he said Michael's name. He took off his glasses and wiped his eyes before continuing.

"Mrs. Hagerman, CeeCee, I am so sorry about your loss. I've been in Cleveland working with . . . with Michael on a very important case. I was on my way down to see him when this happened."

"Did you know this was going to happen?" I asked, almost accusing.

"When you're up to it, we'll talk. In the meantime, I have my best crime-scene specialists on their way down to process the . . . the scene. If there's anything I can do for you, please let me know."

He and the other man, who I assumed was an agent, left the room. I was too tired and too grief stricken to protest or ask any more questions right now. Not that any of this was hard to figure out. Michael had been investigating the Mafia, and now he had been killed by a car bomb. It wasn't difficult to understand. Coping would be an entirely different issue.

Redirecting my attention to the red and blue lights that were reflecting off my bedroom window, I instinctively started to get up.

"CeeCee, you don't need to look outside. Its best you don't. They're still processing everything right now. Eric's outside. Do you want me to go get him?" my father asked.

I nodded. The sheriff, L. Richard Stephens, who had remained silent throughout, began to follow my father out of the room. He was a close friend of my father, so I'd known him since I was a child. He stopped and said a few words.

"CeeCee, I'm sorry, but I'm glad you're not hurt—physically. You let me know if you need something.

Okay, kiddo?" He had a sympathetic smile but sadness in his eyes.

"Thank you, Sheriff."

Naomi and I were the only ones left in the room now. Coop had left earlier to assist the FBI with witness statements and anything else he could, no doubt. He was close friends with Michael, and his face showed that he was hurting. My head continued to throb, which prompted me to ask Naomi if she would get me some aspirin.

"Of course, where are they?"

"Inside the medicine cabinet, in the bathroom."

While Naomi was out of the room, rifling for my pain reliever, Eric came in. He was on duty, wearing his uniform, like my father. Although Eric and Michael had never got along, he wore a pained expression, surely anticipating our daughters' upcoming grief. He sat down on the bed next to me, where my father previously had sat, and took my hand.

"CeeCee, I'm so sorry."

My tears began to well up again. "Eric . . . the girls. Can you keep them one more night? I don't—I don't know how I'm gonna be able to tell them!" I began to sob.

He stayed silent, but nodded. Although we had been through a lot together over the last several years, one fact held true—our love for our little girls. Any parent wanted to protect their child from pain, sadness, and heartache. This was one time we couldn't.

"I think it would be best if we told them together, Cee. They'll need us both." He paused. "I think I'll just tell them you had to go out of town until the day after tomorrow. We'll tell them when I bring them over. Don't worry. You know I'll be here to help you and the girls through this." He leaned over and gave me a tight squeeze.

Naomi stood in the doorway of the bathroom until Eric left. Thankful for the aspirin, I found myself thinking of Sean.

"Naomi, Vanessa's supposed to drop Sean off in the morning—it's our scheduled weekend. Could you call her for me and tell her? I think it's best that she be the one to tell Sean."

"Sure, CeeCee. I'm gonna stay here tonight. I don't think you should be by yourself. Eric said outside, earlier, that he would get ahold of your mom and brother." She paused. "Do you know if the FBI is going to notify Michael's parents?"

For whatever reason, this thought reopened my floodgates. I began to sob uncontrollably again, begging for anyone that would listen to put me out of my misery. I desperately wanted Michael. I wanted to hold him, see him, feel his body against mine, smell his cologne, and look into his eyes. I thought of him, burned beyond recognition just outside the window of the bedroom we shared, and I couldn't take it anymore. Bringing my hands up to my head, I began to scream as loud as possible. I wanted to die, and was so hysterical that my father and Eric had to hold me down while the EMTs shot me with a sedative after Naomi called them. It took less than two minutes for the darkness to overcome me again.

"It's done, Sal."

"Done? I thought we weren't ready for two more days?"

"Cleveland got to him first, Sal. Blew him up in his own driveway."

Salvatore smiled. For the first time, he felt like sending

Cleveland a bottle of champagne. Not only had they taken care of a major problem, but also they'd taken the heat off Youngstown. Fools. Regardless, the FBI would now focus all of their attention on the agent's murder, instead of on them. It couldn't have worked out better.

"So, our glorious Agent Michael Hagerman is no more, eh? Fantastic." He paused. "What about his wife? Did they get her, too? I think I'd have to make a personal phone call offering my thanks for that one."

"No, sir, but she'll no longer be a problem. My source tells me that she's pretty much done upstairs, had to be sedated—the whole lot. I suspect that she'll be too over-come with grief to function from here on out."

"Just as long as she doesn't get 'overcome' with re-venge." He thought while he chewed his bottom lip. "I still want our eye on her—you hear? We still don't know what he's told her about us."

"Yes, sir."

"If that Irish bitch makes one move that looks like she's on our ass . . . take care of her."

CHAPTER FIVE

Sleeping fitfully most of the night, I didn't know if I was awake or dreaming half of the time. I remembered at one point looking over and seeing Michael sleeping next to me. I nudged him a little, he opened his eyes and reached his hand out, touching my cheek.

"I love you, baby," he whispered.

"I love you too, Michael."

I breathed a sigh of relief; my nightmare had been just that. Only when I opened my eyes and saw Naomi sleeping in the recliner did I realize I was wrong. The familiar thud in my chest and the reality of it all crashed down on me again, bringing forth immediate tears. Naomi woke up instantly.

"CeeCee, let me get you something. Do you want some water?" she asked, handing me tissues.

I shook my head. Today was the day I had to start over, the day to begin grieving so I could get it out of the way and make it eventually stop. This was the day to start my new life—without Michael. I don't know how I managed, but I ultimately got out of bed, showered, and dressed. My first priority was to call Vanessa and make sure Sean was okay. Naomi had called her last night. She said Vanessa didn't take it too well, either—not that I was surprised. Not long before, Vanessa had tried to blackmail me into leaving Michael so they could get back together. It clearly hadn't worked. She sounded hoarse when she answered the phone, and just as I suspected, she said Sean wasn't doing well.

"He was up all night, crying off and on. He was crying for you, too, CeeCee." She began to sob. "His father meant the world to him! I don't know what to do!"

It was all I could do not to break down. My own tears flowing like Niagara Falls, I told her one of my reasons for calling.

"Vanessa, if it's okay, I'd like to have Sean with me for the weekend. The girls will be here and help him through it . . . It'll be good for Sean and them to be together." I paused, feeling myself choking up. "It'll be good for me to have him here. Please."

She breathed deeply into the phone. "I'll have him there by three."

As I hung up, it dawned on me that this was the most cordial conversation Vanessa and I had ever had. After the blackmailing incident, we'd hadn't spoken so much as one word to each other.

My next call was to Eric. I would pick up the girls the following morning, but I wanted some time alone with Sean. I became an Academy Award–winning actress when he put Selina on the phone, trying to sound cheerful, until she asked about Michael.

"Can I talk to Michael? I want to tell him about the FBI movie I watched last night!"

I was shaking like a leaf, and my heart sank. "Oh, honey . . . He—he had to run some errands and go pick Sean up." I held my breath. "He'll be back later."

"How come you sound funny?"

My daughter never misses a beat. "I think I'm getting a cold is all. I'll see you tomorrow morning."

I had to be strong for all of my children, Sean included. If they saw me in pieces, they surely wouldn't be able to cope.

Looking at the clock every fifteen minutes in anticipation of Sean's arrival, I both welcomed and dreaded his visit. Being around him, a smaller version of Michael, would both comfort and sadden me. I had sent Naomi home, assuring her I would call later. After she left, I noticed she had taken all of my guns with her. I'm sure she thought she was being careful, but if I truly wanted to commit suicide, there were certainly other ways . . . not that I had any intention of doing so.

Vanessa arrived half an hour early, and by the time I got outside, Sean was already out of the car, and she was standing in the driveway looking at the blackened roadway where Michael's car had exploded. Her eyes were red and puffy, and she was starting to fall apart. The last thing we needed was for Sean to put everything together while watching his mom stare at the road. I let the door slam so Sean would get distracted. It did the trick.

"CeeCee!" He came running to me at full speed.

Seeing the tears well up in his eyes while his face was scrunched up, I caught him and fell to my knees, holding him tightly and sobbing. He cried right along with me.

"My daddy's gone! He's in heaven, CeeCee!" he wailed.

I squeezed him tighter, and he buried his face into my shoulder. Vanessa stood quietly, watching us, her own tears still flowing. Holding Sean was the closest I could get to Michael, and I didn't want to let him go. Nonetheless, both Vanessa and I needed to keep ourselves together for Sean's sake.

"Vanessa," I sniffled, "do you want to come in for some coffee or something?"

"No, thanks, CeeCee . . ." She wiped her eyes. "I need to get going. I have my own grieving to do."

I responded with only a nod, and Sean and I watched her drive away before we went into the house. We sat, talked, and cried for hours. Sean was the best medicine I could've asked for. I knew I had to be strong for him, so I suppressed my own grief enough that I felt able to function. It was a long night, but at least we had each other. The next morning would be another horrible affair, when Selina and Isabelle arrived.

They, like the rest of us, didn't take it well when Eric and I gave them the bad news, Selina especially. She was the oldest and had never experienced the realities of life and death. Michael was the first person she had ever known who had died, and it took such a toll on her I had to put her in counseling within a week.

Michael's funeral was an entirely different issue. The FBI, for reasons they refused to discuss with me, insisted on a small, private service, instead of the full-blown law-enforcement burial. I was furious, to say the least. Alan Keane called me several times and tried to explain. He insisted that while they were searching for Michael's killers, they thought it best to try to give the impression that Michael had not been killed—only injured. Therefore, no obituary was printed, and the incident had not been reported by any news agency anywhere. He felt that if the higher-ups among Michael's killers thought they had failed, the conflict between them would lead the FBI right to them. My opinion of Alan Keane's explanation was that it was bullshit, and I told him as much. They were keeping something from me; there wasn't a doubt in my mind. However, he said, once Michael's killers were caught, a service with all of the bells and whistles would be held. Never in my life had I heard of such a thing.

The weeks that followed were the most difficult of my life. Each time I walked into our closet to pack up Michael's clothes, I walked right back out. The last time in the closet was the day I decided his things would be put away only when I was ready, and now wasn't the time. Vanessa still let me take Sean on the designated weekends, which surprised me. Sean did wonders for me, and I think I did the same for him.

Dreams of Michael came every night in my restless sleep, and I found myself wanting to sleep more, just to see him. When I couldn't fall asleep, several glasses of wine or vodka did the trick. The more I drank, the more I slept, and therefore, the more I saw Michael. Eric several times expressed his concern, taking the girls more than usual, but I found myself caring less and less about anything.

My days went as follows: wake up, drink a bottle of wine, sleep, wake up, drink more, sleep, and so on. When my vacation time and sick leave finally ran out two months later, it was time to go back to work.

My first day back didn't go well. I was hungover and found myself craving more alcohol. Naomi,

Coop, my father, the sheriff—everyone tried to talk me into counseling, but I refused. I told myself to get it together and dive into my work. As easy as it sounded, I wasn't aware of how difficult that would be. Naomi was around me so much it began to get annoying.

"How 'bout Coop and I stop by after work and take you to dinner? You're a skeleton, CeeCee. You really need to eat something." She stood in front of my desk with her arms crossed.

"You guys really need to stop." Sighing, I put my face in my hands. "I know you all are worried, but trust me, I am *not* going to kill myself, so you can stop all of the fucking nightly checkups at my house."

She sat down in a chair. "I don't know that we're really worried about you committing suicide, Cee . . . There's ways of slowly killing yourself, ya know? You're not eating, you're drinking too much, and if you don't get it together, you will eventually kill yourself—whether intentionally or not."

Taking a deep breath, I leaned back in my chair. "I just don't know if I can do this, Naomi." Tears began to fill my eyes.

She leaned forward. "Yes, you can! You're the strongest person I have ever met in my life! You were strong before you even met Michael, and you will be strong now!" She stood up. "This isn't the CeeCee I know. She can overcome anything, even the death of the man she loved, for her children and for herself. Now, take the homeless murders and review the file. Dive back into work and get your mind off all of this! We've had nothing since you've been gone, and maybe you can find whatever it is that we missed."

She pulled a thick brown expanding file from her briefcase and threw it on my desk. It landed with a loud thud.

"Let me know if you find anything, and let me know if you need anything." She left my office.

I stared at the file. For some reason, I had a feeling that if I opened it, it would be like working. That would mean that I was moving on without Michael, making me feel guilty somehow. Still lost in thought, I was jolted back into the present when someone knocked loudly on my door. It was the new detective, Justin Brown.

"Sergeant Gallagher?"

"Yes, Justin. Come on in."

"I just wanted to tell you I'm glad to see you back, and I'm sorry about what happened."

I did my best to smile. "Thank you. So how are your cases coming along?"

We talked briefly before he left. People expressing their condolences was something that would take time to get used to. Flipping through the homeless-murder file was no good. I couldn't concentrate and certainly didn't find anything that might've been missed. There were two murders to be solved, and I was worthless.

The third murder came less than two weeks after I returned to work. Thirty-nine-year-old Jamie Ellerman had hitchhiked his way to Mansfield from Louisville. He had initially thought he had relatives here, but found out they had either died or moved. Finding himself with no money or transportation, he walked to the nearest homeless shelter, where he had been staying for the last five days. His body, minus both kidneys, was found in Ferndale Park, at the end of Harmon Avenue.

Harmon Avenue, also known as "the drive-through," was the street that supplied the majority of the city's crack cocaine. House after house was a crack store. People literally went door-to-door to feed their habit. Ellerman's body was found by a crack addict who had gone to the park to smoke her morning breakfast. Most addicts are so eager for their supply, they can't wait to get home, so they go right to the park. On any given day, one could find ten to fifteen people in the park, smoking crack. All of us deduced at least five to ten people had seen the body and not reported it. Why this addict decided to call the police was anyone's guess.

Pulling into the parking lot of the park, I felt different than I had at other homicides I'd been to. It was the lack of emotion, the hardhearted indifference. I didn't care. Looking at the body, my usual thoughts of compassion were replaced with *So what if another no-good piece of shit was carved like a Thanksgiving Day turkey. Someone ought to give a medal to the killer—he did the world a favor.* That was the day I knew my career in law enforcement was over.

After standing over the body and staring at it for a while, Coop came over and asked my opinion.

"What do you think? It's definitely the same killer. I'm starting to think it's one of the high-end dealers around here looking for a quick buck."

I glared at him. "Does it really matter? All that happened here is the taxpayers got another break from having to support this nonworking, drug-addicted shitbag! Do we really want to find the killer?

Maybe if we let him do his business, there wouldn't be any more welfare recipients in this county."

Coop's jaw dropped ever so slightly as he stared at me, looking as if I'd just announced it was me who was killing the homeless. Raising my left eyebrow, I glared right back at him.

"Alrighty then, I see somebody isn't quite ready to come back to work." He gently grabbed my arm. "I've got plenty of vacation time built up. Why don't you let me donate it to you so you can take some more time off?"

I jerked my arm away. "I'm fine, and I'm perfectly capable of doing my job!" I pointed at the body. "What difference does it make? Huh? If we catch this guy's killer, then next week we'll have someone else putting their baby on the heater or shooting their wife in the face! It goes on and on, Coop! Maybe tomorrow we'll have the mayor getting blown up in his car!"

My reference to the car bomb shocked Coop, especially since the actual cause of Michael's death had never come up in our conversations. Maybe he was right. Maybe it was too soon for me to be back at work, looking at dead bodies.

"CeeCee, try and relax." Coop's voice was quiet, since there were other people around.

"Don't you fucking tell me to relax, Detective! Go start interviewing the residents on the street to see if they saw anything." I nodded toward the houses. "That's an order!"

Coop's face turned red as he pursed his lips and clenched his fists. He was unmistakably pissed. Coop and I had started our careers together from day one, and never had I talked to him like that, until now.

"No problem, Sergeant." He turned and walked away.

I felt like crying again. It was apparent I was falling apart, not getting better. Several feet away, Naomi was looking at me, knowing an altercation had just occurred between her husband and me, but not knowing why.

After confirming with the crime lab that they had the scene under control, I headed for my car. While driving home, I called Naomi on her cell phone and told her I was going home sick, and hung up before she could finish asking for an explanation. I stopped at the store and grabbed several bottles of wine and vodka. I had one of the vodka bottles opened and halfway drunk before pulling into my driveway. Stripping off my clothes and getting into my bed sobbing, I finished off the bottle. Drifting back into the darkness soon after, I knew Michael would be waiting.

"Are you sure he's dead?"

"Yeah, Sal, I'm sure."

"How come nothing ever showed up on the news or in the papers?"

The man smiled and sat down. "Another FBI ploy. They want us to think that the job was botched and Hagerman is still alive. Then we'll start fighting among ourselves and bring the family out in the open."

"You sure?"

"Of course I'm sure. He was blown to pieces in his own front yard."

"And her? You followed my orders, right? Someone's got their eye on her?"

Sal sure was on edge, the man thought. "Yes, Sal, all is

taken care of. She's pretty much gone off the deep end, so again, don't worry so much."

"I can't help but worry. If this gets fucked up, we're all done."

CHAPTER SIX

Calling in sick for five more days after the homicide, I was out of sick leave and wasn't getting paid. Not that I cared. Money was the least of my worries. Michael had always tried to talk me into quitting my job. We were pretty much financially set for life. A while ago, I had written a book on a high-profile serial child murderer I had investigated and had acquired a substantial advance—along with significant sales. With Michael's salary from the FBI, I never really needed to work for the money. I did it because it was in my blood. Now, since Michael had been killed, technically in the line of duty, I would be getting a huge payout by the United States government. At this bleak point in my life, the sheriff could tell me to turn my badge and gun in tomorrow, and I couldn't have given two shits about it.

On the third day of my unpaid sick leave, the phone calls began. I didn't give the first couple of calls much thought. The phone would ring, and I wouldn't answer. Unless the caller ID showed Eric's number, in case Selina and Isabelle wanted to talk to me, or Vanessa's, I didn't want to talk to anyone. Regardless, the number showed up as private. Eventually I decided the phone would just keep ringing until I answered it. When I did, there was silence. Unquestionably, someone was on the other end, but nothing was ever said. After a few seconds and several times of my saying, "Hello? Who the fuck is this?" they hung up.

The long, sleek, black sedan pulled into the empty parking lot and slowly parked in one of the spaces that lined the back row. Minutes later, another sedan, dark blue, rolled into the lot and made its way toward the black car. The man driving the blue car exited his vehicle and got into the other one, facing the boss himself.

"How bad is it?"

"It's getting worse," the man answered.

The boss sighed. "I was hoping it wouldn't come to this . . . I was counting on her."

"Maybe we shouldn't give up yet. There's still time, but we need to be careful. They've got an eye on her."

"I know, I know. The problem is, we're going have to do something soon. He's losing his patience, and I don't know how much longer he'll last." He paused for a moment. "Keep our agent on her, no matter what, and make sure he doesn't blow his cover. If he does, we're all done."

The last day of my sick leave was spent at the park with my daughters. I even managed to stay sober for a day. Doing my best to maintain a smile, my attention was drawn to a man sitting across the park, in the pavilion. He had arrived after we did and went directly to the pavilion to sit at a picnic table and read the newspaper. I didn't think much of him at first, but my suspicion grew when I caught him peering over the top of his newspaper at me. There was something familiar about the man that I couldn't quite describe. I ran through my mental list of local sex offenders I had investigated and arrested. A lot of them frequented children's playgrounds, parks, and such. Noticing immediately that he didn't have any children with him, I put myself on guard, but still couldn't remember where I had seen him before.

Continuing to play with the girls, I did my best to keep tabs on the newspaper man. Only when I took a quick glance and saw him with a black object in his hand did I become alarmed. Knowing he had been caught, he hurriedly put the object behind the newspaper. *I think he just took a picture of me*, I thought, while shuffling the girls to our car.

"Selina, get into the car with your sister and lock the doors. I have to take care of something," I ordered.

"But Mom—!" she began to argue.

"Just do it!" I raised my voice while grabbing my gun out of my purse.

I started walking directly toward the newspaper man. *He had better have one hell of an explanation as to why he was photographing my daughters and me.* Seeing that I was headed right for him, the man jumped up from the picnic table and almost jogged to a small red compact car that was parked by the pavilion.

"Hey! Wait a minute!" I yelled, and began running.

It was no use. He drove out of the lot like a bat out of hell, so fast that I was unable to read the license plate. More alarmed than ever, I ran back to my car in hopes of catching up with him. If I could at least get his license-plate number, that would help, but he was nowhere to be found. It was as if he'd disappeared into thin air.

Both the girls were upset—understandably, since

I shouldn't have done something like that while they were in the car. Michael's death even seemed to have sucked the common sense out of me along with everything else. Isabelle was crying, and Selina was on the verge.

"Mom! Why are you chasing that guy? Is he a bad guy?" Her voice was shaking.

"I don't know, honey, I just . . . We'll go home now. I'm sorry, guys."

"I wanna go to Daddy's house!" Isabelle screamed.

"Me, too!" Selina concurred.

"You guys! Just hang on a minute! We'll go home and order some pizza."

"No! I want Daddy and Jordan!" Isabelle continued.

My heart was crushed. My own children didn't even want to be around me, not that anyone could blame them. Eric seemed confused when I called and told him the girls wanted to stay with him, but he agreed. When we pulled into his driveway, he was standing outside with his and Jordan's son, Brandon. Isabelle jumped out of the car and ran to him, bawling along the way.

"Daddy! Mommy was chasin' a bad guy, and she had her gun, and I was scared!"

Eric caught her and picked her up, letting her cry for a few minutes before he glared at me.

"Oh, for God's sake, Eric, it wasn't that bad!" I tried to convince him.

"Yes, it was, Mom." Selina intervened, not helping matters.

After Isabelle calmed down, Eric told her and Selina to take their brother indoors. Both of the girls came over and kissed me good-bye, but it was more than obvious they were happier here. I quickly launched into an explanation of the events, but Eric held his hand up, cutting me off before I finished.

"I don't even want to hear the rest." The lines in his face deepened. "Go home. I'll be over in a little bit. We need to talk."

He turned around and went inside, leaving me standing in the driveway. I stared at the house for a few minutes before getting in my car to drive home, crying the entire way. I was worried. Eric's face had told me he wasn't happy with me, and he was going to do something about it. My kids didn't want to be with me, bottom line.

My entire life was falling apart. And while I was sitting on my living-room sofa, waiting for Eric to arrive, the thought of putting a gun to my head and pulling the trigger flashed through my mind, the first time a thought like that had ever entered my head. It was terrifying to me. In fact, it disturbed me so much, I had to stand up and walk back and forth across the room, trying to erase the thought altogether.

I am going crazy! my mind screamed. Picking up a picture of the girls and holding it to my chest, I took deep breaths and sat back down. By the time Eric pulled in the driveway, I had calmed down a bit. Not that I expected it to last. He wanted to talk to me about something serious, and I didn't think it was the girls' future college choices.

He sat at the kitchen table while I poured him some coffee that I'd just made. He seemed to have had aged in the recent months. Eric had always been very handsome. In his early forties, his dark hair, skin, and eyes almost gave him a Latin appearance.

But he was German, and Isabelle was the mirror image of her father. Always a fitness fanatic, Eric had arms the size of large tree trunks. But today he looked different, and it worried me. Being married to him for over ten years, I didn't ever remember seeing him like this; he looked stressed. I put his cup of coffee in front of him and sat down.

"Well." I pulled a cigarette out of a pack on the table. "What did you want to talk about?"

"I want to talk about you." He locked his eyes on mine.

I lit my cigarette. To say I had been chain-smoking is an understatement.

"Me? What about me?"

"CeeCee, I know you've been through a very traumatic event with Michael's death and all, but you just don't seem to be getting any better." He leaned forward. "I've heard about some things going on at work, and some of the stories the girls tell me when they stay at my house genuinely concern me. Last week Isabelle wanted to know why you suddenly talk 'funny' all of the time, as if you're sleepy. Exactly how much are you drinking a day?"

My defenses going on red alert, my body stiffened up. "I have a glass of wine here and there, Eric. It's not as if I'm some falling-down, pissing-my-pants lush! There's no problem."

"It sounds to me like there is. I mean, look at you, Cee . . . You look like you haven't eaten or slept in months! I know this has been hard for you, but there are two little girls that need a mother!" He was getting angry. "What the fuck happened to you? You were always able to get through anything—especially for your kids!"

I stood up, walked over to the door, and opened it. "If this is why you came over—to tell me what a piece-of-shit mother I am—then you can just leave!"

He stayed put. "Come over here and sit down. I'm not finished."

My eyes began to well up with tears as I conceded. "Okay, finish."

He scooted his chair next to me and took my hand. "Look, CeeCee. You know I have never stopped loving you. You *know* that! But our daughters are all I have, and I just don't think you're able to take care of them right now."

My heart began to thud in my chest. Beginning to tremble, I sensed what was coming.

"I hate more than anything to do this, but the girls are going to stay full-time with me for a while, at least until you get yourself together."

I was staggered. "You can't do that! I need them!"

"I'm sorry, CeeCee, but I am doing it. If you want to fight me on it, I'll file for temporary custody with only supervised visitation rights for you. You can't take care of yourself right now, let alone those two little girls. Jordan and I feel that it's best."

"Oh, *Jordan* does, does she?" I tore my hand from his and stood up. "What the fuck does that bitch have to do with anything?"

"She's their stepmother and she loves them. You know that."

Seriously beginning to lose my composure, I begged. "Eric . . . please! I need them!"

"I'll let you see them on weekends, but only if your dad is with you." He tried to hug me, but I pushed away. "You need help, CeeCee. For Selina and Isabelle, please, go get some help." His eyes were watery.

"Get the fuck out of my house!" I screamed.

Eric sighed and nodded, then walked to the door. Before he left, he turned around and looked at me with nothing but compassion—and pity.

"If you don't want to do this for yourself, then at the very least do it for your daughters."

"Get out!"

He closed the door behind him, leaving me on the floor in a heap of blubbering self-loathing. Now I had officially lost my children. As for Sean, even Vanessa had been making excuses over the last month about why he couldn't stay the weekend. As I lay sobbing on the floor of my kitchen, the vision of the gun to my head returned, and this time it didn't go away. I crawled over to the counter and stood up long enough to grab a bottle of vodka before slumping back down on the floor. What a pathetic excuse for a human being I was. After setting my bottle down on the floor, I made my way to the cabinet above the desk in the kitchen. I always kept a small revolver in there, one Naomi didn't find, in case I needed a gun quickly. Holding it in my right hand while cradling the bottle of vodka in the other, I took long drinks every other minute. I sat in the corner of my kitchen and began to spin the barrel of the gun, looking at all of the bullets and wondering which one would be the one to end all of my pain.

God must've had me on his watchdog list that night because I passed out before making the decision to take my own life. Dreams of Michael flooded my subconscious, as if he were right there with me. He was caressing my cheek, telling me that things would get better and not to give up. However, when he touched my cheek, it felt so real, I jerked myself awake.

The morning light flooded through the kitchen, so bright, my eyes immediately began to close. My cheek still tingled from where I had dreamed that Michael touched it. Raising my hand to feel it, I realized I was still holding my gun. Horrified that killing myself had even been a option, I tossed the gun across the kitchen floor, trying to get it as far away from me as possible.

Believe it or not, that was the day I decided to go back to work. I couldn't fathom that I had actually contemplated shooting myself. It sent chills through my body every time I thought about it. What if I had done it in my drunken state? My daughters would be grieving right now and probably would be ruined for the rest of their lives.

Even though my head felt like an ax had been embedded in it, I managed to get myself up, showered, and dressed. I didn't bother to call Naomi and tell her of my impending workday, because I would then have to address the hundreds of unanswered messages left by her and Coop checking on my well-being. That was something that could be dealt with later. For right now, getting myself together and driving to the department was the best I could do.

Everyone was shocked to see me. I ignored their stares and whispers, knowing they thought I had gone off the deep end and had left the department for good. Naomi was on my heels the minute I walked into our section of the building and followed me right into my office.

"I have been calling and calling, for Christ's sake!" She was fuming. "We thought something happened to you! Didn't you hear us pounding on your door for the last two days? I almost told Coop to kick it in, but he called Eric, who thankfully told us you were still alive!"

"Where's the homeless murder file?" I was scattering papers across my desk.

Naomi's jaw dropped. "You have been gone for five days without any word, and you want to discuss a murder case? Did you hear a fucking word I've said?"

"I heard you." I crossed my arms and looked at her defiantly. "Are you firing me?"

"Of course not!"

"Then would you please find the file for me? There are some things I need to look at," I said calmly.

She stared at me for a long time before turning and leaving my office. She returned in less than two minutes with the file.

"Coop had it," she said coldly. "Let me know what you need."

I sat in my chair and let out a sigh. A part of me felt bad for how I'd just treated Naomi. We had come a long way in repairing our relationship, and I hoped it hadn't been undone.

After grabbing four aspirin out of my purse and eating them like candy, I pulled the stack of papers out of the file, sorting them by date. Beginning to make a list of things to be done, I stopped long enough to make a pot of coffee. It would take me hours to re-familiarize myself with the case, and I needed to be alert. Making notes along the way, some of the things that hadn't been followed up dawned on me, things that Coop had apparently overlooked. After reading the coroner's report on all three murders, I called him immediately.

What hadn't caught my attention before was that

the first victim, Daniel Huber, had been strangled—
after his kidney and hand were removed. My question to the coroner was what his opinion on that was.

"You can live without a kidney, CeeCee. That
wouldn't necessarily have killed the guy right away,
nor would cutting his hand off, which I believe was
some form of torture. He would eventually have died
from infection and internal bleeding if he wasn't seen
by a medical professional, but based on the time-
tables, he died right after they took his kidney."

"So you determined he was still alive when they
took it? How'd you do that?" I was furiously scribbling down notes.

"He had gouge marks on the palm of his right
hand from his own fingernails, and had bitten the
tip of his tongue off. That tells me his fists were
clenched and he was in excruciating pain. Having
his hand cut off would be instantaneous, but to have
your kidney removed while you're awake would
take some time. I can only deduce that he lost con-
sciousness at some point from the pain, but he suffered up until then, no doubt."

"And the guy who had his liver taken?"

"Instant death. You can live with a partial liver, but
not without any at all. He also showed signs of being
conscious during the removal. He actually broke several of his teeth from his jaw being clenched so hard."

"A partial liver?"

"Some living liver donors can give a partial liver.
The liver will actually regenerate in both the donor
and the recipient, but again, you can't live without
one—period."

"Just like both kidneys?" I referred to the third
victim.

"Just like both kidneys. And he was just as awake as the other two."

I thanked the coroner and hung up. Then I reviewed my notes. Whoever took these organs didn't want these men left alive. There would easily have been ways to take one kidney without killing the donor. Since it was assumed that whoever was performing the actual removal was medically educated, they could merely have knocked him out and sewn him back up. This led me to believe there were time constraints on the part of the killer or killers. They didn't have time to screw around and restitch the victim. They took the organ, dumped the body on their way to wherever, and were done with it. Throwing my pen down, I leaned back in my chair and stretched before I began to type up my conversation with the coroner. In doing so, my thoughts kept drifting to Dr. Esposito and Dr. Schmidt. This new information told me that a trip back to Cleveland was in order. Dr. Schmidt had yet to be interviewed, and now was as good a time as any. Except there was one more phone call to make, and it had nothing to do with my case. It was a call I had been putting off.

"I'd like to speak to Supervising Agent Alan Keane, please," I politely asked the FBI secretary who answered the phone.

"Who is calling?"

"CeeCee Gallagher." I paused and swallowed. "Agent Michael Hagerman's wife." I noticed my hand was shaking.

"Just a moment, please."

She kept me on hold for almost five minutes, which enabled me to change my nervousness to anger.

When the phone clicked back over, it was the secretary again.

"Ms. Gallagher, he's in a meeting right now and asked me to get a number for you. He'll call you back shortly."

"He has my number, and you can go give him another message. Tell him if he doesn't call my office within five minutes, I will call every news station in the country to inform them how the FBI covered up my husband's murder." I slammed the phone down and noticed I was still trembling.

Less than two minutes later, my phone rang. It was Alan Keane.

"CeeCee? I'm sorry. I was in a meeting. Did something happen?"

"No, nothing has happened, which is precisely the point. What the hell are you people doing to find out who killed my husband? No one has called me, and quite frankly, I'm pretty pissed about it."

He breathed deeply into the phone. "I understand you're upset, but believe me, we are working on it. We want to find these people just as much as you do."

"I doubt that."

"Regardless, we've been hitting several dead ends, and we're trying to work around them. It's not easy."

"What type of bomb was used on the car? Was it wired to the ignition system?"

A long silence followed. He didn't expect a question like that, nor did he want to answer it. The FBI was all about secrecy. Alan Keane cleared his throat before he finally spoke.

"Uh, no, it wasn't wired to the ignition. Those

types of VBIEDs—I'm sorry, that's what the FBI calls car bombs. They're technically 'vehicle-borne improvised explosive devices,' VBIEDs. Anyway, those types of VBIEDs haven't been used in a long time. Every once in a while, they'll turn up, but they're pretty rare. They're extremely difficult to install and very easy to detect. With today's cars—their security and computer systems—a bomb wired to an ignition can set off the car's alarm or drain its electrical system. No, this bomb was placed under the fan belt and detonated when the car began to move."

I felt ill. "You can't track it anywhere?"

"Every hardware store in the country sells the stuff to make these. Normal fuel was used, but really not a significant amount. The bomb, in this case, was made to—" He stopped.

"Made to what?" My heart was pounding.

"Stun and burn."

I set the phone down. The bile and familiar lump in my throat began to rise. The warm wetness that filled my eyes came swiftly. Hearing Alan Keane's voice through the phone, I shook my head, wiped my eyes, and continued my conversation.

"CeeCee? CeeCee, are you there?"

"I'm here."

"I'm so sorry. I didn't know how else to say it. I shouldn't have said it that way."

"It's okay. I want to know . . . Who were the people Michael was investigating? I know they were Mafia, but I want family names."

"I can't tell you that, CeeCee. You should understand why, but I can't give you that information right now. Like I said earlier, we've hit a few dead ends, but we're slowly working our way around them." He paused. "This is going to take some time."

"I have to go. Thank you, Alan."

Slamming the phone down, I was both outraged and devastated at the same time. This wasn't right; something wasn't right with their investigation. They knew goddamn well who had killed Michael. They had been close to making arrests in the investigation before Michael died. He had told me he would be wrapping things up in several weeks, so why was everything being held up now?

Knowing I wouldn't get any answers today, I gathered my things and decided to leave for Cleveland early. As I picked up my briefcase, my eyes fell to the calendar that lay on my desk. The holidays were right around the corner. I hadn't paid attention to the changes in weather or the festive lights going up on my neighbor's homes. I had been living in my own distorted reality. We always celebrated Christmas and Thanksgiving in a big way at our house. Our yearly ritual of decorating the house right before Thanksgiving, picking out a Christmas tree, and making Christmas cookies would not come this year. This year, I would be totally alone, and it scared me to death.

I poked my head in Naomi's office and told her where I was going and why. She still seemed a little miffed, but not to the extent that she'd been earlier. She even offered to go with me, but I declined.

During my drive, I called Dr. Schmidt's office and requested an appointment with him. The secretary immediately informed me that she had been told to relay a message that Dr. Schmidt would not speak to me unless he was in the presence of his attorney, and furthermore, that no interview would occur unless he was being charged with a crime.

Expecting the same treatment at Dr. Esposito's office, I was not surprised when his plastic wife glared at me as soon as I walked in the door. The waiting room was full of patients, so she waited until I got to the receptionist's window before banning me from the office.

"You are no longer welcome here, and you need to leave. Unless you have a search warrant or criminal charges against my husband, he doesn't want to speak to you. If you don't leave, I will be forced to contact the local police and have you removed," she ordered.

"How long did you have to practice that little dissertation for you to remember it? Since you probably don't even know the definition of words like *search warrant* or *criminal charges*, I assume you must have all that written down in front of you somewhere. On that note, I'll leave. No need to contact the locals." Smiling, I left the office.

Something had caused the turnaround from the doctors. Of course, they could've simply contacted their attorneys and explained my visit. Any attorney who had successfully passed the bar exam would tell them not to talk to me. I wouldn't either, if I was them.

Since it was nearing the end of the day and I didn't want to go home, I decided to sit in my car and wait for Dr. Esposito to leave again. Maybe this time I'd follow him somewhere that actually linked him to my case. However, when he did leave, I didn't believe that his drive to the nearest hotel to meet a twentysomething blonde would be the thing to do it. Not that his extramarital affair was against the law, but I snapped a few pictures anyway. They might have come in handy down the road if I had to turn his wife against him. If not, I could shove them in her face for the sheer thrill of it. After driving past Dr. Schmidt's already-closed office, I headed home.

It was dark by the time I pulled into my driveway. Seeing my own dark, looming house made me remember how it had once been. It made me remember how I couldn't wait to get home. How when I'd walked through the door, my family barraged me with hugs and kisses. Michael would be cooking one of his specialty dishes in the kitchen, filling the house with wonderful aromas. Now it was cold and unfriendly, and I ached for those times.

I couldn't bring myself to go in just yet, so I sat out on the front porch swing for a while. The air was cold. After living in Ohio most of my life, the smell in the air alone told me snow was coming. Not that it mattered; there wouldn't be any skiing, sled-riding, or making snowmen this year, no sir.

As I prepared to light my millionth cigarette of the night, a very eerie and familiar feeling came over me. It was the feeling that someone was watching me. I put my lighter down, stood up, and walked to the end of the porch to see into the side yard. Nothing. As I walked to the other end, my eyes scanned the darkness and shadows but again saw nothing. Opting not to reclaim my seat on the swing, I stood and looked out at the street before me. Someone was out there—I'd have bet my life on it.

There had been times in the past when I chastised myself for being paranoid when this feeling came, but after learning that my instincts had been right every time, I listened to them. There wasn't a doubt in my mind that it was either the Mafia or someone related to the homeless murders watching me.

I slowly backed up, and when I reached my front door, I turned around and went inside. If it was in fact the Mafia watching me right now, I was in serious trouble.

CHAPTER SEVEN

I couldn't sleep and didn't want to stay alone in my house tonight. On edge, I paced around my kitchen before deciding to leave. Less than forty-eight hours ago, I had contemplated suicide, and now I was standing in my own home terrified someone was going to kill me. As I grabbed the keys to my personal car, a thought stopped me in my tracks—the thought of a car bomb. My car had been there all day. I had used my department-issued SUV when I drove to Cleveland.

I dashed upstairs to my bathroom and grabbed my makeup mirror. Out of the downstairs closet came a roll of duct tape and a broom. After attaching the mirror to the end of the broom handle using the tape, I went into the garage and turned on the lights.

Even though I wasn't experienced enough in explosives to know exactly what to look for, I knew enough that any black electrical tape, colored wires, or any type of clock or watch would be a major clue. Lying on my garage floor, I slowly slid the broom handle with the mirror under my car. Scouring every inch, I found myself soaked with sweat despite the rapidly falling temperatures outside. Once I was satisfied there were no bombs attached to the bottom of my car, I thought about what Alan Keane had told me.

The bomb that killed Michael had been placed under the fan belt in the engine. I needed to look down in the engine from above, since I had already looked underneath. From what I could see, there was nothing but an engine—all was as it should be.

After slamming the hood down and tossing the broom to the side of the garage, I brushed myself off and got inside my car. My hand was slightly trembling as it turned the ignition. When I'd put the car in reverse and successfully backed onto the road, I let out a large burst of air. I hadn't even realized I had been holding my breath. Laughing, my foot planted firmly on the brake, I was overcome by the recognition of how absurd my paranoia was. My laughing stopped when I noticed the fading black spot on the road, a spot that had been purposely ignored over the last several months.

Why in the hell would the mob watch me? I thought. Michael was dead, so the threat was gone. There was no reason for them to watch me. Even if they had in the beginning, they would see that I had turned into nothing more than a washed-up drunk of a detective who was slowly working her way into a mental institution. No threat here.

Nonetheless, my earlier feeling had been real. So whoever was watching me had to be related to the homeless murders, not the mob. Relaxing drastically, I put my car in drive. I decided to continue to my original destination—a local bar.

As if driven by absolute will, I found myself sitting in the same bar where, not long ago, Michael and I had sat before making love for the first time. Remembering that night was not a difficult task, truthfully. Every part of the night, down to the song playing on the jukebox, was as fresh in my mind as if it had just happened yesterday. I remembered our conversation, word for word. I remembered the clothes I wore, I remembered what Michael wore, I remembered what time we left, and lastly, I remembered when we made love.

Each of these memories came flooding through me, side by side with the glasses of vodka I was drinking. By the time the bartender yelled for the last call, I could barely stand up, let alone drive. But I did get into my car, doing my best to drive with only one eye, since closing the other brought my triple vision down to double.

Getting picked up by a member of my own department was the least of my worries. They would simply park my car and take me home. However, if a state highway patrolman came along, I would be looking at a full-blown arrest for DUI. Those guys didn't practice professional courtesy, even to each other. Of course, there was always the possibility of crashing into someone, and hurting or maybe even killing them. This was a possibility I didn't want to consider. Not that I could've dwelled on it for a lengthy amount of time anyway. About a mile from my house, I steered my car in the direction of what I thought was the road. Unfortunately, I chose the wrong side of my double image and wound up hitting a tree.

I sat for several moments, stunned. It took a few more moments for me to comprehend what had happened. How I would get out of it would take much longer. Normally, when a bad situation arose, Michael would be the first, and only, person I would call. Now that he was gone, I didn't know what to do. There was only one choice, and I had to do it quickly before another car came along. Coop.

Attempting his cell phone first, I wanted to avoid a late-night call to his house. He answered sleepily on the third ring, and I prayed the call hadn't woken Naomi.

"Coop! It's CeeCee." I was elated he had answered.

"What is it?" he asked groggily.

"Listen to me, and don't let Naomi know anything. I've had an accident, and I need you to come and pull me out of a ditch. I think my car is still drivable, if I can get it out." I did my best not to slur my words.

"Why don't you just call a tow truck?"

My silence was his answer.

"Oh, let me guess. Because you're loaded out of your fucking mind, that's why!"

"Coop! Please don't let Naomi hear you."

"She's downstairs. She fell asleep watching TV. I ought to let your ass be picked up by the highway patrol. Maybe then you'll get your shit together!"

I started to whine like a small child. "Coop, I know, I'm sorry! Please come down here and help me."

"Where are you?"

"Halfway down Hanley Road, between Lexington Avenue and Middle Bellville Road. Bring your truck and a tow rope."

"I'll be there in a few minutes."

Waiting and praying a state trooper wouldn't drive by, I was thrilled to see Coop pull up less than ten minutes later. He had my car out of the ditch in no time. The front end wasn't terribly mangled. The ditch caught most of my momentum before my car hit the tree, and most importantly, it was drivable.

"How the hell are you gonna make it home?" Coop asked.

"The crash sobered me up enough that I think I can make it one more mile." I avoided his gaze.

"I'll follow you."

"What did you tell Naomi?"

"She was still asleep. If she's awake when I get home and she asks, I'll tell her you hit a deer or something."

"Thanks, Coop," I said softly, my head down.

When we arrived at my house, I said a silent prayer. Coop, who hadn't bothered to pull in the driveway, poked his head out his window.

"You'll be okay?"

I nodded.

"Get some sleep, CeeCee. I'll talk to you tomorrow."

Too embarrassed to say anything else, I gave him a slight wave before going inside and diving on my bed, clothes and all. Morning came quickly, along with a monstrous headache and a queasy stomach. It was when I walked in front of my bathroom mirror that the image looking back at me stopped me cold. To say I looked awful was the understatement of the year. It had been a long time since I'd taken a good close look at my appearance.

My eyes looked hollowed, probably from my protruding cheekbones. The dark circles under my eyes accentuated the pale, deathly white tone my skin had taken on. My teeth, which always had been gleaming white, had darkened from constantly drinking red wine. Even my hair, which had shone and looked healthy, now appeared dull and drab. I looked like I had aged twenty years. Staring at the mirror in disbelief, I began to sob. Naomi and Eric had been right when they said it looked like I hadn't eaten or slept in months. I cried for half an hour straight until I decided that would be it. Taking a handful of aspirin for breakfast, I knew it was time. It was time to live again—if not for me, then for my children.

After doing my best to make my appearance presentable, I made a series of phone calls. I made a hair appointment, a facial appointment, and an appointment with the dentist to get my teeth bleached. This weekend, I surmised, a shopping trip was in order, at least until I could gain some weight. Right now, my clothes hung on me as if they were on a hanger. And lastly, before leaving for work, I took a handful of vitamins.

Coop was waiting for me in my office when I arrived. He obviously wasn't happy and nodded for me to shut the door when I walked in. I took a seat at my desk and braced myself.

"CeeCee, I know you don't want to hear this, and I know you'll want to bite my head off, but the bottom line is that you need some *serious* help. Evidently, the time off you took didn't do the job."

He paused, waiting for a response from me. Receiving none, he continued.

"We were all upset when Michael was killed, but he is gone, CeeCee! Eric told me that he took the girls permanently because of the state you've been in, and it shocked me. This isn't you!" He stood up and began to walk around. "Ya know, I knew you were having a hard time, but I had no clue you had gotten this bad until last night, and I have to ask . . . Have you had any thoughts of hurting yourself? Did you purposely run into that tree last night?"

"Sit down and I'll talk to you." I motioned toward

the chair, which he sat in. "First of all, Michael wasn't killed, he was murdered. I know you don't see much difference in the two, but I do." I kept my voice cool and calm. "Secondly, you're right, I definitely need help, and yes, I have had thoughts of hurting myself . . . even went so far as to take my revolver and hold it to my head while I sat on my kitchen floor for an hour. I had every intention of pulling the trigger, but I was so drunk, I passed out holding the gun."

Coop's face paled two shades at my confession. We had been friends for fifteen years, close friends, and this information upset him greatly. Before he could respond, I kept talking.

"However, I know this will be hard for you to believe, but after last night, I realized that life needs to go on. At the very least, for my kids. I looked in the mirror this morning and cried at what I saw." I paused. "I don't want to be that person anymore."

Fighting back the tears I promised I would never shed again, I finished what I had to say.

"I miss him, Coop."

When he rose from his seat to comfort me in a friendly embrace, I saw Coop's own eyes were teary.

"I know you do, CeeCee. We all do."

My no-crying-allowed proposition had lasted less than two hours. Coop held me while I cried again—with one difference. When I finished, I actually felt better, and even managed a genuine smile.

"So, you're going to be fine, right?"

I nodded. "I think so . . . It's not going to be easy, but at least I'm willing to try."

"This may not be the right time, but how many times have you been to his grave?"

"I haven't gone since the day they buried him. I can't, I just can't bring myself to go there yet."

He nodded. "Why don't we—"

He was interrupted by a loud knock on my door, followed by its opening. It was Naomi and she hadn't come to join the conversation.

"Sorry to interrupt"—she looked at us both strangely—"but we've had another homicide."

"She called you?"

"Yes, she wanted to know why we haven't made any arrests in her husband's murder."

"Did you tell her?"

"I told her the truth—we've been running into dead ends."

The man flipped his pen between his fingers. "They're watching her, you know. They're waiting to see if she makes a move."

"I know that. We have our own people on it, at least for his sake . . . which brings me to him. We're going to have to do something quickly, before he does."

"Judas Priest, Alan! I don't know what else to do! Do you? You're the one that swore up and down she would crack this wide open for us, and all she's doing is drinking herself to death and playing Russian roulette in her kitchen!" He threw his pen across the room.

Alan Keane hung his head down in defeat. "Just give her some more time . . . please. I really think she'll come through for us."

"You'd better be right."

"Another homicide? Where?" I asked.

"North Lake Park, floating in the lake."

Coop and I rode together, since Naomi had stayed back at the office to make some phone calls. All we knew was that the victim this time was female.

The usual suspects were on scene: the coroner, uniformed cops, and crime lab. The city street-department workers had seen the body floating when they arrived to repave one of the lots in the park. They weren't excited about it; North Lake Park was another hot spot. A body turning up there was nothing new. This brought me to another conclusion that I shared with Coop.

"You realize, don't you, that these bodies are being dumped in the absolute worst parts of town? Whoever is doing this dumps them there so the list of suspects becomes phenomenal."

"You're right."

We went straight for the group of people standing on the shore of the lake, actually a large pond. Lying on a tarp on her back was our victim, thirty-four-year-old Alisha Cross. One of the crime-lab technicians told me they had her identified immediately because her driver's license was found in her back pocket. She had only been in the water for a couple of hours, so the body wasn't badly decomposed.

Like the other three, Alisha's side was wide open, her liver taken. But what made Alisha different from the others was that she wasn't homeless, nor was she a drug addict. In fact, she was a suburban housewife who lived on the exclusive south side of the city. Our new detective, Justin Brown, had spoken with her husband just a few minutes earlier.

"He said she left to go grocery shopping. She goes to the grocery store in the Appleseed Shopping

Complex every Tuesday. Hubby's off his rocker, as you can imagine. They had a four-year-old that was in preschool at the time of the murder."

"What does her husband do?" I asked.

"He's a pharmaceutical salesman. Big bucks. She didn't have to work."

This threw a monkey wrench into the entire murder case, as far as a pattern went. But it did tell me one thing: this person, or people, was smart. Most businesses in the south district of the city don't even have video security systems, since crime is so low in that area. It's the wealthy part of the city, so the local thugs don't go there; they feel and look out of place. Our suspects evidently knew this. Taking the victim from the south and dumping the body in the north end made our investigation a nightmare. These people were deliberately trying to throw us for a loop.

"You took from his wife!"

The man nodded.

"What the fuck is the matter with you, Frank? When I told you to take care of him, I didn't mean his wife—I meant him!"

"That makes it all the more sweeter, Sal." The man smiled. "Now he will definitely not make any more waves. With his wife gone, he's got that kid to take care of. Now he knows not to fuck around."

"How the fuck do you know he's not gonna talk to the feds?"

"They just pulled his wife out of a pond. Unless he wants his kid raised in foster homes, he'll keep his mouth shut."

Sal had a frightening thought and grew quiet. Rubbing his temples, he couldn't believe how out of hand this entire situation had gotten. In a low, quiet voice, he asked the man, "Were you watching when they pulled her out of the pond?"

"Sure, Sal."

"Was Hagerman's wife there, too?"

"Well, yeah, Sal, but she's not gonna figure—"

Sal stood up and got within inches of the man's face. "You stupid motherfucker! He's in pharmaceutical sales! Don't you get it? He could lead her right to us! Don't you watch TV? If a woman is murdered, they always look into the husband's background first! Always!" Spit from Sal's mouth was hitting the man in the face.

He backed up slightly. "I think you're making too much of this, Sal. Even if she does connect him to the company, it stops there. There's no way any of that can lead to us— you know that! I mean, the guy was stealing from us, for Christ's sake! You wanted him out! Now he's out!"

Sal walked over to the window and looked down at the street below. He was worried. He had done a lot of checking into Hagerman's wife and he'd concluded that she was just as smart, if not smarter, than Hagerman himself. If anyone could put the pieces together, it would be her. Not to mention, Frank was getting to be more of a liability than an asset. He'd have to give some serious consideration to keeping Frank around.

"Do we still have our people on her?"

"I pulled them off weeks ago. My source said she's more than crazy right now. He said he even expected her to get fired or quit."

Sal was incredulous. "You did what? Did I tell you to pull them off? I want them back on her—pronto!"

"Of course, Sal."

"You sure you covered everything?"

"Down to the penny. I really don't believe she'll even

be able to tie him to the company. I've got my source on it."

"She gets within twenty feet from the front doors of the company, take her out! You got it?"

"I got it, Sal."

While they were loading the body into the coroner's van, a thought came to mind. Seeing Justin by the van doors, I flagged him over my way.

"You said the victim's husband was in pharmaceutical sales?"

"Yeah, that's right." He looked confused.

The husband's profession was entirely too close to the medical field. Keeping my fingers crossed, I was hoping this was the break we needed.

"Get your pen out and write this down," I ordered, and waited for him to grab his pen and notebook out of his shirt pocket.

"Go back and talk to him some more. I want everything on him: his company's name, how long he's been there, his sales district, his annual salary, his financial records, investments, stocks, bonds, whether or not he's fucking around on the side, and most importantly, I want the *exact* names of the companies and doctors he sells to."

Justin was furiously scribbling down my list of questions. Looking at him more closely, I realized he wasn't as young as I'd thought. He might even have been close to my age—in his thirties. I knew he had transferred several years ago from another department north of here and had made quite an impact when he worked uniform. He had been promoted to detective within five years, a very impressive feat. Average looking, he was only a few inches taller than I was and had sandy blond hair and brown eyes. On his left hand I noticed a wedding band.

"Do you have any children, Justin?"

"Huh?" He looked up from his notebook and saw me nod at his ring. "Oh, uh, yeah, Sarge, we have a two-year-old son."

"I'll bet he keeps you busy."

He smiled. "That he does!" He shook his notebook at me. "I'll get right on this, Sergeant."

"What's his name?"

"Who?"

"The victim's husband."

"Oh, it's Troy. Troy Cross."

"Okay . . . and Justin, call me CeeCee, please."

His face turned red as he nodded and walked away. He would go far in his career, as eager—and apparently, smart—as he was. People either make it or they don't in this business. Justin Brown wouldn't have to worry.

On the way to my car to drive back to the department, I was blindsided by Coop. He had a very large grin on his face.

"I see someone is smitten."

I was clueless. "What are you talking about?"

"The new dickie. Justin. The guy is totally in love with you."

"Oh for God's sake, Coop! Where the hell do you come up with this crap?"

"Don't tell me you don't notice him following you around like a lost puppy." He laughed. "And every time you talk to him, his face gets beet red. Probably gets a hard-on, too."

"That's enough." I shook my head. "He's a kid."

"He's older than us."

"What? He couldn't be."

"Yup, he's thirty-eight or nine, around there. I know, he's got that baby face that makes him look like he's still in his twenties, but I saw his driver's license with my own eyes."

"Huh. Certainly doesn't look it. And to answer your question, no, I have not noticed him following me around." I got in my car, not wanting to continue this conversation.

"Well, I have, and so has everyone else."

"Lovely."

The rest of the day was spent in my office finishing the Alisha Cross homicide paperwork. Justin Brown came in my office about half an hour before it was time to go home. Astonishingly, he had already obtained the information on Troy Cross.

His information brought no significant leads. Troy Cross didn't screw around, didn't have any investments or stocks, and only sold to lower-end doctors on Cleveland's east side. There was one discrepancy that caught my interest.

"How much does he make a year?" I asked.

"Seventy-five thousand."

"And how much money is in his savings account?"

"Two hundred thirty-one thousand, six hundred forty-seven dollars, exactly."

That didn't make sense. "Did you happen to ask him where the hell that money came from?"

Justin looked uncomfortable. "I was going to, but I wanted to wait and discuss it with you first. I thought maybe we could use it to our advantage later."

Smart move on his part. I took the thick file on all of the murders and handed it to Justin.

"Take this home, study it, and familiarize yourself

with everything. I'll fill you in on some of it now, so pay attention. I think you're going to do well in Major Crimes."

His face lit up as if I'd told him he'd just been elected sheriff. He started rifling through the file as I briefly went into my findings about LifeTech Industries, the two doctors, and my theory.

"You really think those doctors have something to do with the murders?" he asked.

"There's no factual evidence that connects them, but let's just say I've got a feeling that they are. I still plan on keeping an eye on both."

Justin got up to leave. "Sergeant, um, CeeCee . . . Thanks. I won't let you down, I promise." His face turned red again.

I couldn't help but laugh. "I'm not worried, Justin. Have fun."

Justin's response to receiving the file made me remember my own early days in Major Crimes—how eager I was, putting everything else aside, including my family, to do the best job I could. How I wished I could go back in time.

As soon as I got home, I turned on my computer. There were several topics of interest that needed to be researched. I hadn't had time, or the will, until now. The computer was in Michael's office, a place I had rarely ventured into, let alone touched. His things were just as he had left them the night he was murdered, down to the empty, chipped, purple ceramic coffee cup sitting on his desk. Doing my best to ignore the surroundings, I pushed a stack of papers away and began my research.

Organ donors and trafficking in body parts was my first priority. Looking at the pages and pages of

Web sites, I was dumbfounded. There were hundreds of stories, articles, and medical journals written on the subjects. As I read through some of them, I found myself focusing mainly on the area of trafficking in body parts—a multimillion-dollar black market. There were thousands of people that did nothing but run illegal organs for a living. They were referred to as the "Body Mafia."

The demand was monstrous. Over three hundred thousand people worldwide receive organ transplants. Almost triple that number of people actually need a transplant, therefore generating a black market that spreads across the globe. According to my research, the badly proposed 1984 National Organ Transplant Act set the black market into motion. The act makes it a felony to buy or sell human organs for purposes of transplantation, and essentially set the price on organs at zero. Most people won't give something for nothing—even when they're dead. Had the act not been put in place and the families of the deceased been compensated for the organ donation, the number of registered donors would go through the roof. As it stands now, less than twenty-one percent of Americans are registered organ donors. If the number grew to ninety percent or more, the supply would meet the demand, and the black market would be wiped out.

What sickened me was that a country like China literally executed their prisoners for the purpose of selling their organs. In 1999, China executed more than twelve hundred people for crimes ranging from assault to pig stealing, an average of forty people a week. On the night before the scheduled execution, blood samples were taken so their organs could find a match. The next day they were executed by one bullet in the head, so it minimized body-tissue damage. Throughout the 1990s, China executed more people than the rest of the world combined. China went so far as to have a standard price list for prisoners' organs: $25,000 for livers, $20,000 for kidneys, and corneas and pancreases for $5,000 a pair. Now the kidney has become the golden organ for sale and can fetch $30,000 and up.

As I leaned back in my chair to stretch, my attention was drawn to the clock; two hours had passed since I began. Nonetheless, there was more. The market had taken on such a high-paying demand that some people resorted to murder to sell the organs. I read an article from a South African newspaper. In 2004, a nun at an orphanage reported that the children were consistently disappearing from the orphanage. What had actually transpired was that the children had all been kidnapped and killed for their organs. The nun blamed a nearby farmer and his son, but received so much pressure from the government to keep her mouth shut that she had to leave the country.

There were other stories of people merely walking down the street when someone walked up to them and killed them right there for their organs. I was amazed and repulsed at the same time. Here in America, you have to worry about someone attacking you for your car. In other countries, you have to worry about someone attacking you for your corneas. Considering the elements of my recent murders, it seemed as if the tide may have been shifting our way.

Most of the buying and selling took place in Third

World countries: the Philippines, Nigeria, Uganda, and Vietnam, to name only a few. But the organs could come from anywhere.

I had decidedly had enough. As I went to click out of the Web site I was on, I accidentally hit the history button, which opened up an entire list of sites the computer had been on earlier. Feeling my pulse quicken, I read aloud the Web sites that Michael had visited months ago. Some, if not most, were the exact same ones I had read tonight. He was researching the area of trafficking body parts as well. But why?

My thoughts drifted to the night I found him reading my file on the first murder, in his office. His excuse had been that he was bored and just wanted to take a look. A flood of memories came crashing through my head: of that night, all of the nights he'd acted strangely, the time he insisted I take the kids out of state, and lastly, his reaction when I'd told him I had contacted the doctors.

Michael had always kept a copy of his files at home so he wouldn't have to cart them back and forth to Cleveland. Remembering this, I found my eyes drifting toward his filing cabinets.

CHAPTER EIGHT

Going through Michael's files had never crossed my mind before. I had been so grief stricken over the last several months that going into his office was the last thing I had wanted to do. That changed tonight. Feeling almost euphoric, I went to the metal cabinets. There were three total, each with three drawers. Starting at the top, I began flipping through the massive amount of files. One thing that could be said about Michael, he had always been organized; each file had been color-coded and labeled with the name of the investigation in bold black letters on top.

Evidently, this was going to take some time. One of the drawers had nothing but personal paperwork—our bank statements, the kids' birth certificates and Social Security cards, and so forth. Nearing the last drawer of the last cabinet, I was interrupted by the phone. I wiped the sweat off my brow and quickly picked up the receiver on Michael's desk.

"Hello?"

There was silence.

"Hello?"

I didn't ask again, but listened carefully. There was no sound at all, as if the other end had been muted. Only when I saw my hand begin to tremble did I realize that the phone had rung in Michael's office. It was a separate line, and there hadn't been a call in there since the night Michael died. Confronting the obvious, I dropped the phone, went over to the large window of his office, and quickly closed the blinds. There was no other explanation other than that someone was watching me closely and knew I was in his office. The call also came in before I got to the last drawer, which led me to believe I was getting downright hot. The fear that spread through me was beginning to dissipate from the rising anger I felt.

I turned from the window, strode back over to the cabinet, and jerked the last file drawer. It was locked. None of the other drawers had been locked. My adrenaline at an all-time high, I went to Michael's desk and violently looked for a key. Throwing papers, pens, staplers, and folders all over his office, I was determined to find one. My search proved fruitless. There wasn't a key anywhere, but that wasn't enough to prevent me from opening the drawer. I'd open it if I had to saw the goddamn thing in half.

Soaked with sweat and almost hysterical, I went into the garage and grabbed a large screwdriver, a hammer, and a crowbar. Back in Michael's office, I tipped the cabinet onto its back. As heavy as it was, I had to use my entire body to do it. I worked on the drawer for forty-five minutes. I put the screwdriver into the lock and hammered with every ounce of muscle I had, which wasn't much. When I finally disabled the lock, I had to stand on the crowbar and jump up and down to bend the steel bar that attached the lock to the drawer until it eventually snapped in half.

There were five files inside, red, and each about an

inch thick, except for the last, which was about three inches thick. Spreading them on the floor in front of me, I looked at the labels on each one: "Iaccona," "Filaci," "Philippines," "LifeTech Industries," and the last one, "CeeCee's Murders."

I set the last file to the side and grabbed the Filaci file first. Michael had been investigating the Niccolo Filaci murder, something I had suspected long ago. Inside were photographs, tape transcripts, copies of airline tickets, a sketchy family biography and family tree, and copies of deeds to various properties. There were numerous typed reports by Michael, along with newspaper articles focusing on Leon Filaci, who, according to the family tree, was the boss. Photographs of Leon with his two sons, Joseph and Niccolo, were attached to the articles. The paperwork on Niccolo's murder was placed in the back of the file, which told me Michael had been investigating the Filacis long before Niccolo was murdered. But there was nothing in the file that told me why.

Several unmarked folders in the file sat empty, the labels on top cut off. Michael knew I would never have looked through his files, so why would he have taken out key information? None of this made sense. The Iaccona file was similar, and again, empty files, with no reason for the investigation in the first place. The LifeTech Industries file was filled with their corporate earnings, employee information, distribution centers and surgical sites (including Quinn-Herstin Funeral Home), and a photograph showing the outside of the company building. Nothing substantial, other than that Michael was investigating them, which brought me to the file with my own name on it.

My growing trepidation of what awaited me inside the file became insurmountable, and with my thoughts in complete turmoil, I opened the folder.

Michael had copied my entire case file on every murder, down to the handwritten notes on scraps of paper. At the back of the file was a smaller folder marked "Confidential." Expecting the folder to be empty, I was surprised to see three handwritten pages of notes, a typed transcript, and a microcassette tape. Each of the handwritten notes had dates and times, along with several sentences of what appeared to be threats against Michael, me, and the children. They were too scattered to understand directly. Common sense directed me to the cassette tape. I knew all the answers would be on it.

I always carried a microcassette recorder in my briefcase for interviews and interrogations. After retrieving it and sitting on the sofa in Michael's office, I put the tape in and pushed play. It began with voices in the background that couldn't be understood, followed by a man coughing loudly. Next, loud scrapes, as if a chair was being pushed across a floor, came blaring through the small speaker. And finally a man began to speak clearly.

"You got everything ready?" one man said.

"Yeah, Sal, it's in place" another man said, with a deep scratchy voice.

"Let's hear it."

"We've got one of two. The first is, she leaves the office every day at five, and usually gets home before he does, at least an hour. If we plant Tommy and Henry in the garage and wait for her, they could probably get her out the back door without being seen." He coughed. *"We'll knock her*

*out and bring her up here, make the tape like we planned,
and mail it off to Hagerman. When we're finished, we can
always stick her under the construction site on Brushman
Road. He'll spend most of his time looking for her, so that'll
take the heat off. I've already got it tagged to the Filacis, so
he'll be on them heavy. If that doesn't do it, we can start on
the kids, too."*

"And the other?"

*"The other is taking him out altogether. Hell with his
wife and kids."*

"He's a federal agent. That'll bring a lot of heat."

*"I know, I know, but if he's done, he's done. We won't
have to worry about him anymore, period. I can take care
of him just like I did Niccolo. I think that's our best bet,
Sal. I can tie that to the Filacis easy, as well."*

There was a long pause before Sal, who I assumed
to be Salvatore Iaccona, boss of the Iaccona family,
according to the file, made his choice.

"What are you planning, if it's Hagerman?"

*"Henry's got it all ready to go. He said he can stick it
under the fan belt in less than five minutes. So what's it
gonna be, Sal?"*

"Give it two weeks, and then do the wife."

The click on the tape told me the conversation was
over. My hands were shaking so bad that I was having a hard time finding the stop button. Good thing,
since the tape wasn't over. A separate recording and
another man's voice, different from the ones in the
first conversation, came over the tape. This time, in-
troductions were made.

"Leon Filaci, this is Vincent Vicari."

Several how-do-you-dos could be heard before what
sounded like three men started their conversation.

"Sir, I'm very sorry to hear about Niccolo. They'll pay, don't worry."

"Thank you, but they're second to someone else, which is why you're here. It's Hagerman. He had something to do with Niccolo's death, I just don't know how. Not that it matters. I want him erased right off the fucking map."

"He's a federal agent. It could cause trouble," the unnamed third man said.

A long pause followed before Leon Filaci disclosed his disdain for Michael and the Iacconas.

"I don't give a fuck what kind of heat it brings. He's already trying to take us down, for fuck's sake! Tag it to the Iacconas. That'll kill two birds with one stone. Salvatore Iaccona got Niccolo wrapped up with Hagerman in the first place, that greasy motherfucker! Vince? Who do you plan on bringing down for the job?"

"Tony Bertola. He's done a couple jobs for me in New York and could easily tag it on the Iacconas. He's retired NYPD. We put him on our payroll three years ago, and he hasn't failed us yet."

"How long?"

"Give me three weeks to get everything together."

"I'm sorry, but I think you're making a big mistake," the unnamed man said quietly.

"Mistake or not, consider it done."

The tape clicked and I pushed the stop button feeling so nauseous I actually ran to the bathroom to throw up, but nothing came. You can't throw up what isn't there, since I still hadn't been eating much. Michael *knew*. He knew he was going to die, which explained his odd behavior the few weeks before his death. He was also worried about me; that's why he'd wanted me to take the kids and leave.

They had the evidence! Why the fuck didn't they have

*the indictments ready within twenty-four hours of the tapes,
and arrest them all?* my head screamed. They had a
perfectly recorded conspiracy to commit murder of a
federal agent and had done nothing.

One of those two families had murdered my husband. Either Salvatore Iaccona changed his mind
about me and went with Michael, or Tony Bertola got
to him first.

Someone was going to pay, and they would pay
with their life. A rage on a level that I had never
known before rose up in me so quickly it was frightening. They killed my husband and planned to kill
my children and me. I'd be damned straight to hell
and back if I would let them get away with it. In my
mind, the FBI had botched the investigation from the
beginning, so they could no longer be trusted. From
this point on, I would be on my own.

But the creeping question of what all of this had
to do with my murder investigation kept coming up.
Michael had obviously been onto something substantial, as far as my case went. But how did it involve
the two families? Or did it?

The remainder of the night was spent listening to
the tape over and over, making copies, looking at the
files again, and thinking. Things were starting to
become clearer now, the fogginess I had experienced
over the last several months starting to fade. No one
could argue about anger and hatred being two of
the most volatile emotions in a human being, but one
thing can be said: they'll keep pushing you no matter
what.

"Hell hath no fury like a woman scorned" was
not only a quote that I could identify with, but also
one that I would live by for the rest of my life.

Scorned I was, and these people were going to pay hell for it.

When the sun started to poke through the shadows in the early morning hours, I found myself wide awake. With many loose ends to tie up in the next couple of weeks and much preparation to do, time was running out.

"Have you found the mole yet, Alan?"

"We're still working on that, but we've got a bigger problem." Alan Keane dreaded telling his boss the bad news.

"I assume I should remain seated for this?"

Alan nodded. *"Hagerman had files and tape recordings that we didn't know about. She found them."*

The boss closed his eyes and groaned. *"How in the hell did that happen? I thought we checked his office!"* He shook his head. *"Not that it matters now, but he wasn't supposed to be copying any goddamn files anyway."*

"There was a locked file drawer. We didn't think he had anything but family information in it. There really wasn't an opportunity to get in there without her knowing, sir. She is a police officer, you know."

The boss slammed his fist on his desk. *"I know that! You know what this means, don't you?"*

"As far as I know, their bugs are still in place, along with ours. If we know . . . then they know."

"Right! This now means we have to watch her 24-7 to make sure they don't whack her! The Filacis and the Iacconas probably have their people on the way to her now." He paused before asking the inevitable. *"Does he know?"*

"I'm afraid so, sir."

"This wasn't the way it was supposed to happen. She was only supposed to link LifeTech to them and be done

*with it." The boss stood up. "Get our eyes on her, now. And
for God's sake, don't let her out of our sight! If we lose her,
and he finds out, you know what that means."*

*Alan Keane nodded before leaving the office. His first
stop was to his secretary. Looking out the window at the
Lincoln Memorial, he wondered if this was the end of the
road for his career. What his boss didn't know was that his
own plan was working. God forbid he was caught.*

*"Nancy, I need you to make an airline reservation for
me. I need to leave tonight for Cleveland, Ohio."*

*Before Alan Keane went home to pack for his trip, he
stopped at the nearest mailbox and dropped in the video-
tape. Its destination: Erie, Pennsylvania.*

Most of my workday was spent organizing the
homeless-murder file and making copies of everything for my own use. Earlier, I had instructed Justin
Brown to call Troy Cross and schedule him for another interview. The clock on the wall told me that
he should be arriving any minute. Grabbing the large
brown box I had taken from our storage area, I began
putting all of my things that had been gathered
into it.

"Moving out, are we?"

I looked up and saw Justin in my doorway. "More
like winter cleaning. I accumulate so much junk, I
can't find my own name," I lied, and smiled.

"Troy Cross is here. He's in the interview room."

"I'll be there in just a sec. Oh, Justin? You want to
sit in on it?"

"You sure? I mean, I'd love to . . ." His trademark
redness returned.

"Go on and ask him if he wants a cup of coffee or
something, and I'll be there shortly."

Justin and Troy Cross were sitting at the interview table discussing the weather when I walked in. Around thirty-five years old, Cross appeared extremely nervous and agitated. By the time I sat down and set my tape recorder on the table, he had shredded his Styrofoam cup into pieces.

"Excuse me, but are you going to tell me what this is about?" he asked defensively.

"Mr. Cross, I'm Sergeant Gallagher, and before we begin, I want to express my condolences to you for the loss of your wife." I could certainly feel his pain. "I can assure you that the reason we're here today is simply procedural, and you are by no means considered a suspect in this case."

He began to relax, which was the point. Getting the "not a suspect" out and on the table first usually makes the rest of the interview go that much smoother. Essentially, I went through everything Justin already had, confirming his answers on tape, before I got down to Cross's salary and savings account.

"Mr. Cross, you stated your salary is, on average, approximately seventy-five thousand dollars per year. Is that correct?"

"Yes, that's correct."

"Your savings account is showing a balance in excess of two hundred thousand dollars. Where did that money come from?"

He stiffened. "What does that have to do with anything?"

Wrong answer. Whenever someone answers a question with a question, they're hiding something. This is a standard rule in police questioning, along with "I swear to God" or "I swear on my children."

"It's just a discrepancy is all, Mr. Cross. I'm sure

once you clear it up, that'll pretty much be it." I smiled, calm and cool.

"I, uh . . . I go to Las Vegas a lot, gambling," he stuttered. "Most of that was made there."

Another lie. "When was the last time you were in Las Vegas, and do you have any receipts proving you were there? Airline, hotel, restaurants, anything?"

He pushed his chair back. "Look, no, I never keep that stuff. I swear on my child, that's where the money came from. I just lost my wife! Can you please tell me what any of this has to do with her murder?"

"I'll move on. Have you ever heard of LifeTech Industries?"

He tried to hide the shock on his face, but it was too late—I had already seen it. He clearly had heard of LifeTech. Before he answered, I saw a small bead of sweat run down from his left temple.

"LifeTech? Uh, no. What is it? Does it have something to do with Alisha's murder?" He fidgeted.

"I'm not sure. You're sure you've never heard of it?" I locked my eyes on his.

"Yes . . . I mean, yes, I'm sure I haven't heard of it." He looked down at the floor.

"Okay. I guess that wraps it up, Mr. Cross. I'm all done here. Do you have any questions for me?"

"No, I don't."

Justin showed him out while I played the tape of the interview. Troy Cross was on the payroll of LifeTech; there wasn't a doubt in my mind. And that was where his money had come from. This all confirmed that LifeTech had a large, if not the sole, role in the murders. Which brought me back to the doctors. Troy Cross had not even asked if we were close to finding his wife's killer. That's because he didn't want us to be. If we did, his own life might have been in jeopardy.

"What do you think?" Justin asked when he came back in.

"I think my hunches were right. I think this guy is on the payroll of LifeTech, and those doctors have a hell of a lot to do with our murders."

"Now what?"

"Now"—I looked at my watch—"I have other things to do. Do me a favor and start a more thorough background on both doctors and LifeTech. Keep at it until you find something. I have to leave early today, so if you need anything, call me at home."

Most of my appointments were that afternoon, and I had every intention of keeping them, with the exception of my teeth-bleaching, which was the following morning. Feeling considerably better after my appointments, I started toward home. There was a lot of planning to do.

CHAPTER NINE

Before going home, I stopped at a nearby pay phone. The phone call I'd received the night before had me more than paranoid. Any and all of my arrangements would be made outside of my home and preferably not on my cell. The call was to my father, who I instructed to leave immediately and call me back from a pay phone near his house. Being in law enforcement for over thirty-five years, he didn't argue and knew why I was asking. Fifteen minutes later, my own pay phone rang.

"What's going on, honey?" He sounded concerned.

"I remember, sometime in the early eighties, you worked a case involving the Mafia when you were in Major Crimes, am I right?"

"Yeah, what's this about?"

"Please believe me when I tell you that right now, I can't get into much. What I need is someone on the inside. Did you ever have any contacts? Anyone that's still around you could hook me up with?"

There was a long pause. "Let me think . . . Hon, let me call you back, I need to make some phone calls first."

"All right, call me at this number, and use the pay phone. Don't call from your house."

"You think you're talking to some two-year patrolman? For crying out loud, CeeCee, I was doing this job before you were even a thought!"

I laughed as my dad huffed and hung up the phone. Sometimes it's hard for me not to be so bossy—even to my father, whose experience puts mine to shame. A little more than five cigarettes later, the pay phone rang.

"Nine o'clock tonight, go down to the Wiener Castle restaurant and park across the street—"

"You mean the rumors are true!" I interrupted.

Since I was a child, there was a fast food restaurant named Wiener Castle that sat along Lexington Avenue in the city. In all of my years, I had never seen one person go inside, but it miraculously remained open. On any given day, one could drive by and see someone working the counter, but never a customer. The rumor throughout law enforcement over the years was that it was a front for the Mafia; they owned it, and it was their meeting place. We all laughed about it. I clearly would never laugh about it again.

"Just listen, CeeCee. There's a guy named Jimmy Garito who'll meet you in the back. Nine o'clock sharp! I knew he was still around, but I'd heard he got out of his Mafia dealings in the late eighties. I guess he has, but he keeps in touch with family in Cleveland and still knows what's going on. He's owed me a favor for the last twenty years, and I just cashed it in. He's in his early sixties now, so look for him."

"Thanks, Pop."

"I don't know what's going on, but I'll tell you

something. I've dealt with these people more closely than I ever cared to, and they are dangerous. Please be careful."

"I will. I'm going to have Eric bring the girls to your place tomorrow evening for my visit. Even though I talk to them on the phone every night, I miss them like hell."

"See you then."

My next series of phone calls, also made from the pay phone, were to make my upcoming travel arrangements. More calls would be made from home—a smokescreen to confirm if my paranoia was warranted. I had about three hours before I was to meet Jimmy Garito, so I stopped and grabbed something to eat, forcing it down before grabbing a few things at a nearby shopping center. By the time I got home, there was just enough time to make my other calls before leaving to meet Jimmy. Taking my personal car, I left a half hour early to drive around and make sure no one was following me.

Standing at the back door of the closed restaurant at approximately eight forty-five P.M., I was startled when the door opened behind me. An older, heavy-set man with black and gray hair, wearing a black velvet sweat suit, poked his head out.

"CeeCee?"

"Yes, sir. Mr. Garito?"

"It's Jimmy, not sir. Come on in here—quickly, before someone sees you."

He led me directly down a flight of cement steps into a large room that was situated underneath the restaurant. For the most part, the room was empty, with the exception of a large metal folding table with metal chairs around it in the center. Jimmy pulled a chair out for me and motioned for me to sit. He chose the chair at the opposite side of the table. Reaching into my coat pocket, I pushed the record button on my hidden tape recorder.

"I've known your father for a long time. He's a good man," he began. "He's the only reason I agreed to talk to you. Now, he didn't tell me much, but it sounds like you've gotten yourself mixed up with some bad guys."

I filled Jimmy in on everything, since there was no other option but to trust him. When the part about Michael's car-bombing came up, I felt myself fighting back tears. After giving him the names on the files, my theories, and the information on my murders, I sat back and waited.

He took it all in, remaining silent for several seconds while he tapped his fingers on the table.

"Before we get to anything, you must assume that your home is wired and they can hear everything you say and do. Trust me on that. Since your father told me you called him from a pay phone, I can presume you've already figured that out."

I nodded and swallowed. My paranoia was sufficiently confirmed, at least by Jimmy. Sitting here with him now, I realized how nervous I'd been.

"Now, what is it that you want from me?" he asked directly.

"I need all the information I can get on these families. As I said before, some of the files were missing. I need a history of some sort—where they came from, what they're into, and why they hate each other."

"May I ask if this information is for personal or professional use?"

"Strictly personal."

He nodded. "Before we begin, I have to say this. Whatever happens, or whatever you do with this information, nothing came from me—understand? We have never met. Got it?"

"Of course."

"You're dealing with two of the most dangerous organized-crime families in the country, especially the Filacis. They are directly connected to the Vicari crime family in New York, one of the top five, understand?"

I nodded.

"I have to tell you, if they have any idea you've come upon this information, they will see you as a major problem, and they will not hesitate to take care of it. They have connections in all factions of law enforcement, including the FBI, so even they can't help you. Get it?"

"I got it."

"Probably got people on their way down here now. God forbid they find out you met up with me. Not a good thing . . ." He looked uncomfortable for a moment. "You want a drink? I keep a bottle of scotch stashed in the cabinet over there."

"I'm fine, thanks." I was anxious to hear what he had to say.

He clapped his hands together. "All right, here it goes. I'll start with the Filacis first. In the 1920s, a successful Cleveland businessman named Alfred Basilici started supplying corn sugar to area bootleggers. It was prohibition, and if you didn't know, corn sugar was a legal ingredient used for making whiskey. Basilici's top guy turned to the competition, the Agliata brothers, and had Alfred Basilici killed. At that point, Frank Agliata took control of the corn-sugar business and essentially became the Cleveland boss. Then came the 1930s, when Basilici's son Tony avenged his father's death by having both Agliata brothers killed, which turned control back over to the Basilicis. You with me so far?"

"I think so."

"During the forties and fifties, the Basicili sons brought in a couple Jewish gangsters. When this happened, Cleveland became one of the most potent crime operations in the nation. By the late fifties, Cleveland had more than sixty made members, and many, many associates. These were the people that saw Cleveland's move into Las Vegas. So that brings us up to the Cleveland Mafia wars in the midseventies.

"At that time, the Mafia was led by Alfred's grandson, Leonardo Falaci, Leon, the son of Alfred's only daughter. He did a piss-poor job in keeping tabs on everyone, and basically let his guard down. A competing mob faction rose, led by Irish gangster Kenny Giblin. What followed that was the bloodiest mob war the nation has seen since prohibition. There were over forty car bombings and hits in Cleveland within a two-year period. Same with Youngstown, since Giblin was playin' the two against each other, but we'll get to that. The war ended when Giblin went to a doctor's appointment and was blown to pieces in his car. The Filacis put a bomb in the hollowed-out section of his passenger door. To this day, the Filacis are still run by Leon, who they call Leo the Lion, and his two sons, Joseph and Niccolo—well, now only Joseph, who I hear was heavily involved with Vincent Vicari's daughter. Word is he hooked up the two families not that long ago—a very bad combination."

"How's all of this play into Youngstown?"

"Giblin was a greedy Irish fuck, that's why. He wanted control of both cities, so he was fighting 'em both at the same time. The Iacconas have always controlled Youngstown, and no one ever thought about taking them on. They're Italian Catholics who came over in the early twenties to a neighborhood everyone called Hunkeytown. A lot of badasses came from that part of town, including Larry Beneditto, Salvatore 'Singin' Sal' Iaccona's cousin. Ever hear of him?"

"The state senator?"

"Yup, that's the one. Before that, he was the county sheriff. A guy by the name of Mono Rigati bribed him with thirty thousand dollars during his campaign and threatened to expose him afterward. He disappeared and was never found. Now along comes Rigati's wife, who breaks the vow of *omertà*. This is a code of silence that all mobsters and their wives live by, no matter what. So Mrs. Rigati takes tape recordings that her husband made between him and Beneditto to the feds. They try him on all kinds of shit. The guy winds up representing himself in court, is found not guilty, and goes on to be a fucking state senator." He shook his head in disgust.

"Youngstown is also known as Murdertown, USA, by Mafia and law enforcement. In the fifties and sixties they had over seventy-five car bombings and murders. There's no end in sight for that place. In 1999, a new county prosecutor took over, Edward Narillo. He shot his mouth off all over town about

how he was going to rid Youngstown of corruption
for good, and reopens the Mono Rigati case. On
Christmas Eve of the year he was elected, he was
almost shot to death in his own home. He survived
and is still out there trying to bring everyone down.
The guy's got some balls, I'll give him that. Suppos-
edly, Salvatore Iaccona arranged the hit on Narillo
to protect his cousin. Salvatore is still the boss, and
has his sons, Damien, Antonio, and Petey running
things for the most part. His lieutenants are some
of the worst in the business, including Frank Trapini and Tommy Miglia. I swear Frank Trapini is
Satan himself. That is one bad dude. If it was the
Iacconas that killed your husband, Frank and Tommy
would've been the ones to do it, no doubt about
that."

"Do you know why my husband was investigating
both of these families?" I rubbed my eyes, trying to
absorb everything.

"Not for sure, no. The Iacconas build shopping
centers and office buildings, which of course are all
a front for something else. They've had their own
offices bombed five times in the last ten years. The
Filacis are to blame, I suspect. The word is that the
Iacconas were trying to move in on a lot of the Filacis' business contacts. Now this is where it gets fuzzy,
and I don't know nothin' for sure, but lately I've been
hearing a lot of grumbling from up there."

"About what?"

"About what the Iacconas are involved in. Alleg-
edly, it's something big. Only Sal's closest captains
and lieutenants know about it—no one else, and no
one dares ask—but it's big money. The rumor is that
Niccolo Filaci tried to get a piece of it but was turned

down and threatened to overthrow the business. That's when he was killed."

"It has to be LifeTech Industries," I thought aloud.

"Could be."

"What are the Filacis' main businesses?"

"They control most of the banks in Cleveland. They also hold most contracts to the high-end construction in the city. And they happen to be co-owners of the Cleveland Browns football team."

"Wonderful." I sighed. "Jimmy, if you don't mind me asking, how were you involved with these families?"

"I worked directly for Leon Filaci himself," he said matter-of-factly. "I met your father when a cousin of Leon's set up shop here in Mansfield. The guy was a fucking idiot—even Leon knew that. He was bringing in a substantial amount of money, so Leon let it go. Your father caught me with my hands in the cookie jar, so to speak, and let me go if I rolled on him. Your father promised me the guy would never know where the information came from, and he kept his promise. I'll always thank him for that. If not, I'd be in prison or dead. What my exact role was, I'd rather not say."

I understood, and really didn't want to hear it. I had a feeling if I looked into Jimmy Garito, I'd probably find out he'd been one of Leon Filaci's top hit men.

"How'd you get out?"

"I walked right up to Leon and told him I was finished. He knew me well enough to know I'd take my secrets to the grave, but I had children, and the feds were all over me. We still talk every once in a while, but not about business." He paused. "I'll tell you something, and remember it. If you find out the people responsible are the Iacconas, you're going to need some help. And as bad as it sounds, the person that could help you is Joseph Filaci. Known him since he was a boy, and he's really not that bad of a guy. I do know the tension is rising since Niccolo's death, so I expect things to come to a head real soon. But also remember this if you're dealing with the Iacconas: they have contacts that go right into the United States Justice Department. They'll be difficult to break."

"Do you know any of the places where the Iacconas meet? Where they do their business?"

"There was an old warehouse on Washington Street, downtown, where they used to meet once a week. Keep in mind, that was years ago, but it's a start. You got a pen?"

I gave him a pen and piece of paper, on which he wrote several addresses, including some in Cleveland.

"You'll want to check these, but again, be careful, young lady. These people are not stupid. The phone number I wrote down is how you can get ahold of me directly. Memorize all of those and burn that paper."

"I can't thank you enough, Jimmy, really."

"If you're anything like your daddy, you'll be just fine. Good luck to you, CeeCee."

We shook hands before we left. As I drove home, my mind was in turmoil trying to sort out everything that Jimmy had told me. At home, I went outside, on my porch, and made two copies of the tape made at the restaurant. One of the copies was placed in my gun safe, and the other I put inside my purse. The original was placed at the bottom of an opened can of coffee in my cupboard. The copies of the tape I'd found in the file were placed with the others.

Now it was time to prepare for my trip, and there was a lot to pack. Grabbing suitcases and bags out of various closets, I threw them all on my bed and divided them down the middle. Since I would be in two different climates in less than a week, I needed my summer and winter clothes.

It was getting late, so I finished packing and tried to sleep, knowing that I needed to be well rested for my day tomorrow.

"She knows, Sal."

"What do you mean, she knows?" He anticipated the worst.

"She found some tapes Hagerman had about us, and apparently some files, too. I don't even think the feds knew about 'em," the man said uneasily, knowing his boss was about to explode.

Sal stood up, knocking over his chair, and walked over in front of the man, grabbing one of the lapels on his designer suit.

"I ought to fucking kill you right here. She was your responsibility, and you fucked up! You know what we have to do, don't you? I don't need this fucking snag right now. The Filipinos are pissed as it is that we didn't make the order last month, and this is the last thing we need to fucking worry about!" Sal shoved the man backward, letting go of his jacket.

"Look, Sal, it may not be as bad as it seems. She just

made reservations in Florida to spend three weeks there. I think she's still off her rocker and is going away for a while. She's not acting like she really cares that much."

"You think, huh? Bullshit!" He couldn't believe this had happened. "Do the Filacis know yet?"

"I don't think so, but it's only a matter of time. I'm sure they'll send their own people on her . . . probably Bertola."

"We can't count on them to take care of it, since we're not sure they even know yet. You and Tommy personally keep her in sight every minute from here on out. When is she leaving for Florida?"

"Her reservations were made for an afternoon flight out of Cleveland the day after tomorrow. She reserved a condo in Siesta Key for three weeks, paid in full already."

"Wait until she gets to Florida, and do her there. Throw her ass in the fucking Everglades for all I care—just get rid of her, and soon!"

"Sure, Sal. Consider it done."

"You're on thin ice, Frankie. This is your last chance to make it right."

After leaving the dentist's office the next morning, I ran around doing more errands, which included stopping my mail and newspaper for a month. If things didn't go well, they would be stopped permanently. I had called in sick leaving a message on Naomi's voice mail. The days after would be taken care of tomorrow. The last stop was to my bank, where I rented a safe-deposit box. The copies of everything I had, along with copies of both tapes, were placed inside. The key to the box was mailed to a close friend of mine in Atlanta. The note wrapped around the key had a date on it with a message that told her to call the FBI and turn over the key if I didn't call by ten P.M. on the date given. The date was exactly one month from today. Everything in the box was probably not enough to take both families down, but I would be getting more information, and it was better than nothing. At the very least, it would be leverage.

Lastly, I headed to my father's for my visit with Isabelle and Selina. Since I was early, I took the opportunity to call Sean and say good-bye.

"When will I see you again, CeeCee?" He sounded like he was going to cry.

"Oh, honey, you'll see me soon enough." I prayed that was true. "Hopefully you'll be able to come down around Christmas and open all the neat presents I bought you!" I lied.

Christmas was the last thing on my mind, since we hadn't even gotten to Thanksgiving yet. In the best-case scenario, I would be back in plenty of time to shop for the kids. Worst case, they would be opening the letter I wrote telling them how sorry I was, and to go on with their lives as best they could without me. Without a doubt, it was one of the hardest letters I have ever written. Saying good-bye to the girls at my father's house would prove to be even more difficult, since it was highly possible it would be the last time I would ever see them.

Most people might consider me downright pathetic for doing what I was about to do. They would say my children were given no consideration, but how wrong they would be. Everything I was about to do was for my children. I looked at it in one way only. My life had hit rock bottom and would continue that way if I didn't do something about it. Yes, I could put everything behind me and move on, but now I was pretty confident the Mafia was looking for me, and I would not live in fear. I could either take them head-on or wait to die. Either way, it was about protecting my children. For me to leave and try to take down the men who killed my husband would put them out of harm's way. There was no other choice.

When Eric arrived with the girls, I had to fight back tears just looking at them. They were happy to see me, and I was bombarded with squeezes and giggles. Eric wasn't aware of my upcoming travel plans, so I motioned for him to step outside with me. He was visibly not thrilled.

"Three weeks!"

"Things just aren't getting better, and I decided to take your advice. You were right. I need to get my head together for the girls' sake, and the only way I think I can do that is to be by myself for a while, with no distractions, including work." I avoided eye contact with him.

"Don't you think that's more of running away? I mean, if you stayed here, at home, facing your surroundings every day, I think that would be better medicine." He paused and kicked a small stone around with his foot. "Not to mention, I think I might've jumped the gun a little as far as the girls are concerned. You can see them again, alone."

I dreaded what was to come next. "Eric, please don't ask me any questions when I tell you this, okay? But if . . . if something were to happen to me, there's a large envelope in my kitchen desk drawer with your name on it. Inside is a letter to the girls, and a list of other arrangements I've made."

..

He was stunned. "You're not going to Florida, are you?" He grabbed my arm, hard. "You better tell me exactly what you're up to, CeeCee!"

I jerked it away. "Of course I'm going to Florida! Ever since Michael died, I realized how we can all drop dead at any minute! It scares me, Eric! I just want to be prepared is all. Nothing is going to happen, I know that . . . I think. How do I know my plane's not going to crash or something?"

"Your plane is not going to crash." He grabbed my chin to face him. "Look at me directly and tell me you are not lying. You are the mother of my children, and I still love you, so if you're in some kind of trouble I want to know about it."

I almost told him. Eric would be a great asset to take along with me to confront the Mafia. He was a SWAT team member and one of the best police officers I knew. Regardless, my daughters couldn't lose both of their parents at once.

"I'm not lying, I promise, Eric." I tried my best to smile. "C'mon, let's go inside so I can tell the girls."

He didn't believe me, not that I expected him to. We'd been married for over ten years, and he knew me as well as anyone. The girls took my trip fairly well, except for Selina trying to talk me into taking them with me.

"Why can't we go, Mom? You're gonna be all alone on Thanksgiving!"

"I have to, honey. You'll be with Daddy and Jordan, so your Thanksgiving will be great, and I need to be alone right now—understand? When I get back we're going to make it a fresh start." I pulled her close. "How about during your spring break, me, you, and Isabelle head down to Clearwater Beach for a week or two? Maybe we could even take Sean—does that sound okay?"

They both squealed in excitement while my heart skipped. I could only pray I would be around in the springtime. Eric left while we enjoyed the last few hours of the evening together. Dropping them off later, I couldn't hold back my tears at the thought that this might be the last time I ever saw them.

"Why are you crying, Mommy?" Isabelle looked alarmed.

"I'm just going to miss my baby girls. You guys listen to Daddy and I'll try and call you both every night, okay?" I wiped my cheeks.

They both hugged me tight before going inside. I noticed Eric was at the window, watching. There were a lot of things I would've liked to say to him, too, a lot of things I'd never said when our marriage ended. Even though I still cared for him deeply, I felt it was best to let it lie.

Back at home, the rest of the night was spent loading up my car and walking around my house. Michael was everywhere, it seemed—the kitchen, the family room, our bedroom, and his office. Each place held its own memory of him, and as I shut the light off in each of the rooms, I stood for a few moments, remembering.

My last project was typing up the important letter I had put off writing all day. As I sealed it in an envelope and wrote the name on the front, I felt the warm tears run down my cheeks. None of this seemed fair. Wallowing in my self-pity, I pondered the shitty hand of cards life had dealt me, how it all changed in a matter of minutes.

Lying in bed, doing my best to get some sleep, I almost had second thoughts, until searching for other options proved fruitless. After several hours of tossing and turning, I finally drifted off, only to be awakened less than two hours later by the telephone.

"Hello?"

Silence again. Repeating "hello" two more times, I knew I wouldn't get an answer. My anger was reduced to sobs. I was exhausted.

"Who is this?" I cried. "Please! Leave me alone!"

I slammed the phone down, fell onto my pillow, and cried myself back to sleep.

"The hit has been put out on her, sir," Alan Keane said into the phone from his hotel room.

"From both?"

"Just the Iacconas for now. I'm sure once the Filacis get wind of it, they'll follow suit."

"Did we get this on one of our wires? Is it enough to drag them in now?" There was eagerness in his voice.

"No, sir. It came from one of our snitches, but I'm fairly sure it's solid." Alan sighed into the phone. *"Her plane leaves tomorrow night. She's flying into Sarasota, but has arrangements made south of there, in Siesta Key. What do you want me to do?"*

"Send Mark Sanders and Gary Nicholas down there immediately and watch her at all times. Salvatore will probably have his people do it while she's in Florida, so they can't take their eyes off her for a minute!"

"Yes, sir. I'll have them on a plane first thing in the morning."

"Alan, do your best to make sure he doesn't know about this. I'm afraid this might be the one to do it . . . if you know what I mean."

"Yes, sir."

Alan hung up the phone, his chest heavy. The problem his boss didn't know was that it was too late. He already knew.

I slept less than three hours and was up before sunrise. A full day lay ahead of me before my scheduled flight. After quickly taking a shower and getting dressed, I grabbed the rest of my things before lingering in the doorway between the garage and the kitchen. Feeling the familiar surge of emotions, I forced myself to ignore them before shutting the door for good.

Once I arrived at Richland Metro, I thought it best to park in front. The main entrance was an easy way to get to the sheriff's office, and I didn't want to take the chance of running into Naomi or Coop. They had called several times in the last couple of days—at home and on my cell—and had been ignored every time.

When I saw the sheriff's car parked in front, a silent thank-you came through my head. No one ever knew when and if the sheriff would be there. He usually had a full schedule of meetings daily. After parking in the spot next to his, I ran inside and skipped steps going up to his office. His secretary told me to go on in. He was seated behind his desk, listening to voice mail.

"CeeCee!" He shut his phone off and stood up. "Where have you been? Naomi has been in and out of here worried about you."

"I know, Sheriff, I'm sorry. Look, I don't have much time. I wanted to give you this personally." I took the envelope out of my purse and handed it to him. My hand was shaking.

He took the envelope. "What is it?"

"It's my resignation, sir, effective immediately."

CHAPTER TEN

He looked at me as if he was in a state of shock, turning the envelope back and forth to make sure he was really holding it. After a few moments, he thrust the envelope back at me.

"Take this. I will not accept it."

I had expected this, but there was no other way. Sheriff Stephens looked crushed and very worried. He would do everything in his power to talk me out of it, but there was no going back now. Ignoring the envelope, I took my badge and duty weapon out of my purse, set the badge on his desk, and unloaded my gun before setting it and the magazine down as well.

"I'm sorry, Sheriff, but it's done. I have to go."

"CeeCee, wait a minute! Look, per your union contract, I can grant you up to a year of unpaid leave of absence. I know you've been having a rough time, but don't quit! I'll give you all the time you need!" he pleaded.

I shook my head. "You don't understand. I have to do this. I cleaned out my office several days ago. Justin Brown and Coop can handle the homeless murders, and the rest of my cases can be assigned to the other detectives. It will all work out. Please understand."

"I'm not worried about the fucking cases right now!" he barked, and then lowered his voice before walking around his desk and facing me. "CeeCee, you're the best detective I've got. I've known you since you were a little girl, and I know this is all you've ever wanted to do. Please tell me what to do. What can I do to help you and change your mind?"

"Nothing," I whispered, my eyes beginning to fill with tears.

"Does your dad know?" he said, just as quietly.

Shaking my head again and closing my eyes, I answered, "You're the first. Please don't make this harder than it is. I wish I could explain it better, but please, trust me."

He let out a long sigh. "All right, but I'm not filling your spot for a year. The union can file every grievance from here to China, but they can kiss my ass, you hear me? If you change your mind, it'll be here waiting for you."

I nodded, letting my tears fall before I hugged him and said good-bye. He surprised me with what he said as I walked out the door.

"CeeCee, whatever you've gotten yourself into, please . . . be careful." He looked somber.

I didn't respond but merely did my best to smile as I walked out of the Richland Metropolitan Police Department, no longer a civil servant, but a civilian. And that was exactly how I wanted it.

My flight wasn't scheduled to leave for four more hours, which would give me just enough time to get to Cleveland and check into my motel room. All I really needed to do was pay the clerk for the two weeks I planned to stay, and put my things inside with the DO NOT DISTURB sign on the door. If all went well, I would be back in three to four days.

The clerk didn't pay much attention to me—not that I expected him to. Not many people would give a second look to a dark-haired beauty-supply sales-woman checking in under the name Michelle Faulkner. As he handed me the room key, his eyes were still focused on the television that sat on the desk, blaring a twenty-four-hour news channel. It couldn't have been more perfect.

It took less than five minutes to grab my suitcases out of my trunk and throw them in the room. Then I drove to the airport. After acquiring the plane ticket reserved in my own name, I was finally sitting on the plane, slowly sipping a vodka and orange juice as the plane roared through the sky. My previous fear of flying had significantly been squelched. Dying in a plane crash was the least of my worries right now, and I felt that if it was meant to be, then it was meant to be. Three hours and fifty-five minutes later, my plane landed in Sarasota, Florida.

"She's here, Sal."

"Good. Now watch her for a couple of days before you do anything. Make sure the Filacis or the feds aren't watch-ing her as well, and for Christ's sake, don't let them see you if they are!"

"We won't. We know what we're doing."

"Have you figured out what you're gonna do with her yet?"

"I have a contact here. They're building a new high-rise hotel in Fort Myers, and he said they're pouring the

cement in three days. I figure we'll do it the night before and have her in there before the morning."

"Can this contact be trusted?"

"Sure, especially after I paid him ten g's for the info."

"I want to be informed the minute the cement is poured, and I don't care if you have to tear her room to pieces, I want those tapes found and buried with her, you got it?"

"I got it."

Sal slammed the receiver of the pay phone down before telling his driver to pull away. For whatever reason, he was nervous. They'd done several hits like this before, and it had never been a problem. Nonetheless, on this one, he had a bad feeling . . .

It took longer than expected to get my rental car. They'd screwed up my reservation and didn't have a car ready, so while they scrambled to find a replacement, I called the girls to tell them I had arrived safely. When I eventually made the thirty-minute drive out to Siesta Key, it was late. Normally, I would've been somewhat miffed to be driving a late-nineties model rusted-out car around the upscale island, but since nothing was normal anymore, I couldn't have cared less. By the time I pulled into my parking space at my rented condominium, exhaustion overcame me.

Since the condo was located in the heart of Siesta Village, on Ocean Boulevard, I would've loved to take a quick stroll along the beach, but my fatigue wouldn't allow it. The village streets were always adorned with art vendors and flower vendors, and generally had a festive atmosphere. Tossing my bags on the floor of the bedroom, I dove onto the bed fully clothed and slept for twelve hours.

When I woke up and looked at the clock, I silently

chastised myself for sleeping so late, since there was so much to do. My first stop was the grocery store. Technically, I was staying in Siesta Key for three weeks. It would be obvious that I wouldn't eat out the entire time, so I had to have enough food there to prove it.

After the shopping was taken care of, I unpacked all of my suitcases and put everything in drawers and my toiletries in the bathroom. Some of the clothes I balled up and threw in a pile on the bathroom floor, while others were put in a laundry hamper. The condo needed to appear lived-in. In the kitchen I made several frozen dinners, only to dump them in the garbage disposal and throw their boxes in the trash.

When making the reservations, I had requested the condo be a second-story beachfront with a balcony facing the beach. I took two large beach towels and hung them over the balcony, where they began to flap in the wind. It was a beautiful day, and because I was feeling caught up with everything, I threw my bathing suit on and headed to the beach for a couple of hours.

Later that evening, I was walking to my favorite oyster bar in the middle of the village for dinner when I noticed the men. Had they not made such a purposeful move not to be noticed, I would never have given them a second look. They were too sloppy looking to be feds. Even undercover, federal agents still have a clean-cut appearance. No, these were Mafia, no doubt about it.

I was passing an outdoor bar and grill when my attention was drawn to a man who was seated at the bar, drinking a beer. The only reason I noticed him was that he was wearing an Ohio State Buckeyes hat. Whenever I'm out of state and see someone wearing Ohio garb, I automatically notice it for no reason in particular.

The problem happened when he noticed me, out of thirty people walking down the street, and made eye contact. Even then, I may not have been alarmed, but when he quickly looked away and made eye contact with another man across the street perusing the art vendors, my heart rate skyrocketed.

The man looking at the art was wearing a white-collared shirt, khaki shorts, and boat shoes in an attempt to fit in with the locals. An intimidating looking man, he was scummy as well. He locked in on my stare, and we both looked away at the same time. Praying they didn't think I had just discovered them, I stopped at a flower vendor with a large smile on my face and bought several peach roses before strolling down to the oyster bar.

It was difficult to eat, and I had to fake my way through an otherwise-enjoyable dinner on the patio, trying to conceal my fear and trembling. At one point, I dropped my fork on the floor and was able to take a quick glance down the street as I picked it up. There was no sign of the two men anywhere. The only positive side to the incident was that I now knew what they looked like and could keep my eye out for them. The negative was that they might have decided to bump up their scheduled time to take me out.

They could have been waiting for me back in the condo for all I knew. If they were, there wasn't a whole lot I could do. My gun was in the motel room in Cleveland. There had been no way for me to get it through airport security and bring it here. I seriously thought about going to a pawn shop and buying whatever I could get my hands on, but there was a waiting period, and hopefully I would be out of Siesta Key by tomorrow night. If I could survive that long.

"Salvatore's got his men down there, sir. Agent Nicholas spotted Frank Trapini watching her on the street today, and Sanders thought he saw Tommy Miglia sitting at a bar."

"Damn . . . What about the Filacis?"

"No sign of them anywhere, sir. They're all accounted for in Cleveland. No one's missing, even Bertola. I don't think they know about her yet."

"Do you think she knows?"

"I don't know. They saw her slow down and look at Trapini a little strange, but she kept walking and stopped and bought some flowers. I don't think she picked up on it."

"Did you find the tapes?"

"We searched Hagerman's home office after she left, and they weren't there. I'm assuming she has them with her." Alan Keane hoped that wasn't true.

"That's bad if she does. If we know about the tapes, so do they. They're all we got, Alan. Those tapes are gold to us right now, especially with Hagerman gone."

"I know . . . I have some more bad news. Richland Metro just discovered another body today, missing both kidneys."

"Jesus fuck!" his boss's voice screamed through the receiver. *"God damn it, Alan, how did that happen? I thought we had people watching everybody involved?"*

"Yes, sir, we do, but we haven't found the mole," he grumbled.

"I don't know what's taking so long to find him, but you'd better do it soon!"

Alan Keane sighed as he hung up the phone.

Since I had understandably worked myself into a state of paranoia, I stopped at a souvenir shop on my way home. All I could find was a six-inch-long letter opener with a bright green handle that had "Siesta Key" stamped on it. It was better than nothing, and it was also sold in every souvenir shop in Siesta Key—a good thing. If I would ever have to use it, the investigators would be at a dead end as far the letter opener went.

Nervous as hell while opening the door to my condo, I braced myself for anything. The door didn't appear to have been tampered with, and I had lodged a broom handle in the sliding glass door that led to the balcony. All was still in place. Semiconfident that no one else was inside, I searched the place anyway. My heightened awareness and instincts were telling me that I might have to move up my departure date. Instead of leaving tomorrow night, I would have to leave tonight. There was no other way. Each time I thought back to my nonverbal exchange with the man on the street, I became more positive he knew I had blown their cover.

Because my original plans on how I would leave had been botched, I had to take my chances another way. I grabbed my duffel bag, which contained everything needed for my trip, quickly soaked my bathing suit in water, threw it over the shower rod in the bathroom, and turned on the television. Just before I left, my eyes drifted to the letter opener that was on the counter. I grabbed it.

Leaving my condo and walking toward my car, I noticed that one of the towels that had been hanging on my balcony had fallen down to the beach below. For whatever reason, I walked over to pick it up and throw it in my duffel bag. It was while I was bending over to grab the towel that I saw the shadow.

The hat gave him away. As my hand reached for the towel, a dark shadow appeared instantly on the sand to my right—a tall figure wearing a baseball hat. I waited just a split second longer until I knew he was directly behind me to strike. With my letter opener still in hand, I dropped the towel and stood up, quickly spinning around before driving the blade directly in the left side of the man's neck. It was the man I had seen earlier sitting at the bar.

Evidently, he had not expected me to see him or react so quickly, but he had underestimated me. A look of shock washed across his face as his hands dropped the wire he was holding and reached up to grab the letter opener I had just put in his neck. Since I had struck him directly in his carotid artery, blood was literally spraying out of the wound all over the sand and me. The man was making loud gargling sounds as he fell to his knees, and I instinctively pushed him backward, putting both of my hands over his mouth and holding them there. Furiously looking around, I could see no one in the area or anyone else on the balconies. It was less than a minute of the man's thrashing about, trying to pull my hands off his mouth and moaning, before he became still.

I was now in the midst of a full-blown panic and tried to get myself together as I felt the dizziness rush in. Taking long, deep breaths, I looked around some more. Where was the other guy?

I didn't know and didn't wait around to find out. This was a monstrous glitch thrown into my equation, which I clearly hadn't planned for. I stood up, ran over to my rental car, which sat less than ten feet away, and opened the trunk. My hands were shaking so badly I could barely turn the key. Almost on the verge of hysterics, I ran back over to the body and wrapped the beach towel around his head to prevent any more blood from coming out. It was everywhere. And then, with every ounce of strength I had, I dragged the body over to my car. He was so heavy, I didn't know if I'd be able to get him up into my trunk, but adrenaline took over and I managed. I slammed the lid down and began kicking up sand to cover the bloody trail where I had dragged him, including the pool of blood that lay below my balcony.

Like a sand crab, I was on my knees, digging a two-foot-deep hole violently with both hands. Packing the bloody sand inside of it, I smoothed clean sand over the area. The enormous amount of sweat that poured down my face mixed in with the blood that had splattered. My clothes were soaked in it as well. My only option was to dive into the ocean to clean myself off. The salt water would help; it would at least clean me enough so that I wouldn't draw attention if seen getting a fresh pair of clothes out of the duffel bag in my car.

There was a large garbage can in the parking lot that had been emptied for the day and only had a few empty cans in it. I grabbed the plastic garbage bag out of it and put my soaked clothes inside before tying it up and throwing it in the trunk with the body. Standing by the side of my car, I felt ill and had to sit on the nearby curb for a few minutes, trying to get myself together and think.

I had a dead body in the trunk of a rental car, registered in my own name. Fantastic. Then I had an idea. I drove out of the parking lot, got on Midnight Pass Road, and headed for Little Sarasota Bay.

There was a secluded pull-off area just between Turtle Beach and Casey Key with a small wooden pier. Fighting the oncoming numbness in my arms, I dragged the body from my trunk to the edge of the pier and pushed him off. There wasn't a doubt in my mind that the body would be found within the next day or so, but it would be in the water long enough to wash away any evidence I hadn't thought of, and was far enough away from Siesta Key.

After ripping the carpet out of the trunk and placing it inside the garbage bag, I pulled onto the road, then got back out to see if any tire tracks were left. The pull-off was mostly gravel, so I was in luck. Stopping at a public beach area, I threw the bag containing the carpet, clothes, towel, letter opener, and wire that apparently he had planned to strangle me with into a large Dumpster before going to a nearby car wash to spray out the inside of the trunk.

Finally finished, I got back inside my car and began to cry. It was justifiable homicide, without a doubt, but when you factor in the lengths I had taken to dispose of the body, a prison term was guaranteed. If I had called the police, the entire reason for my trip would be blown, and I would be back to square one—even worse off, since the mob would definitely know I killed one of their own. Now, when the body was found, they would only be able to speculate and might possibly blame the other family for getting their revenge.

Again, I had an insatiable urge to feel Michael's arms around me right now, reassuring me that all would be okay. Knowing that wouldn't happen, I stopped at a pay phone and called for a taxicab to pick me up at a restaurant near the condo. My rental car had to remain in the parking lot. Others had to view the situation as if I were still in Siesta Key, in my condo.

Once I got there, I left the keys in the car and saw that I had some time before the cab would arrive at the restaurant down the street. I noticed a child's sand bucket sitting by the pool entrance. Filling the bucket several times with water, I soaked the sand where the buried bloody sand was, over and over. As I felt myself relax somewhat, I went through a checklist of anything I might've forgotten. When I was confident everything was covered, I walked on the beach toward the restaurant.

"What's the emergency?" Alan Keane grumbled sleepily into his phone.

"You're not gonna believe this, sir, but she just killed Tommy Miglia."

Alan Keane, now wide awake, sat straight up in his bed. He wanted to make sure he heard Gary Nicholas right.

"What do you mean, she killed him?"

"He was going to strangle her, so we were about ready to move in, but she got to him first. She stabbed him in the neck." Gary Nicholas sounded out of breath and panicked.

"Right now, she's loading him into her trunk. What should we do?"

Alan Keane thought for a moment. "Don't do anything."

"Sir?"

"I said, don't do anything! Let her be. Just keep a tail and see what she does with him. If we move in now it will fuck everything up, and they'll kill her anyway. We'll deal with this after the fact. Understand?"

"Yes, sir, I understand." Gary Nicholas swallowed loudly, which Alan Keane could clearly hear through the phone.

"Agent Nicholas, neither you nor Agent Sanders are to tell anyone about this, do you hear me? No one!"

"Yes, sir."

"Call me in the morning with an update."

Alan Keane slammed the phone down and fell back on his bed to stare up at the ceiling. He would have to call Erie, Pennsylvania, and inform him of this. It was a phone call he dreaded.

I stopped inside the pool house and put on my dark colored wig, a floppy hat, and a large sweatshirt. With my duffel bag slung over my shoulder, I went out the back door that led to the beach. The cab would be at the restaurant waiting to take me back to the Sarasota airport.

The ride to the airport went quickly, and after several glances behind us, I concluded that the cab wasn't being followed. In addition, the car ride gave me the chance to settle down somewhat.

I rented another car at the airport in the name of Michelle Faulkner and showed "Michelle's" identification and credit cards. When a law-enforcement officer works undercover, the Bureau of Motor Vehicles will allow them to obtain a driver's license in that name. Of course, the paperwork is horrendous and has to be signed by the sheriff, etc.

Using the driver's license of Michelle Faulkner, one I had used on numerous undercover operations, I'd been able to obtain credit cards in that name. I had committed a felony just by obtaining the cards, let alone charging anything to them, which I had no intention of doing.

The drive to Miami International Airport gave me a lot of time to think and put things into perspective. Feeling exhaustion like I had never felt before, I was asleep before my flight left the ground for Cleveland. Only when I felt the flight attendant gently shake my shoulder did it dawn on me the flight was already over.

More than groggy, I made my way to the rental-car desk, then made the drive to the motel I had checked into less than forty-eight hours before. A sense of déjà vu came over me as I tossed the duffel bag to the floor and fell onto the bed fully clothed with my wig still on and into a deep sleep. Like my first day in Siesta Key, I woke up almost twelve hours later, in the middle of the afternoon.

It was a dreary, cold, overcast day outside, and I wanted nothing more than to stay in bed and sleep. Unfortunately, the events of the last two days flooded my memory, and I immediately felt sick as I dragged myself to the shower to wash away my sins. Then I dressed casually, brushed out the long, dark wig and put it on, and set out to find the Filaci family.

The suitcases that I had put in the room days earlier contained not only clothing and toiletries but also a complete set of high-tech surveillance equipment that I had purchased with my own money. Some of the items were top of the line, even better than what we had at Richland Metro. Grabbing the night-vision goggles and video recorder, a camera that could record pictures and sound from up to a thousand feet away, I started for the Filaci offices. Jimmy Garito had told me most of them worked out of their offices during business hours on weekdays. He had described Joseph Filaci at our meeting, so I recognized him immediately when he emerged from the office building an hour after I'd begun watching it.

Joseph Filaci was an extremely handsome man. Unlike Michael's clean, pretty, model good looks, Joseph had a rugged appeal about him. In his early forties, he had the Italian dark hair and eyes, with two to three days' worth of stubble on his face in the shape of a goatee. Wearing an expensive blue suit with a black overcoat, he looked very intimidating. He wasn't overly tall, maybe five nine or five ten, but he was stocky.

I began filming him as soon as he left the building and continued as he walked down the street and into a local diner on the corner. I jotted the time down in the notebook I had with me and logged the time Joseph left the diner and went back to the office building.

For the next three days, I watched as Joseph Filaci went to that diner every day at the same time. On the fourth day, I decided it was time we met.

"She's gone, sir."

"She's what?" Alan Keane couldn't believe what he was hearing.

"She disappeared. We—we last saw her walking toward

the pool at the condominium. When she didn't come back around the building, Sanders went to check, and she was gone. We looked down the beach and all, but she just vanished."

"Oh, dear God," Alan mumbled. "Did they get her?"

"I don't think so, sir. That's what's so odd about all of this. After she dumped Miglia's body in the bay, she went back to the condo. When Sanders saw that she was gone, we saw Frank Trapini pulling into the parking lot. He's been sitting there for hours. I think he's waiting for Miglia, not realizing he'll be waiting for eternity. But regardless, I don't think they had anything to do with it. I think . . ." Agent Gary Nicholas paused.

"Go on. What?"

"I think she figured all of us out and gave us the slip— the Iacconas included."

Alan Keane closed his eyes and sighed loudly. The ramifications of this night may prove fatal, he surmised. Knowing the phone calls he would have to make, he gave Agent Nicholas his last order.

"Find her. Now," he said, before hanging up.

He immediately made the phone call he dreaded, and waited until morning to inform his boss in Washington of what had transpired.

"You know what this means, don't you?" the boss said in a calm voice that frightened Alan Keane.

"Yes, sir, I do."

"Do what you have to, but don't let him find out."

Alan sighed again. *"It's too late, sir. He's already on his way to Cleveland."*

The day I decided to meet Joseph Filaci, I put extra time into my appearance. I wanted to look good, but not to the point where it was distracting, or remembered. I styled the wig to where soft dark curls framed my face before cascading down my back. Before dressing in a casual black pantsuit, I put in the brown contact lenses purchased a week ago. I grabbed my tan overcoat and set out for the diner, arriving ten minutes before Joseph.

Taking a seat at the counter, I ordered a cup of coffee and lit a cigarette. As I took it out of my pocket, my hand was sweating, like the rest of me, from nerves. The dark green Pontiac parked on the street two buildings down from the diner had caught my attention days ago—including the federal agents that sat inside of it. As I strode past the car, I kept my head down and my face hidden by the large scarf and dark glasses I wore. They didn't even glance at me.

When I heard the door to the diner swing open, I knew it was Joseph Filaci even before he sat directly to my left. In my previous surveillance, I'd noticed Joseph sat in the same seat every day. The waitress, obviously familiar with his routine and orders, had a cup of coffee waiting for him as he sat down.

"Here you are, doll." She shoved the cup toward him.

"Thanks, Ginny. I'll take a menu today."

I noticed my hand shaking horribly as I stirred my own coffee and looked down at the counter.

"No BLT today, Joey? What's the world coming to? Here ya go, handsome." A homely woman in her thirties, she was clearly infatuated with him.

I was so overcome with nerves, I didn't even hear him when he spoke directly to me. It took a couple of seconds to realize what he wanted.

"Ma'am? Excuse me, but can you slide the cream down my way?"

He was smiling at me, a smile that faded instantly when he saw the look of contempt on my face.

"Sure, here you are." I slid the bowl full of creamers toward him.

"I'm sorry, but do I know you? You look awfully familiar. You come in here a lot?"

My pulse quickened, and I found myself beginning to panic. In a quick slip of grace, I managed to knock over my coffee. Jumping off the stool, I began grabbing napkins to wipe up the mess.

"Here, let me help . . ." He was eyeing me curiously as he started wiping the counter.

"No, that's okay, I got it." I tried to smile.

The only good thing about my coffee spill was that I had managed to evade his question, which he didn't ask again. It didn't matter; it was time for me to leave. I slid the item I had held in my hand under a napkin and pushed it toward him.

"Here you go. I think I might've splashed some on your suit. Sorry about that."

Throwing a dollar down on the counter, I hurriedly walked out of the diner. My car was a block away, and I was hoping that once Joseph Filaci read my note, he wouldn't come running after me. The note gave him enough information to tell him it would be a bad idea.

It read,

There is a green Pontiac four-door parked outside, two buildings away. In it are three FBI agents watching you. I have important information that you want

about your brother Niccolo's murder. Meet me at the
Pink Floyd exhibit in the Rock and Roll Hall of Fame
in EXACTLY thirty minutes. Whatever you do, make
sure you are not being followed. It is very important
that you come alone.

There wasn't a doubt in my mind that Joseph
Filaci would show up.

CHAPTER ELEVEN

It was going to take every ounce of self-control I had to present a cool demeanor. Finding the Pink Floyd exhibit in the museum wasn't difficult; they were Michael's favorite band, and I had a photograph of him standing right in front of it. It seemed Michael was everywhere.

My watch showed that Joseph Filaci was due to arrive in ten minutes. There weren't many people in the museum, much to my dismay. I was hoping we could blend in somewhat, but it clearly wasn't going to happen.

At that precise moment, my prayers were answered. Walking in my direction was a large tour group, followed by Joseph Filaci. I could feel my heart rate quicken. I knew meeting with him was a huge risk. I'd heard the tapes, including their plan to kill Michael, but something in my gut told me that it was the Iacconas who were responsible. God help me if I was wrong.

"Tommy's dead, Sal."

"What!" He wasn't sure he'd heard Frank right.

"They fished his body out of the bay this morning. I don't

know the particulars, but they already had him identified and on the news."

Frank was nervous, an emotion he wasn't accustomed to. He had dreaded making the phone call to Sal and spent over an hour rehearsing how he was going to break the news. He screwed up, letting Tommy go alone to take care of the woman, and he knew there were no more second chances as far as Sal was concerned. The quiet response on the other end of the phone made his nervousness worse, and he saw his hand was beginning to tremble.

"How did this happen, Frankie?" Sal's voice was dreadfully calm.

"He wanted to go alone, Sal. He said he could take care of her with no problem. When he didn't show up, I went and sat in front of her condo, but there was no sign of him anywhere. I spent all night looking for him until I saw the news . . ."

"And her?"

"I don't know. After a coupla hours, I broke into her condo to see if maybe Tommy had already done her, but she wasn't there. Her car, clothes, cell phone, and stuff is still inside, so she either was out late, or Tommy got her first."

Another long moment of silence.

"I think it's safe to assume that Leo and Joseph just got their revenge for Niccolo, eh Frank?"

"I thought that too, but how in the hell did they know we were here? Or her? Last we heard from our source, the Filacis weren't even onto her."

"That's right." Sal paused and had a frightening thought. "Maybe it was her."

"Who?"

"Gallagher. Maybe she killed Tommy. Maybe she was onto you two fuckups long before you arrived. And maybe . . . she planned this trip to set us up."

Now it was Frank's turn to be silent. Sal might have been right. She must've caught on the day she made eye contact with them in the street. Sal obviously read his mind.

"She saw you on the street that day, didn't she, Frankie? Where are they on the murder investigation?"

"I don't think they have a clue, Sal. Whoever is responsible covered their tracks real well. The cops haven't even connected Tommy to Siesta Key yet, and I don't think they will either."

"Stay there a few more days and see if she turns up. If she doesn't, get your fucking ass back here."

"Sure, Sal."

I braced myself as the tour group passed by. Joseph Filaci stopped approximately two feet away from me, a hardened look on his face.

"Here I am. Now, do you want to tell me who the hell you are and how you know so much about my brother?" He spoke low, but strong.

"I'm Michelle Faulkner." My head bowed, I avoided eye contact. "That's all you need to know about me. I don't have proof right now, but I believe Salvatore Iaccona killed your brother, or at least one of his employees did. Have you ever heard of Frank Trapini?"

"Of course."

"I think he was the one personally sent to kill Niccolo." My eyes locked on his.

"How do you know that, and why do you care? You're going to have to give me a little more information about yourself before I continue this conversation. I can't help but get the feeling I know you from somewhere."

I turned away from him and faced the exhibit, my thoughts in turmoil. I couldn't come out and tell him I had a recording where Frank Trapini and Salvatore Iaccona confessed to Niccolo's murder. This wasn't going to be easy.

"Mr. Filaci, all I can tell you right now is that Salvatore Iaccona is responsible for the death of someone close to me. Jimmy Garito told me you might be able to help," I whispered, and turned to face him, forcing tears to my eyes. I needed to appear delicate.

"You know Jimmy?" His face softened.

"Yes."

He began to look around. "Let's get out of here. There's a warehouse at the corner of Chester Avenue and—"

"The FBI is watching it. We can't go there," I interrupted.

"How'd you know that?" His eyes narrowed suspiciously.

"Two blocks from here is a small bookstore." I ignored his question. "There's some tables and chairs in the back. We should be able to sit and talk without worry."

He looked at me oddly before walking away. I waited ten more minutes, then followed. Walking to the bookstore, I used my convenience-store prepaid cellular phone to check the messages on my regular cell, which was still in Florida. The phone I was currently using couldn't be traced.

As I suspected, there were numerous calls from Naomi and Coop regarding my resignation. They were worried and wanted to know why I quit. There were three messages from Justin Brown, too. There had been another murder, and he urgently wanted my help. I called him back, knowing I wouldn't have to answer the intimate questions that Naomi and Coop would ask. He answered on the first ring.

"Justin, its CeeCee."

"CeeCee! How are you? You know everyone here is all worried about you. Hang on a minute, I'll grab Coop and . . ."

"No! Don't do that, Justin, please. I don't have much time. I was just calling about the other murder." I tried not to sound panicked.

"Huh? Well, okay then. Um, let me look here . . ." The sound of papers shuffling came over the phone. "Yesterday morning we had another one. This time it was both kidneys, and the liver."

Happening to walk by the Cleveland Browns stadium, I could barely hear him as the score of the current football game was being announced. Quickly, I stepped inside a nearby tobacco shop.

"You said both kidneys and liver?"

"Yup."

"Any leads?"

"That's what I wanted to talk to you about. I found out where all that money in Troy Cross's account came from. All I know is, it was some type of stock, but I can't determine how to find out for sure."

"Ask him."

"What?"

"Ask him, Justin. Bring him in, and ask him directly if he had stock in LifeTech Industries. If he doesn't want to answer, threaten to put him on the polygraph. He'll talk. But you might be surprised. He'll probably just come out and tell you. Remember, he denied knowing anything at all about LifeTech during the first interview, so if he comes out and admits it, you'll at least have an obstruction charge to hold over his head and threaten him with."

"I feel pretty stupid for not doing that in the first place."

I laughed. "Don't worry about it. Sometimes it's easy to make things more complicated in the detective business. I'm assuming no leads on the recent murder?"

"Not a one."

"Stay on Troy Cross and hammer down on him about the two doctors, if he knows them and such."

"All right, I'll keep in touch, CeeCee. How's Florida? I'm jealous, the weather up here sucks, and they're calling for more snow."

"It's wonderful. I'm basking in the sun daily," I lied. "Listen, Justin, I have to go, but do stay in touch."

I hung up before he'd have a chance to put Naomi or Coop on the phone. Not to mention, Joseph was waiting for me at the bookstore. As I walked to the front door, I briefly checked around for any suspicious cars or people. Seeing none, I went in and headed straight for the back of the old, smoky bookstore where Joseph Filaci sat and waited patiently. He stood up as I sat down. He was undeniably a well-mannered mobster.

"I took the liberty of getting you a cup of coffee, with cream, which I already added so you didn't need to risk spilling it again." He smiled.

"Thank you. Do you mind?" I shook my pack of cigarettes at him.

"Absolutely not. Light up."

I lit a cigarette and took a long sip of the hot coffee before taking a deep breath, not knowing where to begin. As I reached into my purse to put my lighter back, I pushed the record button on my hidden tape recorder.

"Mr. Filaci . . ."

"Call me Joseph."

"All right then, Joseph. Honestly, I'm not quite sure where to begin."

A strange look came across his face. He stood up and grabbed my purse off of the chair. I was frozen, unable to act. Pulling out the tape recorder, he slammed it on the table, breaking it. The few people perusing the bookstore looked our way. My gun was in my purse—not that I thought he would kill me in front of three other people. Nonetheless, I was terrified. Even more shocking, he sat calmly back down in his chair before he took a sip of his coffee.

"How about we begin this conversation with the truth? Do you agree, Mrs. Hagerman? Oh, that's right. You go by the name Gallagher."

He set his cup down and locked his eyes on mine. My mind was in pure chaos in an attempt to establish my next move. Out of my element, I determined the best thing I could do was comply with Joseph's request. I was going to tell him everything.

"You don't understand," I said quietly.

"The only thing I understand is that the detective wife of a dead FBI agent is secretly meeting with me to gather evidence against my family. You are on dangerous ground here, Ms. Gallagher. You see, I couldn't remember where I had seen you, but then it hit me. Jimmy Garito lives in Mansfield. You know as well as I do that we keep tabs on law enforcement, just like you do on us. I've seen your picture several times, when you were on the news—minus the black wig and dark contact lenses. Frankly, you look much better as a blonde."

"Please, listen to me. If you don't like what I have to say, I'll never contact you again."

He leaned back in his chair and folded his arms. His nod was the only form of communication that enabled me to continue.

"I'm not a detective anymore. I resigned over a week ago. I'm here on my own personal business. Not for the feds, not for local law enforcement, only for me. Please believe me." I breathed deeply. "Before I go on, there's an important question I have to ask you, and you can choose whether to answer it or not."

"Go on," he said without hesitation.

"Mr. Filaci, did you or your family kill my husband?" Now the tears that filled my eyes were genuine.

His body relaxed as he leaned forward. As if this day could get any more shocking, he gently took my hand before he spoke, looking directly in my eyes.

"No, we didn't. The persons responsible for killing your husband were none other than Salvatore Iaccona and his family."

"But you planned to, didn't you?" I pulled my hand away, tears flowing down my cheeks. "I heard you! I heard you, your father, and Vincent Vicari planning to kill him!" My voice rose.

He looked shocked. "How do you know that? You heard? How?"

I shook my head furiously. "It's not important how, but why? Why would you do that?"

He sighed. "It's true, my father wanted your husband dead. But believe me when I tell you, I didn't agree and even talked him out of it later on."

Remembering the recording of Joseph telling his father it was a bad idea to kill Michael made me believe him. Surprisingly, I felt better. Hearing it come directly from Joseph Filaci seemed to put me at ease.

"Can you tell me what happened?" I wiped my eyes with a tissue.

"I'm not sure what all you know, but most of this is mere speculation. We think that the Iacconas are into something very profitable, something my brother wanted a piece of. When they shut him out, we think your husband brought him on board with the FBI, as an informant, to bring down Sal's business. Obviously, Sal found out and took care of Niccolo before he could pass along any information." He took a sip of coffee. "You need to understand my father. Niccolo was his golden child, and when he died, my father wanted to take it out on everybody, including your husband."

"Do you know what the business is?"

"No, but we've been trying to find out. I'll tell you straight that if I get solid proof that Sal killed my brother, there will be hell to pay."

"I have a tape recording, where Frank Trapini and Salvatore confess to killing your brother. The business they are involved in is called LifeTech Industries, and I'm not positive what it's about, but it's a medical company here in Cleveland." Ignoring the look of shock on his face, I continued. "I've been watching you for the last four days and wanted to meet with you to make a deal."

"A deal?"

"Yes. The deal is this: you help me gather evidence and bring down Salvatore Iaccona and his entire family, and I will give you every file the FBI has on your family. Not to mention the revenge you are so desperately looking for," I said defiantly.

He slid his chair back. "Look, this is a lot to take in. I'm gonna need some time—"

"I need an answer now. Yes or no."

His eyes scoured the walls lined with books. Then he looked down at the floor and finally back at me.

"Okay, I'll do it."

"Fine. And Joseph? Call me CeeCee."

The call that came in for Alan Keane was urgent. "Well?" *Alan asked breathlessly.*

"We haven't found her yet, but we got a hell of a good lead," Agent Nicholas said calmly.

Alan's heart sank. "I was hoping you were calling to tell me you found her. Is she dead?"

"I don't think so. We checked all of the cab companies and found that one picked up a thirtysomething, dark-haired female at an oyster bar up the road from the condo the night we lost her. He drove her to Sarasota International and dropped her off at the rental-car place. From there, she rented a car, which was turned in at Miami International."

"Why would someone rent a car from one airport and drive to another?"

"Well, get this, the name used for the rental cars took an immediate flight to Cleveland."

"It's got to be her! It's got to be! What was the name?"

"Michelle Faulkner."

"Get your asses back up here and start checking every goddamn motel and hotel in the city for anyone registered in that name."

"I'm already on it. Nothing so far, but we still got a shit-load more to go."

"Let me know the minute you find her. What's going on with Miglia? Are they going to be able to tie him to her?"

"Nah. She did a damn good job of covering her tracks. We talked to a source at the police department, and they don't have a clue."

"Good. Keep checking in from time to time to see if anything turns up."

"Will do. Alan, you know that if Salvatore thinks she's responsible for Miglia, they're gonna come at her harder and harder until they find her."

"That's what I'm afraid of."

Joseph suggested we meet later for dinner to go over some plans. Little did he know, I had a daily itinerary mapped out for the next week or two.

He wasn't overly surprised that he was being followed by the FBI; he had suspected as much. But now that he knew what kind of car they were in, it was easier for him to give them the slip. We agreed to meet at a parking garage downtown. He would pull in, park, get into my car, and hunker down while I drove back out.

Predictably, the green Pontiac was parked on the street about a block down from the parking garage. They didn't even glance my way when I pulled out. When I gave Joseph the okay that we were safe, he chuckled to himself as he crawled from the backseat to the front passenger seat. Once we were several miles away from the waiting Pontiac, I took off my wig and sunglasses. I hadn't bothered with the contacts today. Joseph smiled.

"Definitely better. You know, you're a very attractive woman, CeeCee."

"Thanks." His compliment made me uncomfortable. It made me feel guilty somehow.

After circling the block of the restaurant several times, I was satisfied no other cars were tailing us, so I parked. We chose a small, quiet table at the back of the dimly lit room, and Joseph ordered a bottle of wine. Even though I knew our meeting was strictly business related, my guilt began to grow rapidly. I missed Michael more than ever at that very moment.

Joseph wanted to know definitively what I had planned, down to the minute, regarding our newly formed partnership. I had a few questions for him as well.

"Did you tell your father about me, Joseph?"

"Absolutely not. He would've become unglued and sent hit men out for you and Salvatore both."

His response startled me a little. "Why would he want to kill me?"

"You don't know my father."

Apparently not, and the more I heard, the more I realized I didn't want to get anywhere near Leon Filaci. Before we got into details, I learned a few minor facts about Joseph.

He was forty-three years old, and surprisingly, like me, he was widowed. His wife had died two years ago from cancer, and they'd had no children. He had been seeing someone off and on for the last year, but I got the impression she was more serious about him than he was about her. Joseph didn't seem to be as interested in the family business as his brother Niccolo had been, a fact that made Niccolo the favorite in Leon's eyes. Not resentful of the superior sibling like one would see in most families, Joseph clearly loved his deceased brother.

"What about you, CeeCee?"

"What about me?" I knew I appeared defensive.

"You seem so mysterious, hardened." He paused. "You must have loved him very much." He referred to Michael.

"More than life itself." I didn't like the direction the conversation was going, so I quickly redirected it. "Let's get down to business. I think we need to go to Youngstown first thing in the morning."

He smiled, openly amused at my avoidance of personal questions.

"That's fine, but one of the things I don't understand is how you can gather evidence against the Iacconas? How will any of it be admissible?"

"I'm a private citizen now. I don't have to abide by the rules of search and seizure. I can gather all the information I want, drop it off anonymously on the FBI's doorstep, and they can use all of it. They won't even know where it came from."

"So that's why you resigned."

"Yes, it is."

"I have to tell you, these are some pretty dangerous characters we'll be dealing with. You're obviously familiar with Frank Trapini, but there are others: Tommy Miglia and—"

"Tommy Miglia is dead."

"He is? How?" Joseph put down his glass of wine.

"Let's just say it was an unfortunate accident." My face was expressionless.

"I see," he said quietly, while grasping the underlying confession I had just given. "I've heard stories about you, CeeCee, a strong-willed, tough cop, but mostly brilliant. I guess Tommy Miglia didn't know who he was up against."

Looking down at the table, I twirled my fork in between my fingers.

"You realize they'll be looking for you, CeeCee?" Joseph said.

"They've been looking for me for quite a while already. In fact, they'd already ordered Tommy to kill me in Florida when I had to defend myself, which resulted in his ill-fated swim in the Gulf of Mexico." I was sullen. "You know, Joseph, they may think your family is responsible, as an act of revenge for Niccolo."

He put his face in his hands and sighed before taking another drink of wine. We were interrupted by the waitress, who was ready to take our order. Since my appetite was still on a permanent vacation, I ordered a light salad.

"CeeCee, why are you telling me all of this? You didn't have to tell me about Tommy. How do you know I won't turn you in?"

"Because I have a tape recording of you and your family ordering the murder of my husband, that's why. Call it collateral. As long as I'm alive and a free citizen, that tape will never surface. Understand?" I asked stiffly.

"You certainly play hardball."

"I wasn't aware there was any other way. You help me, and you can have the files, *and the tape*, as promised."

From that point on, Joseph and I had an understanding. He knew where I stood and where I was coming from, and most importantly, I trusted him. There was no one else to turn to.

We agreed to meet the following morning in front of the diner where we had first met. From there we would drive to Youngstown and check into a motel Joseph was familiar with. He would rent out both rooms under an assumed name. After that, we would be trailing the Iacconas night and day.

Arriving back at my own motel room, I quickly called Eric and talked to the girls. Hearing their voices on the phone brought me immediately to tears. How I missed them. Next, I grabbed my laptop computer so I could go online and check the Florida newspapers for any word of Tommy's murder investigation. I already knew they had found the body almost a week ago, but as each day passed, the articles grew smaller and were printed farther toward the end of the paper.

Today, there was a small article below the weather, asking anyone with information to call the detective bureau. I breathed a sigh of relief. I knew that meant they had absolutely nothing to go on, as far as his murder went. The evidence I had put in the trash bin was long gone by now, and other than that, there was nothing.

Next, I read an article in the Mansfield paper about the recent murder Justin had told me about. The victim, thirty-three-year-old Christopher Albert, had been out walking his dog in a middle-class neighborhood when he had been abducted. His body was found a mile and a half from his home, in a nearby park. I felt disconnected, reading about murders in my own jurisdiction in the newspaper, having to constantly remind myself I was no longer a police officer. One thing the article told me is that the killer or killers were getting desperate. They were no longer targeting homeless, displaced citizens, but had moved on to whoever they could get—the last two, Alisha Cross and Christopher Albert.

I turned off my computer and undressed to get ready for bed. I had a long day tomorrow, and probably each day after that. Regardless, whatever questions that remained unanswered today, I was sure I would find the answers to all of them in Youngstown.

Frank Trapini dreaded meeting with Sal. As he walked down the long hallway to his office, he prepared himself for a verbal lashing. Sal was already pissed at him before he went to Florida. Now, with Tommy gone, whom Sal had looked upon as a son, he was sure this was the last time he would walk down this particular hallway. He knocked lightly on the closed door and opened it when the loud, gruff voice told him to come in.

"Sit down, Frank."

Frank complied, nodding at Henry Mastragna and William Petrosino standing against the wall. Sal's own sons, Antonio and Petey, stood behind Sal's desk with him.

"She's in Cleveland," Sal announced.

Frank was shocked. "But how?"

"Because you fucked up, that's how." Sal rose from behind his desk, walked around it, and stood in front of Frank. "I've done a lot for you, Frankie. You've been at the top of your game for a long time, but lately . . . lately, I don't know what's going on with you."

"I'll fix it, Sal!" Frank pleaded. He knew what was coming. "I swear, I'll fix it! She won't be hard to find, I know it!"

Sal had never seen Frank so weak. He had always been such an intimidating man, but as Sal knew, even the strongest of men had their breaking point. It was too bad. He had hoped Frank would eventually be able to help Sal's son Antonio take over the family when Sal was dead and buried. But it wasn't meant to be. Frank could no longer be trusted.

"Why should I give you another chance, Frankie? You know I don't give second chances." Sal crossed his arms and stared at Frank.

Frank stood up, facing Sal. "Because! I promise, Sal, I promise! I won't fuck up this—"

The blast of the gun came from the right. Henry Mastragna walked up from behind Frank and was able to angle the gun about six inches from his temple. Frank never saw it coming. As his body fell to the left, the blood, brain matter, and bone fragments sprayed against the farthest wall before Frank, eventually, hit the floor. All of them stood looking over Frank's body as the smell of gunpowder permeated the room. Finally, Sal spoke.

"Petey, Billy, clean up the mess and dump him under the construction site." Petey Iaccona and William Petrosino moved immediately. "Henry, you're now in charge of the deliveries. The truck will be there first thing in the morning for you to pick up the shipment and deliver to the Philippines."

Sal sat down again behind his desk and watched as Petey and Billy wrapped Frank's body in large, industrial-size garbage bags. He decided to warn each of them.

"Let this be a lesson to all of you. Don't fuck with me or fuck with my business. We're already behind on orders, and I'll be damned if I get cut out because of simple incompetence like Frank's." They all nodded. "Tony, you and Billy, as soon as he's done dumping Frank, have a job. That job is *to find Gallagher and finish what Frank fucked up. If you don't, you'll both be lying next to him. You got it?"*

"We got it."

"My source tells me that she's using an alias, Michelle Faulkner. She's checked into a room at the Days Inn on Lake Road, just outside the city limits, in Lakewood. As soon as you're done, get your asses to Cleveland and take care of it."

CHAPTER TWELVE

Joseph thought it best if we met early in the morning at a coffee shop just outside of downtown. We would drive my new rental car to Youngstown. I had taken the old one back, claiming it wasn't running right, so they replaced it. Joseph had our motel rooms reserved, and we would go there first to get settled in before setting out on our surveillance of the Iacconas.

The looming black and gray clouds in the sky above us were full of snow. The weather forecast was calling for several inches, and it was unbearably cold. Joseph was verbally thrashing my rear-wheel-drive rental.

"If this snow hits before we get there we're gonna have to find some dogs or something to pull this goddamn car." He looked up at the sky through the windshield as he drove.

"I asked for an SUV, or at the very least a front-wheel drive, but they didn't have any available," I explained.

"Let's just keep our fingers crossed."

It must've worked, because we had no sooner crossed the Youngstown city limits than the sky opened up and unleashed six inches of heavy, blowing snow. We were able to find our motel, but we wouldn't be leaving it for a while. It was well into the following day before the snow began to subside enough for road crews to get their own trucks and plows out. In the meantime, Joseph and I took the time to go over every little detail of our mission.

"Our best bet is to get the recording devices you have into Sal's personal office at the warehouse. I've been doing some checking, and it seems that all of the confidential meetings take place there. Sal keeps another office to throw off the feds; they apparently don't know about this one. But we do." Joseph looked at the blueprint of the warehouse he was referring to.

"What makes you think that the feds don't know about it? You came across it easy enough."

"Trust me, CeeCee. If we're going to work together, you're going to have to trust me." The frown on his rugged face deepened as he looked at me. "I have people that know people that know people, you get it? I can always find something out, except the main part of their business. They're all being tight-lipped about that."

Joseph was sitting on my bed with the blueprint spread out before him, marking off areas that we would be able to enter without being seen. He evidently had been to the warehouse before, because he told me that no one was there until at least ten in the morning, but they stayed very late. I had learned not to ask Joseph too many questions. While he worked on our entry plan, I started gathering all of my recording equipment to make sure everything was running properly. I was in the process of hooking one of the pieces into my laptop when I found Joseph staring at me.

"What the hell is that?" He referred to the

checkbook-sized black and silver contraption I was currently holding.

"It's kind of like a pen register, but better."

"What the hell is a pen register?"

Realizing Joseph wasn't wise to police lingo, I explained. "A pen register is hooked up to someone's phone line and traces every call that goes in and out. The main box, which would be at the police station, spits out the numbers on a roll of paper. It looks a little like cash-register tape." I held out the small machine. "This one will not only trace all of the calls, but it will actually record the conversations."

"Let me see that so I can make sure one of those things isn't hooked up to my own goddamn phone line at home." I handed it to him, smiling. "You know how to hook this up, CeeCee?"

I nodded. "The phones will be a piece of cake, since the phone cable is on the outside of the building." I picked up a larger, heavier piece of equipment about the size of a brick and held it out. "This is going to be a little harder."

"What is it?"

"The FBI uses something called a pole camera. It's hooked up to an electrical box or something directly across from the building they want to watch. They use it to get license plates, facial close-ups, etc. But the bonus of the pole camera is that you can operate it using nothing but a telephone keypad—zoom, directions, focusing, night vision, anything you can think of. It'll even take still photos. That's what I have, but better. It goes inside."

"Yeah, but where are you going to put it so they don't see it? You've never been in there before."

"I'll find a place, believe me. And the beauty of the

whole enchilada is that we can watch and hear everything from my laptop. Record it all, too."

"I don't want to burst your bubble, CeeCee, but there's a pretty good chance that Sal doesn't have a phone in there. He's not an ignorant man."

"If he doesn't, I have these, too." I held up two small silver microphones that looked like dimes, only a tad thicker. "They record sound up to thirty feet. I can put these anywhere."

"The rumors were true. You *are* brilliant." Joseph smiled and looked at me in a way I didn't like.

We had been spending a lot of time together. Under different circumstances, for Joseph or me to develop feelings for the other would not be unthinkable. Unfortunately for Joseph, under these circumstances it *was* unthinkable to me. Maybe in another life, but not this one. I surmised it would take years, if ever, to get over Michael. The thought alone terrified me. Joseph, clearly sensing my apprehension, began slowly folding up the blueprint.

"It's late. I'm going to head back to my room to get some sleep. You should do the same. Tomorrow, we'll watch the warehouse, if we're able to drive anywhere. If we can't get out before ten in the morning, we'll just follow everybody later." He avoided eye contact.

"Good night, Joseph."

After he had gone, I spent the remaining hours of the night lying on my bed and staring at the ceiling. There were so many thoughts, with no place to put them all. They ran about, frantically searching every last corner of my mind, looking for somewhere to call home. My thoughts crowded each other, a cyclone of images and voices compressed together in my head with such ferocity that I thought it would explode. I sat up, craving a drink and desperately wanting Michael.

Sleep decided to play hide-and-seek with me tonight. In an attempt to stay positive, I figured I might have slept close to three hours. In reality, it was closer to two. I went over and over all of my plans to ensure there wasn't anything overlooked or left out. It was this particular night that I decided dying was not an option. I would see my children again, no matter what I had to do. All of my previous fears would be filed away. They were there to keep me on my toes. The last few months I had been weak, but no more. As hard as it was to imagine, my life would go on without Michael—for my children, and for myself.

"She checked into a room at the Days Inn on Lake Road, but it doesn't look like anyone's been there for a few days."

"Are you sure it's her?" Alan Keane was hopeful.

"Pretty sure. The front desk has security cameras, and we pulled the tape from the day she checked in. She had a dark wig on and a hat, but I'm confident enough to say I'm one hundred percent sure."

Alan breathed a sigh of relief as he nodded at the man who was sitting in a chair directly across from him, having come from Erie two days ago. At this moment, he looked like a rocket ready to take off. Alan's nod made him relax considerably.

"Alan, there's something else that I don't think you're gonna like," Agent Nicholas sighed into the phone. "Joseph Filaci is gone, too. We think they're together."

Alan stiffened. "Together as in he took her, or together voluntarily?"

"We think voluntarily. Keith and Steve saw someone matching her description go into the diner Filaci goes to

about fifteen minutes before he went in. They sat together. They saw the same woman pull out of a parking garage later on that Joseph drove into, but they didn't see him with her. He might've been crouched down in the seat or something."

The man across from Alan stood up and faced him, fists and jaw clenched. His relaxation was short-lived.

"Now relax," Alan coaxed him as he hung up the phone. "It may not be a bad thing. If she's with Joseph, she may have a better chance of getting the information."

The man walked out of Alan's hotel room, slamming the door behind him. This wasn't good, Alan thought. If she was with Joseph, she might be giving him information as well. Alan picked up the phone again and called Agent Nicholas back.

"Go to Youngstown," he ordered.

"Huh?"

"I think they're in Youngstown trying to get the Iacconas. Grab Keith and Steve if you need to. Don't worry about surveillance on the Filacis right now. Just get your asses there and see if you can find them. Remember, don't let them see you!"

"We're on our way."

"Gary, wait. What have you turned up on the mole? If we know she's here or in Youngstown, they will soon enough."

"Didn't I tell you, Alan? We haven't identified him yet, but we know where he's at. The mole is in Mansfield."

Because of the snow, Joseph and I didn't get going until after two the next afternoon. We decided to go directly to the warehouse, and I wasn't the least surprised to find it located in a run-down, deserted-in-daylight part of town. Then again, what part of

Youngstown wasn't? Almost all of the buildings and shops were boarded up or had bars on the windows. Only a handful of cars lined the litter-strewn, pot-holed street, and a sole homeless man sat on the steps of a long-since-closed-up convenience store. The building Joseph pointed at was one of the smaller warehouses on the street. Lined with broken windows and gray chipped paint, it resembled an old assembly shop.

"Is that it?" It didn't look to me like a living human being had ventured into the building in years, and I stress the word *living*.

"That's it."

"Eeks. How do we know who's inside?"

"Usually it's janitorial services and such, but I don't see their trucks here. Sal comes rolling in around four or five," he said matter-of-factly.

"How do you know—?" I stopped. I didn't want to hear it.

"It looks like we might be in luck, CeeCee. The snowstorm probably kept everyone else at home today. We might be able to get in there right now."

"What are you waiting for, partner?" I raised one eyebrow at him.

Joseph smiled and began slowly circling the building to confirm no one else was there. When he was satisfied, he parked on the street that faced the rear of the building, almost a block away. He had already determined that the way into the warehouse would be through one of the loading docks. The door on the dock had its hinges rusted out, and according to Joseph, flapped back and forth like a rubber pet door. We would be able to get in with no problem.

Taking one last glance around, we started for the warehouse. As cleaned up as we were, and wearing our dark trench coats, we would probably be mistaken for real-estate agents by most people. The black duffel bag that harbored the electronic equipment was over my shoulder, concealed under my coat.

Getting through the dock door was, as predicted, a breeze. Finding Salvatore Iaccona's secret office was not.

"I'm fairly sure it's on the second floor. I watched them once before and saw a light on in the rear corner," Joseph said as we climbed the two flights of stairs.

The second floor was enormous. Small offices, closets, inventory rooms, and file-storage rooms were everywhere. We searched for at least half an hour before Joseph called out to me.

"I found it!"

Following his voice, I found him standing in the doorway at the end of a long hallway in the front of the building. He had been wrong about the office being in the back.

"Are you sure it's the one?" I asked, out of breath as I jogged toward him, taking off my coat.

"I'm sure." Joseph's voice was flat and he was looking at the floor.

As I made my way to the doorway, Joseph stepped aside so that I could walk into the small office. I looked at the large bloodstain on the floor that he was staring at.

"Is that what I think it is?" I asked, my trepidation growing.

"Yes, it is. Someone pissed Sal off again." Joseph looked at me intently. "We need to hurry up and get out of here. They would never leave this stain unless they had something else to tend to. They'll be back to clean it up—and soon."

He had me terrified as I anxiously looked around the mostly empty office for a place to conceal the camera. As Joseph had predicted, there was no phone. Taking the small, dime-size microphones out of the bag, I placed one underneath a lonely plastic plant that sat in the corner. The other was placed inside one of the tears of a chair that sat facing the desk. I manipulated it as far into the foam of the chair as possible. The camera was going to be a problem. I needed to think, and Joseph wasn't helping.

"CeeCee, hurry up! We need to go!" he urged.

My heart, which was already racing, kicked up to breakneck speed. I was sweating from nervousness. My eyes veered to a hole in the wall that was directly in front of the desk. It wasn't big enough to hold the camera, but it could be widened. I grabbed a switchblade from the duffel bag and began to dig out the wall.

"What are you doing? They're going to see all that drywall and shit on the floor!" He almost looked panicked.

"Don't worry, I'll clean it all up. You just keep watch."

Digging violently, I needed to keep the hole the exact same size on the outside, but make it deeper. By now, even though it was below freezing outside, I was soaked with sweat. Joseph made it worse when his face turned to sheer horror.

"Jesus Christ! Someone's coming! Forget the camera, CeeCee, let's go!" he whispered loudly.

"Just two more seconds." After placing the camera in the hole and flipping the switch on, I brushed all of the broken pieces and chips of drywall into my hands and dumped the mess into my pockets.

I blew the drywall dust and scattered it with my hands, then grabbed the duffel bag as Joseph grabbed my arm.

"Hurry!"

He pulled me down the hallway and toward the staircase before jerking me behind a large filing cabinet. He put his hand over my mouth, but I slapped it away and tried to quiet my breathing. We had been running, and as the sounds of the men's voices and footsteps grew near, I took his hand and held it to my mouth again. We could hear them as they walked by.

"Just cut that section of carpet out and we'll burn it out at the lot," a man with a deep, gruff voice said.

"We could probably just burn it out back here. None of these local degenerates are gonna say anything," the other man said.

"No! Sal said we're not taking any chances. That's why he wanted Frankie buried out at the construction site." The man with the gruff voice started to laugh. "Man, if Frankie only knew, he'd shit! I wish Sal would've left him alive long enough to tell him he was gonna be buried underneath the Pelican condos full of old people shittin' in bags and flappin' their gums!"

The men's laughter faded as they walked down the hallway toward the office. Joseph pulled his hand away and led me toward the staircase, putting his finger to his lips to signal me to be quiet. As if I needed to be told. Once inside the safety of our car, Joseph pulled away and shook his head. He looked rattled.

"Unbelievable," he mumbled to himself.

"What?"

"You know who they were talking about, don't you? Sal killed Frank Trapini. That's hard for me to believe. Frank was Sal's closest captain, and he must have done something outrageous for Sal to whack him." Joseph slowed the car down and looked at me. "I'll bet it has something to do with the little stunt you pulled in Florida with Tommy."

I was stunned at the accusatory nature in his voice. "Little stunt?" Now I was fuming. "Little stunt? The guy tried to decapitate me with a fucking wire. I had to defend myself, and you call it a little stunt? Are you defending the Iacconas now, Joseph? Maybe we should just split up today and cut our losses!"

He stopped the car and put his hand on my arm. "Look, CeeCee, I'm sorry, I didn't mean it like that. It's just that, well, Salvatore Iaccona just murdered Frank Trapini. In my eyes, and I know you don't fully understand, that means things are bad—really bad." He caressed my cheek with his hand. "I couldn't bear to see something happen to you. I feel protective of you somehow."

"You don't need to be." I pulled my face away, determined to keep my distance. "I can handle myself just fine, with or without you, Joseph."

He sighed but remained silent after that while he drove back to the motel. We went into my room to see if the camera and microphones were working. They were; they had recorded everything the two men had done inside the office, audio and all. After setting the computer on the desk so we could both see, Joseph and I watched as the men, whom he identified as Petey Iaccona and Henry Mastragna, cut out the bloody section of carpet and placed it in a garbage bag. We also heard a useful piece of information. The next meeting to take place in the office would be in two days.

At that moment, I came up with a glorious idea that we hadn't planned. Joseph was less than enthused.

"You want to what? Are you crazy? We can't go digging around a construction site in Youngstown looking for Frank's body!"

"Of course we can. We already know where it is. He said the Pelican Condominiums. This will be one more way to fuck with them. Please, Joseph."

"How the hell are we going to find it, with all the snow?" He looked incredulous.

"The more snow, the better. The snow will tell us exactly where they buried him."

Joseph shook his head. "All right, I hope you know what you're doing. We'll need to stop and buy some shovels."

"Let's go."

The majority of the Pelican Condominiums were already built and being occupied. There was a small section to the west of it that they were expanding; that was where we needed to start our search. Since it was nearing dark, I instructed Joseph to pick up a couple of flashlights as well. He began to pull the car off the gravel construction driveway and onto the snow-covered paved road.

"No! Don't!" I yelled.

He slammed on the brakes. "Why not? The construction's over there. That's where we'll need to check."

"Because the snow on the gravel is gone, but not on the asphalt. We'll leave tire tracks. We'll have to walk, and we're going to put tape on the bottom of our shoes first."

I had personally worked with several of the Youngstown homicide detectives, and they were no amateurs. With the number of murders the city had, some of their detectives were at the top of their field. I would take no chances leaving shoe tracks in the snow. Always prepared, I grabbed a roll of duct tape from the glove box and ripped several strips off to stick on my shoes before handing it to Joseph. We put on gloves and warm hats, and we were on our way.

"With the heavy snow, it's easy to assume no construction workers have been out here in the last twenty-four hours," I explained to Joseph. "So any tire tracks, footprints, or drag marks can easily be associated with the Iacconas. Start looking, and remember where you've walked."

Finding the tires tracks wasn't hard. I found a set coming out of the woods within ten minutes. They had driven off the road through the woods coming up on the rear of the construction site. Common sense told me they had one hell of an SUV to be able to maneuver through the thick snow and mud. The tire tracks had stopped near the last set of condos when I found the footprints.

A halfhearted attempt had been made to cover them up. They led me to the basement of the second-to-last condo on the street, one that hadn't had the cement poured yet. The footprints stopped at the cement sidewalk, but since only the basement had been dug, it was safe to assume Frank Trapini's final resting place was in there.

What they had done was walk around the entire basement floor, kicking up snow and spreading it around in an attempt to make it look like someone had been there working or kids had been playing. The back corner, where the snow was uneven, was a good place to start. I whistled to Joseph and waited for him to walk over. We needed to help each other down the wooden temporary stairs.

"I'm surprised they didn't break their necks carrying a body down these steps," I said.

"Let's just get this over with."

We went over to the corner and I started walking around. Only when I felt the ground sink ever so slightly did I convince myself we had found Frank's burial site.

"Here." I pointed. "They probably dug a significantly deep hole. But even if they tried to pack the dirt in, it's still going to be a little soft, unlike the rest of the dirt. It's winter, so most of it should be frozen."

Joseph took a deep breath as he jammed the shovel into the ground. I didn't dare ask how many times he'd done this—another detail of his life I didn't want to know. The snow and the dirt were heavy. After a while, my back was screaming.

"You guys make this look so easy in the movies," I said.

Joseph, clearly unamused, kept digging. Two hours later and three to four feet deeper, I felt my shovel hit something hard.

"Shine your flashlight down there and hold it." I

got on my knees and leaned into the hole, brushing away the dirt and exposing a black garbage bag.

Tearing a small portion of the bag away revealed Frank Trapini's elbow. Feeling my way down his arm to his hand, I tore apart that portion of the garbage bag and pulled Frank's hand out, letting it stick straight up into the air.

"What the hell are you doing?" Joseph was out of breath and leaning on his shovel.

"Just making it easier for the cops is all. We're done here. We only need to find a pay phone."

I found a long piece of wood with a bright orange piece of tape around it and stuck it upright in the snow to the left of Frank's body. Joseph was already at the top of the steps, reaching his hand out to help me. He had been quiet most of the time. Ever since his semi-admission of his feelings for me in the car, he hadn't said much.

About two miles from our motel, Joseph pulled up next to a pay phone at a gas station. Looking through the phone book hanging by the silver wire, I found the nonemergency number for the Youngstown Police Department. It would take longer for them to trace the number than if I called 911. The dispatcher answered on the second ring. Lowering my voice to the level of a prepubescent boy, I gave the dispatcher the information.

"In the Pelican Condominium construction site, the second to the last condo on the west side of the street, there is a body buried in the basement. The grave is exposed and marked with a wooden stake and an orange ribbon. The body is Frank Trapini, and Henry Mastragna is responsible for his murder."

I hung up the phone and instructed Joseph to drive away. When he pulled into the parking lot of our motel, he finally spoke, looking confused.

"Why did you tell them it was Henry? I figured you would want to give up Sal first?"

"I'm just getting Henry out of the way. I want Salvatore Iaccona to myself." I was driven by pure rage.

Joseph whispered a solemn good night to me as he went into his room and I went into mine. After taking my suitcase and throwing it on the bed, I pulled the inside flap down and grabbed the thick cache of files and the yellow envelope containing the tape. My arms full, I went over to Joseph's room and used my foot to knock on the door. His face told me he was surprised to see me.

"CeeCee? What's all that?" He nodded at the pile of folders in my arms.

Not waiting for an invitation, I brushed past him and walked into his room, letting the files spill all over the bed.

"These are the files on your family, and the files on the Iacconas. Here's the tape." I held the small envelope out to him.

He was stunned. "I thought you were going to turn those over *after* we were done. Are we done?"

"You are. I'm not." I sat down and ran my fingers through my hair. "I don't want to put you in any more danger, Joseph. I care about you—please believe that—and I don't want you to get hurt because of me."

His face softened into concern as he sat down next to me. Now that he had the files, he could walk away easily. He certainly didn't have to stay and help me. Joseph gently pulled my face toward his and kissed me. Instantly, I pulled away. To say I cared about him was true, but as a close friend, and nothing more.

"Joseph . . . ," I began quietly as I looked at the floor.

"You don't need to say it, CeeCee. I know, and I'm sorry." He stood up and walked to the window. "I know you don't feel for me the way I do you." He turned around. "Never in my life have I met someone like you, someone I admire and respect."

"You are a good person, Joseph, I know that. It's just that . . ." I felt tears brimming. "I can't begin to explain how much I loved my husband or how much I miss him. I don't know that I'll ever get over it."

He walked over and knelt before me. "I do understand, and I'm not trying to make this harder than it is. What you're doing right now to find his killer tells me how much you loved him." He paused. "I met him once, you know."

"You met Michael?"

He nodded. "I followed Niccolo, right before he died, to see what he was into. I was the one that discovered his allegiance with the FBI. Niccolo and Michael met in the Metroparks once. After Niccolo left, I confronted him."

I stood up. "You confronted Michael? Why?"

"It was no big deal, really. I just told him he was putting my brother's life in danger by bringing him in. He looked at it differently. He said he was probably saving my brother's life. I guess he was wrong, huh?"

"I guess so." I paused, looking at the spread-out files. "There you are. They're all yours, the only copies," I lied, though I had every intention of destroying the other copies on the Filaci family. "So I guess you'll be leaving now?" I asked, my voice almost inaudible.

"Of course not."

His answer staggered me. "I just figured now that you have the files and tape, you'd leave."

"And miss the impending fall of Salvatore Iaccona? You're kidding, right? Not to mention, I have a vested interest in all of this—you. My new closest friend, who I have to watch over, and make sure stays safe and sound." He grinned at me and winked.

"Thank you, Joseph." I hugged him tightly before kissing his cheek. "You sure? You don't have to do this."

"Sure as I'm gonna get. Now go get some sleep."

Walking back into my own room, I felt elated. Joseph was sticking with me. I had been trying to prepare myself for his imminent departure after he got the files, but he'd certainly surprised me. He'd surprised me by uncovering my own desire to have him around. It had been a long time since I'd been in daily contact with a close friend, and I missed it.

The day before the scheduled meeting at the warehouse was a long one. Frank Trapini's body had been discovered, and the story was all over the news. I couldn't wait to hear what Singin' Sal had to say about it.

"Alan, it's Agent Nicholas. Frank Trapini is dead."

"Jesus, don't tell me she killed him, too!" Alan Keane felt light-headed.

"No, we think she called it in, but we can't say for sure right now. We're assuming Sal knocked him off for letting Tommy get killed. He had him buried under this new

condo construction site, and an anonymous phone call was made. Someone had dug him up and left a little landmark showing the cops where to go. It had to be her."

"I can't believe he'd kill Trapini," Alan thought aloud. *"Things must be getting worse. Anything on Richland Metro's last homicide?"*

"Nope, but we know that Cross guy is connected to LifeTech Industries. We found a shitload of its stock he had invested in, but I don't think Richland Metro knows yet."

"Keep on it. Where is she?"

"We don't know, sir."

"Dear God, whatever you do, find her before Sal does."

According to Joseph, the meeting in Sal's office was a who's who of the Iaccona clan, and Sal wasn't happy, to say the least. We watched the scene unfold on my laptop.

"Somebody better start talking!" Sal screamed from behind his desk.

Present in the room were Henry Mastragna, Petey and Antonio Iaccona, William Petrosini, and three other men that neither I nor Joseph recognized. None of the men spoke, but only hung their heads as if they were small children being admonished.

"Somebody better start telling me how the fuck the cops got the body! How the fuck did they find it, and who the fuck tipped them off?" Sal stood up and knocked everything off his desk. *"I better hear some talking, God damn it!"*

"Pop, listen . . . Settle down! We don't know how they could've possibly found him. Someone must've followed us or something. Maybe it was the Filacis," Antonio Iaccona said.

Joseph's jaw clenched as he heard this. Putting my hand on his arm, I gave it a slight squeeze while we continued to watch.

"Filacis my ass! It was that goddamn Gallagher! I swear to Christ, when I get my hands on that Irish Mick bitch I'm gonna rip her fucking throat out!"

Now it was my turn to have a clenched jaw. Having my throat ripped out by the man on the computer screen was not something I looked forward to.

"We should've taken care of her the same time Hagerman was! And Niccolo! Should've taken care of all the motherfuckers at the same time! I'm surprised Frank didn't fuck up Niccolo's murder, too! Fucker left the goddamn ball bat behind when I told him not to. It was Frank! Goddamn Frank! I wish he was alive so I could blow his goddamn brains out again!"

The admission I'd been waiting for. They had killed my husband and Niccolo Filaci. Salvatore Iaccona was going to pay with his life. But by the look on Joseph's face, I saw that he might beat me to it. Sal continued blasting his employees.

"The cops get ahold of you yet, Henry?" Sal fumed.

"No, Sal, I haven't been home since the news broke."

"You are going to the Philippines, and plan on staying there until the heat's off. There's another delivery waiting at the warehouse on Washington Street. My inside guy is waiting for you. He'll take you to the airport and check in the delivery. You know where to go once you get there?"

"Sure, Sal, I went with Frank a coupla times."

"Good, get your ass moving. The Filipinos are threatening to pull the project because we're behind, and Mansfield is gonna be on my chopping block soon if they don't get their shit together. The fuckin' Chinks are also threatening to make some heads roll, and it ain't gonna be mine!

Our other investors aren't happy either! You got that? What the fuck—?"

Sal looked directly at the camera and began walking closer, his image on the computer screen growing larger.

"Oh shit, CeeCee, he fuckin' found—"

"Just wait. Maybe not!" I interrupted, and prayed.

He stopped right in front of the hole. We still had audio.

"What the fuck is this shit, Petey? We got fuckin' rats or something? Get a fuckin' exterminator in here tomorrow. It looks like something was crawling all inside that wall. I fucking hate rats."

I knew the feeling, but breathed a sigh of relief that he hadn't located the camera yet.

"Petey, you and Antonio find that bitch tonight! If not, go get her fuckin' kids and do them. That'll bring her out. I'm tired of fuckin' around."

"Oh, hell no, he did not just threaten my children." I stood up with every intention of driving directly to the warehouse and blowing a hole through the middle of Salvatore Iaccona.

"Hold on, CeeCee, just wait. I think we should go to the warehouse on Washington Street. We'll be able to find out what his business is. Did you hear him mention Mansfield?"

"I heard him, and I think it's coming together for me right now. Let's go to the warehouse, so I know for sure."

Alan Keane and the other agents watched the same scene unfold that CeeCee and Joseph had. The FBI had found the office three weeks ago and had their own cameras in place— illegally. Another man watched, too, but stayed silent.

"We've got him," Alan announced.

"It's no good, Alan, you know that," Gary Nicholas said. "We can't use these tapes."

"We can't use ours, but we sure as hell can use hers! I have a feeling those tapes are gonna make their way to us soon, a week at the max."

The other man stood up and finally spoke. *"We don't have a fucking week. Didn't you listen? Get your asses to that warehouse on Washington Street!"*

We arrived at the warehouse just in time. We'd had a slight delay when I had to put a copy of the video of the Iaccona meeting into a mailbox. I was mailing it to my friend in Atlanta, while keeping a copy with me. During the fifteen minutes that we waited, something strange happened. At least it seemed strange to me.

Clearly getting antsy while we sat and waited, Joseph reached over and turned the radio on. I had been thinking about Michael and wasn't paying attention until Joseph started to sing the song that was currently playing.

My hair stood up on end, and it wasn't from Joseph's earth-shattering singing voice, either. He was singing a Pink Floyd song, and one of Michael's favorites.

"Isn't that funny? We were just at their exhibit less than three days ago, and I haven't heard one of their songs in ages. CeeCee? What's wrong? Oh, come on. My voice can't be that bad . . ."

Quickly reaching over and turning the radio off, I tried to cover the look of despair on my face, but it was too late. Joseph had seen it.

"Do you want to tell me what's wrong?" His voice dripped with concern.

"Nothing. That was Michael's favorite song is all." I was rattled.

"*That's* why we met at the exhibit." He paused. "Oh, CeeCee, I'm sorry. I didn't know . . ."

Holding my hand up, I attempted to lighten the mood a little while getting my thoughts back together.

"Don't apologize. But, Joseph, could you do me a favor?"

"Of course."

"If you're smart, you'll stay a mobster and forgo the singing career." I smiled.

I looked at the warehouse and saw that a large white van with the name LifeTech Industries on the side of it had arrived. It was backed up to one of the doors on the south side of the building.

"Heads up, they're here," I announced.

This wasn't a loading dock, and it was close to three in the morning—definitely not a normal delivery time. Taking my night-vision goggles and binoculars out, I gasped aloud when I saw Dr. Donovan Esposito standing alongside the van. Another man, who looked somewhat familiar, had his back to me. I desperately wanted to see his face. As they loaded a small cooler into the back of the van, I chastised myself for not putting everything together sooner.

"Holy, shit! Body organs. How could I have been so stupid?" I asked.

"Care to fill me in?"

"They're running body organs, a multimillion-dollar business. That's why Michael was looking at my files. They were taking the organs in Mansfield from the homeless. Esposito was removing them, and someone else was transporting them here to get shipped to the Philippines, all run by the Iacconas." I took a deep breath to let it all sink in. "They killed Niccolo because he knew and was going to tell Michael. They killed Michael because they thought he already had evidence against them."

"Jesus . . ." Joseph mumbled. "Those motherfuckers." He sat up straight. "Heads up again, they're leaving."

The van began to pull away but got stuck in the soft ground. Since they were trying to pick up the organs covertly, they hadn't used a regular loading dock. Instead, they tried to drive on the soft snow-covered ground. We watched as they spun the tires, spewing mud everywhere, until the driver got out of the truck. I still couldn't see his face. He placed something under the tire as Esposito drove it out of the rut, throwing mud all over the man. While we watched them drive away, Joseph startled me.

"Listen to me carefully. There's a club in the Warehouse District in Cleveland. It's called Club Siesta, at the corner of West Sixth Street and Saint Clair. In the back, there are several VIP rooms. Meet me in the one next to the restroom tonight at eight sharp." He opened his door to get out. "Make sure you're not being followed."

"Wait a minute! Joseph, what are you doing? Get in the car!" I was panicked.

"Trust me, CeeCee. Don't worry, I'll get back. Just be there! Now go!"

As I drove away from the warehouse, Joseph ran toward it. I couldn't imagine what he was doing.

When I was almost a mile away, I heard an explosion in the distance. I saw the large ball of fire rise into the air in my rearview mirror.

Chapter Thirteen

Not knowing if it was safe to go back to my motel room, I took my chances and left the car running as I ran inside and grabbed my things. All I could think about was Joseph and if he was okay. The large explosion would've destroyed the entire warehouse. I just hoped he'd made it out in time. The Iacconas and their business practices had been revealed tonight, and it made me angry. Everything that had happened to the unfortunate victims in Mansfield, to Joseph's brother, to my children, Sean, and to me was all due to nothing but the insatiable greed of Salvatore Iaccona.

Crazy mad, I pulled out of the motel parking lot while my eyes fell to a file on my passenger seat. The file contained the home address of Singin' Sal.

He was running toward the fiery remnants of the warehouse on Washington Street when Agent Gary Nicholas ran up on him from the right.

"Wait! What are you doing? You can't go in there!"

"Get the fuck back, I'm going in." He started walking now. "You fucked up and waited too long! I told you to get here quickly, and now . . ." He didn't want to think about the possibilities.

"They're not here!"

He spun around, facing Agent Nicholas, making sure he heard him right. Agent Nicholas was breathing hard, the cold air making his breath look like large puffs of smoke.

"How do you know that?"

"We found their motel rooms. Keith and Steve are there now. We just missed her by a few minutes when she checked out. Filaci's things are still in his room, so we don't know where he's at, but he'll probably meet up with her later."

"Keep on that goddamn room and see if he comes back. If he does, don't lose him! He'll take us right to her, I'm sure of it." He paused. "Something must've gone wrong, so they had to split up."

Not an overly religious man, he found himself praying like he'd never prayed in his life.

Salvatore Iaccona lived in a modest neighborhood on the west side of the city. I turned my headlights off and circled the street several times before parking a few houses down from his. Sal's house was dark, but that was fine. I would wait.

Carrying only my gun, I miraculously found an unlocked back door. Beyond caring if any evidence was left or if I was seen, I strode into the darkness of the kitchen and took a few minutes to allow my eyes to adjust. It was a ranch-style home. I walked down the sole hallway, opening doors in an attempt to find Sal's bedroom. It was the last room at the end. I unscrewed all of the lightbulbs in the room, opened a window, removed the screen, and took a seat in a comfy chair by the bed. Then I waited.

It was over two hours, and almost daylight, when

I heard the garage door open. Stiffening in my chair, I prepared myself for a confrontation like no other.

Sal came right to his bedroom. As the door opened, light from the hallway flooded in, but not on me. Sal was feeling for the light switch along the wall while I held my breath. Finding the switch, he began flipping it up and down, cursing as the room remained dark. Now it was my turn.

"Have a seat," I said calmly from the darkness of the room.

"What the fuck? Who is that?" He began to reach inside his coat pocket.

Racking the slide on my gun loud enough for him to hear it, I gave my second order.

"If you don't want a hole in your head, take your gun out slowly and slide it across the floor toward the sound of my voice. Then have a seat in the chair by the dresser."

Sal did as he was told and slid his gun toward me, where it stopped at my feet. I didn't move. After he had taken his seat, I pulled a cigarette out of my pocket and lit it, providing enough light for him to see my gun . . . and my face.

"Mrs. Gallagher, I presume." He gritted his teeth.

"It's Hagerman, Mrs. Hagerman, the wife of the man you killed," I said while blowing out a substantial amount of smoke at him.

He began to laugh, which infuriated me to the point my finger found the trigger of my gun. But I wanted some answers first, and I wanted him to know what I'd done.

"Tommy certainly didn't laugh like that when I

stuck a letter opener in his neck and dumped him in the bay. I wonder if you'll still be laughing when I do the same to you."

He stopped laughing and leaned forward. "I don't know what you think you're doing, lady, but I really hope you enjoy that cigarette. It'll be your last."

"You didn't plan on me finding Frank, did you, Sal? Nor did you plan on your warehouse going up in flames. It's a shame really. As pissed off as you were in your office yesterday, I thought for sure you'd take out Henry, too. Especially since I told the cops he was the one that killed Frankie boy." I let my cigarette drop on the floor and stamped it out with my foot. "Unfortunately, for you that is, your business is over. No more organs for the Philippines, no more homeless murders, and no more Iacconas. You see, Sal, the feds will have everything by tomorrow. You're finished. Not that you're going to be around to see it all, because I'm going to kill you, here, shortly."

He smiled again. "Did you enjoy watching your husband burn, Mrs. Hagerman? I know I did—"

We were interrupted by the sounds of footsteps walking down the hallway. I hadn't expected or planned for anyone else.

"Petey! In here, my room! Hurry!" Sal screamed before diving behind his bed fast enough that I couldn't get a shot at him.

The footsteps quickened, and I was at the window as the large figure loomed in the doorway. With no time to aim, I fired a shot toward the figure, who ducked behind the door frame. Wood fragments and splinters sprayed the room from where the bullet hit. Before anyone could react, I was diving through the window, falling onto the snow-covered ground.

"Pop! You okay?" Petey Iaccona yelled, making his way to his father.

"I'm okay, I'm okay!" Sal sat up and brushed the wood fragments from his coat.

"I'm going after her." Petey started toward the door.

"No! Wait!"

"Wait? Why? Who was that?" Petey found the light-bulb next to the nearest lamp and screwed it in before turning it on.

"It was her." Sal was out of breath and sat on his bed. "It was Gallagher. She knows everything. We're in trouble, Petey."

Petey went to the bedroom window and closed it, then took a seat next to his father.

"We're not in trouble, Pop. We found her room and we know where she's going."

Sal looked confused. "How?"

"She's hooked up with Joseph Filaci, and they were staying at a motel about five miles from here. She's checked out, but he hasn't."

"Filaci? That motherfucker!" Sal stood up.

"We can't get close enough because the feds are all over the motel, but I'm pretty sure she was at the warehouse and watched the pickup. They're the ones that blew it up, too. Anyway, I suspect they're gonna follow the van to Cleveland to get them at the drop-off."

"She's got a room there too, doesn't she?"

"Yeah, but the feds are on it. We can watch from a distance and see where she goes from there."

"Take your brother and leave now. You'll need to beat

her there. I want her brought to me—you got it? I'll make
the arrangements. She killed Tommy."

"She did?"

"Yes, and she's the one who got to Frank's body. We'll
deal with the Filacis later, but for now, I want her. And
remember, we've still got Paulie on the inside."

Running like I'd never run before, I circled several
houses before making my way back to the car. They
weren't following me and I didn't know why. As I sat
in my car with my hand on the ignition, I saw a car
back out of Sal's driveway like a bat out of hell. I
flung myself down on the passenger seat as it passed
by and waited a few minutes before pulling away.
My hands were shaking terribly and it was hard to
catch my breath. My chest seared in pain from the
cold air I had breathed while running. Finally, turning onto the interstate, I pushed the gas pedal to the
floor and sped toward Cleveland.

"He's back in Cleveland, Alan. Keith and Steve followed
him from his motel room in Youngstown."

"That means she'll be there soon, too. Keep the agents
on her motel room there, and keep the other ones with Jo-
seph. They'll meet up soon. I'll let him know the update."

"Yes, sir."

"Before you hang up, things have changed. When you
get the opportunity, take her into custody."

"What? Are you sure?"

"Yes, I promised him. If we don't, she'll be dead by to-
morrow."

It was safe to assume my motel room in Cleveland
was being watched. Regrettably, I had no other

choice but to go there. I didn't think the Iacconas had found it yet, only the feds. At this point, I was almost grateful they were watching, but I would have to lose them later.

Back in the room, I took a hot shower. I had less than an hour to meet Joseph. I was trying to stay positive and assume he hadn't been injured or killed in the explosion. After throwing all of my belongings in the trunk of my car and donning my black wig and trench coat, I headed toward the bar. Underneath the coat, I wore a gold sequined tank top and black slacks. I was going to a nightclub and didn't want to stand out.

I parked in the three-level parking garage down the street from Club Siesta. I went up to the third level before taking the elevator back down. I then cut down several alleys, going away from the club, before I was satisfied that no one was following me. As I neared the entrance, I saw the doorman holding a weapons detector. Several of the patrons stood with their arms stretched out as he ran the wand up and down them. Of all places for Joseph to pick, he chose one I would be unable to take my gun into.

A blue postal-service mailbox was a few feet from me on the curb. I walked next to it, bent down, and pretended to fix something on my shoe while sliding my gun underneath the box. This was when I saw the men.

There were two of them across the street, and I recognized them immediately: Petey and Antonio Iaccona. They made no attempt to conceal themselves, but merely stood and stared. Cursing to myself, I stood up, ignoring their glares, and continued to the entrance, where I calmly allowed the doorman to wave his wand around me. Out of the corner of my eye, I could see the two crossing the street and heading directly toward me. Once inside, I threw money at the window and barely allowed the woman to stamp my hand before I hurried to the women's restroom. The club was packed full of people dancing to the loud thumping music, lights flashing on and off. I saw the VIP rooms that Joseph had told me about. I ran into the restroom, pulled off my wig and coat, threw both into the garbage can, and fluffed out my hair.

Even though the two Iacconas knew what I looked like, they thought I had my wig on tonight. They'd be watching for a brunette in a dark coat amid the crowd of people. Keeping my head down, I exited the bathroom and went immediately to my right, pulling back the curtain to the VIP room. Joseph sat before me on one of the couches.

"Joseph! You're okay!"

"Hurry up and close the curtain."

After I closed the curtain, I couldn't help but give him a big squeeze. He was nervous.

"How did you get back?"

"I have some contacts in Youngstown. One phone call and I had a ride. Are you okay?" He looked concerned.

"Yeah. Petey and Antonio are out there right now. They must've followed me, but I was careful! I took my wig off, but I don't know how long that'll keep them away." I peered through the curtain and didn't see them. "Joseph, what happened at the warehouse?"

"One flicker to the propane tank took care of it. As you can see, I got away in time. Were you worried?" He smiled.

"Of course I was worried!" I wasn't smiling. "Joseph, I have to tell you something. After I left the warehouse, I was angry. Angrier than I have ever been, so"—I paused—"I went to Sal's house and confronted him."

His jaw dropped to the floor. "You what?"

"Actually, I had every intention of killing him right there, but Petey came home, and there were some shots fired. I got out through a window. I'm okay, but as you can imagine, he's highly pissed." I gave a fake smile.

"Holy Christ, CeeCee! He won't stop until he kills you. God! What the hell were you thinking?"

Before I could answer, Joseph had peered through the curtain again.

"Fuck, they're here."

"What should we do?" I was beginning to panic.

"Just wait—I think they're leaving." He turned around. "We'll wait here for about five minutes and then sneak out. I'm driving you directly to the FBI. They'll be able to protect you."

"What about you?" I didn't want anything to happen to him.

"I'll be fine, don't worry. You have access to those files and tapes you mailed?"

I nodded.

"Good, they'll be able to help you."

After waiting for ten minutes, instead of five, we made our way to the front of the club. Neither one of us saw the men anywhere inside, so we held our breaths as we walked out the front door.

"Stay here. I'm parked down the street. I'll get my car and—"

Joseph was thrown backward the same time I heard the shot. He fell to the ground as the large red stain began to spread across the front of his shirt.

"Oh, Jesus!" I screamed, kneeling beside him, and put my hand against the hole in his chest.

"Run, CeeCee!" He was choking on his own blood. "Run!"

Sobbing, I fell to the ground as another shot rang out. People were running out of the club, screaming and trampling each other. I half crawled, half ran to the mailbox to retrieve my gun, leaving Joseph behind. As another shot hit the mailbox, I stood up and started shooting, backing into an alley that ran alongside the club. I couldn't even see who I was shooting at; my eyes were blinded by tears and hundreds of people running around.

I had forgotten to bring extra magazines for my gun and was out of ammunition after my first round of shots. As I threw the gun into a nearby Dumpster, I saw Petey and Antonio at the end of the alley, running toward me.

I kicked off my heels and launched into a dead run. I turned the corner as they fired another shot at me. I ran down alley after alley, avoiding Cleveland police cars that came screaming through with their lights and sirens on. I couldn't ask for their help, since everyone at the club would've told them a blonde in a gold sequined shirt was responsible for part of the shooting. They would fire at me on sight. Somehow, I managed to find myself in an area that was familiar to me—the flats.

The flats used to be the place where the clubs were lined up and down the Cuyahoga River. But since the Warehouse District emerged, most of the businesses in the flats closed up, leaving a few strip bars here and there.

Standing on the wooden dock that lined the river, I heard running footsteps and voices. It was either the cops or the Iacconas, neither of which I could allow to see me. With no other choice, I sat on the dock and slowly lowered myself into the freezing river. Honestly thinking my heart would stop, I went underneath the water as the footsteps walked above me. I emerged up under the dock, held on, and waited, knowing I was on the verge of hypothermia. My bare feet, already numb from running in the cold, were most likely purple by now as I floated in the icy waters under the dock.

When I couldn't take it anymore, and no longer hearing any voices or footsteps, I pulled myself from the water onto the dock and curled up into a ball, shivering from the cold. Knowing I needed to move, and quickly, I got up and headed for a strip club on the other side of the parking lot that was in front of me. My feet screamed in pain from the cold.

I barreled through the front door of the strip club, almost falling down, before I was immediately stopped by a large bouncer.

"Hey! You can't come flyin' in here like—"

"P-P-Please!" I shivered. "My—My boyfriend's chasing me. I—I need a phone!"

"I'll just call the cops, lady. Come on in here and get warm."

"No—no! You don't understand. He's—he's a cop! Please. I need to make a phone call and I'll leave."

The man walked me back to the office just inside the front door and set the phone in front of me.

"How come you're all wet?"

"He pushed me into the river." I grabbed the phone and began dialing Naomi's phone number.

"Fuckin' asshole. What's he look like, in case he comes in?"

I described Petey and Antonio Iaccona to the bouncer, and he walked out, leaving me to listen to Naomi's voice mail, which kicked in after she didn't answer the phone. Coop's did the same. *Where the fuck is everybody?* my head screamed. Keeping my fingers crossed, I thought of Justin Brown and dialed his cell-phone number. Thankfully, he answered.

"CeeCee! Hey! Long time no talk. How's Florida? I was just thinking—"

"Justin! Listen to me, I need your help!" I was hysterical.

"CeeCee, what the hell's going on? Are you okay?"

"No! I'm not! I can't get into right now, but I need you to come get me."

"In Florida?" he gasped.

"No, no, I'm in Cleveland." He started to ask questions again, but I cut him off. "I'll explain it all later. Do you know where the Bermuda Triangle strip club is—in the flats?"

"Does a bear shit in the woods?" he chuckled.

"Pick me up behind it. How long will it be?"

"Oh, give me half an hour or so. Will you be all right?"

"Yeah, for now. Just bring a warm coat if you have one."

After hanging up with Justin, I did my best to warm up and calm down. I tried several more times to call Naomi and Coop, but neither one answered. Putting my face in my hands, I began to cry. Joseph was dead. He had died trying to save me, and it was my fault. A father out there had now lost both sons. Even though their choice of professions was less than respectable, no one deserved that. Thinking about it led my thoughts to my own children. I called Eric. Understandably, he wasn't happy.

"What do you mean, get the kids out of here?" His voice rose. "CeeCee, God damn it, what's going on? Are you okay?"

"For now, please, Eric. I can't get into details, but the Mafia is after me. I know it sounds crazy, but they're going to try to get at the girls to get to me. Please, please, get them out of there and go somewhere until you hear from me."

"Tomorrow's Thanksgiving, CeeCee." His voice quieted down.

"I know that. Please, Eric."

Surprisingly, he agreed. "All right, I'll take them to my parents tonight and call off of work." He paused. "Please, Cee, be careful. These little girls miss you. Don't make me have to tell them something happened to their mother."

"I'm doing my best, believe me."

After hanging up the phone, I checked my watch. Justin should have been arriving any minute. Sneaking past the bouncer, I was elated to see the taillights of a truck behind the building. I ran up to it, opened the passenger door, and almost started to cry when I saw Justin sitting in the driver's seat.

"Justin, thank God!" I said as I got into the truck. "Just go, now."

He pulled away. "CeeCee! You're soaking wet! What the hell happened?"

I let out a deep breath while I laid my head back on

the seat and put my hands up to the heater vents. The heat felt wonderful.

"Head toward the FBI office downtown, and I'll fill you in. Please, give me a minute first."

Closing my eyes, I realized I had made it. Now I would be safe. As soon as I got to the FBI office, I would contact Alan Keane, give him the files, videos, and tapes, and allow him to do the rest. I was so tired.

Music from Justin's radio was blaring throughout the truck. I smiled. Sitting upright, I was about to comment on his music when I saw him—specifically, his shoes.

Justin's boots, pants, and shirt were covered with mud. My smile faded and my mind flashed back to when he'd picked me up. As I ran toward the truck, I had quickly glanced at the plate, not giving it much thought. Until now. His plates were from Cuyahoga County, not Richland. And come to think of it, the drive from Mansfield to Cleveland was at least forty-five to fifty minutes, not thirty. I had been so excited to see him that I hadn't paid attention.

Everything started to come together, including the scene at the warehouse, when the delivery truck got stuck in the mud. The man driving, a man who looked so familiar to me, had gotten out to dislodge the van and was covered in mud in the process. With my chest heaving and my heart skipping, I did my best to remain calm, even as Justin drove right past the FBI office. I pretended to not notice. *This couldn't be!* my head screamed. *Not Justin!*

In my last attempt to prove my instincts wrong, I sat upright and spoke to him.

"You really helped me out. Thanks, Justin."

"No problem."

"It looks like both of us took a roll with nature tonight." I smiled. "What'd you do? Enter a mud-wrestling match?"

He smiled back at me as he got onto the interstate. "You know, don't you, CeeCee?"

"Know what?" I pretended to look confused, as my hand found the door handle.

His smile was replaced by a look of pure contempt. "You stupid cunt. I told them you'd fuck everything up, but they didn't want to listen to me. Nooo, not Justin! I told them to take care of you right from the get-go."

"What are you talking about?" Still playing dumb, I pulled on the door handle in an attempt to open it.

Unfortunately, Justin was a step ahead of me. Before I could jump, the barrel of his pistol was staring me right between the eyes.

"Shut the door and stay still."

"Justin, think about what you're doing. You're a cop, for Christ's sake! I don't know what they're paying you, but I'm sure I could get you out of this if you just think for a second!"

He began to laugh, the gun still pointed at me. He pulled off to the side of the highway and stopped the truck. I thought for sure he was going to kill me right there. But instead, he made his own confession.

"You're right, CeeCee, I'm a cop." He laughed. "But there's one little piece of information you overlooked. The one little piece of this whole puzzle that you didn't factor in, and it worked out wonderfully!"

"Really?" I was almost hyperventilating in anticipation of the shot, but had to ask, "What exactly is that?"

He grabbed the back of my hair, jerked my head forward, and kissed me, an act that almost made me sick. Allowing me to pull away, he laughed again.

"You stupid bitch. Here's where you fucked up and missed it all! You see, CeeCee, my name isn't Justin Brown. It's Paul, Paul Iaccona. I'm Salvatore's youngest son."

Chapter Fourteen

Even repeating his words back to him still didn't allow what Justin had confessed to sink in. I was flabbergasted.

"Salvatore Iaccona's son? But how . . . how can that be?"

"That's right, CeeCee." His expression was smug.

"You're a police officer!" I exclaimed. "You were a police officer before you even came to Richland Metro! I saw your file. There—there are background investigations that are done before anyone gets hired! How is that possible?"

Tilting his head back, Justin began to laugh. Not the laugh that comes at the end of a joke, but the laugh of someone completely insane.

"Because we're smarter than you, that's why!" His laughter and smile faded. "This is what I was raised for, sweetheart, a life on the inside of law enforcement. My father knew it would take years, but he is the most intelligent man in the world—and patient."

Still in shock, I began shaking my head back and forth in an attempt to deny the information. It didn't work, since Justin continued his family history.

"Most people knew Sal had a younger son, but thought he was killed in a car accident a few days after his twenty-first birthday. Actually it was some poor college kid that was reported missing and never found. That was the day Justin Brown was born and entered the Cleveland Police Academy. It wasn't hard. We threw enough money around, especially at the low-paid cops. It bought my ticket in, and their silence." The smug look returned. "What I'm telling you, CeeCee, is that I *am* a cop. I put my time in just like everybody else to get to where I am now. When I was a child, my father had plenty of cops on the payroll, but they would get too scared and back out when it came down to it. But not me, no ma'am. I get off on it."

His words wreaked havoc in my mind, and I attempted to fire off more questions, mainly to keep him occupied talking instead of shooting me.

"But why Mansfield? Why Richland Metro?"

"We started to draw some heat in Cleveland. People started paying attention and asking questions about me. None of it was documented at the time, just people being suspicious, ya know? How come no one ever saw my wife and kids, my parents, this and that? . . . questions you all would have eventually started to ask. I needed to leave before anything was put on paper to prevent me from transferring to another department. Pop thought it was best that we move the operation to Mansfield, where my cousin was assigned. You know him, don't you, CeeCee?"

I shook my head slowly. "I don't think so. Do I?"

He laughed again. "Of course you do! Dr. Donovan Esposito! Everything was put on hold until I made detective. It took five years to do it, but I did it, and it was all to keep an eye on you." His smile faded again. "I guess I didn't do a good enough job now, did I? If

I had, you wouldn't have tried to kill my father and brother tonight, right?" He became angry and slapped me across the face, causing my head to bounce off the passenger side window. "Now you're going to pay for it."

The realization of what Justin had done hit me like an oncoming train.

"You killed them, didn't you? All those people! You killed them and took them to Esposito to remove the organs. After you dumped the bodies, you transported the organs to Cleveland, didn't you!"

"Covered my tracks pretty damn good, didn't I? Of course, I was trained by the best of the best—CeeCee Gallagher. She took her time going over every detail of the case and was stupid enough to turn the entire thing over to me." He looked in his rearview mirror and then at his watch. "We need to go. They're expecting us."

"This can't be happening," I muttered while I closed my eyes and hung my head forward. "Michael . . . why Michael?"

Justin pulled back onto the highway. "Michael? That faggot-ass husband of yours almost fucked up years worth of work and millions of dollars in cash, that's why! If he hadn't gotten Niccolo to turn on us, he'd still be alive." Justin reached over and tousled my hair. "You know I tried my best to console the grieving widow. That was part of the plan. I figured I'd fuck you for a while so I could watch you every minute. Since you blew me off, maybe I'll make up for it tonight."

He reached across the seat, violently shoving his hand inside my shirt and grabbing my left breast, hard. Instinctively, I grabbed his wrist with my right hand and struck him in the side of the face with my left, causing him to slam on his brakes. He struck back, punching me square in the nose.

"You stupid bitch! All right! That's the way you want to play, we can do it your way." He started driving again. "You're going to suffer. You're going to suffer like you never have before."

My nose poured blood as I tried to pinch it shut. "Yeah? Tell me something I haven't heard a dozen times before."

We were headed toward Mansfield. I'd learned from past experiences to do everything humanly possible to help myself, and that was exactly what I did. Disregarding my bloody nose, I dove across the seat toward Justin. Grabbing the steering wheel, I jerked it aggressively toward me, causing the truck to lose control.

Justin quickly grabbed the wheel, pulling it back toward him, but he pulled too hard. We crossed the median, driving into oncoming traffic. Justin attempted to point his gun at me again, but I held it up toward the roof and away from my face with my free hand. He was stronger, and he pushed the gun back down and pulled the trigger. The shot missed me but blew out the passenger side window, along with my eardrums. With my last ounce of strength, I threw all of my body weight on top of him while I began to claw at his face and eyes with my fingernails. With one hand on the wheel and one fighting me, Justin managed to cross the median again and spin us around in the middle of the southbound lane, then brought the truck to a stop. While we were spinning, he'd managed to hit me in the back of the head with the gun, hard enough that my grip on him loosened.

A large knot began to rise where I had been hit, and I started to get dizzy.

"Okay!" Justin was breathing hard and sweating. "I can see you aren't gonna make this easy."

He reached behind him and pulled out a pair of handcuffs, while I bent over and held my head. Forcing both of my arms behind my back, he handcuffed my hands together and looped the nylon seat belt through them.

"Buckle up for safety!" he chuckled.

He took a few deep breaths and wiped his forehead as he continued to call me every obscenity in the English language. He turned the inside dome light on and looked in the rearview mirror to inspect the damage I had done to his face. Not much, just large scratches and red marks.

"Fuckin' cunt," he whispered, as he lightly touched a swelling scratch.

While I struggled and attempted to jerk my hands free, Justin began to drive again. We were moving for less than five minutes when I felt myself overcome with exhaustion or the effects of a concussion, or both. Whatever ailed me at that point caused my eyes to close as I drifted into pure darkness, sobbing along the way.

"They're on their way to Mansfield!" he said into the phone.

"How do you know?" Alan asked.

"We've been monitoring all of the police channels in case the cops found her first. A report came over the radio for the highway patrol to check I-71 for a reckless vehicle south of the city in the southbound lane. We didn't give it

much thought, until they read back the license plate and who the vehicle was registered to."

"Who?"

"We found the mole, Alan. The truck returned to none other than Justin Brown."

"The new detective at Richland Metro? How?"

"We're still digging, but apparently several other drivers called in the complaint. They said it looked like a domestic situation, a male and female fighting inside the truck. It crossed the median and went into oncoming traffic. Last report had the vehicle still headed south, toward Mansfield."

"It has to be her," Alan thought. "She probably called him for help. Do you have any idea where they might be headed?"

"I have a good idea, and if I'm right, we don't have much time."

Justin let me know we had reached our destination by slapping the side of my head.

"Sit up! I said, sit up, CeeCee!"

Raising my head slightly, I tried to focus my blurred vision on the glove compartment in front of me. My head throbbed horribly, and I felt nauseous and groggy. I needed water terribly. So terribly, it was difficult to swallow.

"Justin," my voice croaked as I begged. "I need water. Can I please get some water?"

"Not to worry." He grabbed my hair and sat me upright. "Water will be the last thing on your mind in a few minutes."

Now that I was sitting up straight, our final destination came into view. Blinking my eyes rapidly, and finally able to focus, I was horror-struck to see that we were sitting in the parking lot of the Quinn-Herstin Funeral Home.

"Here we are, CeeCee, home sweet home." He began to undo my handcuffs. "This will be the last place you ever see on earth. Kinda depressing, isn't it?" He giggled. "Now move."

Once my handcuffs were off, I didn't move, fearing what waited for me inside the home. Again, I frantically looked around for an escape.

"I said, move!" he ordered, placing the barrel of his gun against my temple.

"Go ahead, Justin," I said weakly, calling his bluff. "Shoot me here, right now. You won't do it, will you? Your father has plans for me, doesn't he? Shooting me here in the parking lot will fuck up his glory, and the satisfaction of seeing me die. Won't be happy with you, will he?"

Justin smiled. "You're right, CeeCee. I'm not going to shoot you here, but you're going with me just the same, and there's no way out of it."

A large figure stepped into the light to Justin's left. It was Antonio Iaccona.

"You've met my big brother, right, CeeCee? I don't think formally, though. Here, let me introduce you: CeeCee Gallagher, Antonio Iaccona." He nodded his head toward Antonio.

Antonio, evidently having missed any and all etiquette lessons, failed to shake my hand. Instead, he reached into the truck and grabbed my hair in a death grip. With no amount of exertion on his part, he pulled me with one hand out of the truck and onto the ground. Knowing it was late, I found what little voice I had left and screamed loudly. Hearing a female screaming in the early hours of morning would surely bring a patrol car or two. Where the hell was everybody?

"Shut the fuck up." Antonio lifted me up and placed his hand over my mouth.

He was too large and strong for me to fight, though I did give it a hell of a try. He basically jogged to the door of the funeral home while holding me in his grip, his hand still over my mouth. Justin strode in arrogantly behind us. Antonio allowed my feet to touch the ground, but he still held me tight, although he did uncover my mouth. His hand was so large it had partially covered my swollen, bloody nose, making it hard for me to breathe. I began gulping large amounts of air, my chest heaving in and out. Swallowing the bile that began to rise in my throat, I closed my eyes and breathed deeply.

Standing there in the foyer of the Quinn-Herstin Funeral Home, I realized a blatant fact: I had failed. I had failed my children, I had failed Michael, I had failed Joseph, I had failed everybody—and I had failed myself. Being this close to death was nothing new to me. Nevertheless, I recognized that on each one of those occasions something had been different than it was here. There had always been an out, a saving grace. Each incident carried with it a hope that I would be rescued, the *potential* of being saved. Not tonight. Tonight there was no hope. No one knew where I was. I had done a superb job of covering my tracks. Since I was no longer a law-enforcement officer, I couldn't count on the brilliant minds of my peers to come to my aid. I was in Florida, basking in the sun, trying to get my mind and body together after the untimely demise of my husband. Or so everyone thought.

But here I stood, ready to face the epitome of evil, the highest crime figures imaginable, who would relish the screams of my pain and suffering, and there was no possibility of being liberated. My last hope was lying in front of a nightclub in Cleveland with a fatal bullet hole in his chest—Joseph.

"Bring her down here, Paulie," a voice beckoned from a stairwell to our right.

The voice, I recognized immediately, was that of Salvatore Iaccona. Even before he stepped out of the stairwell and into the light, I knew it was him. It was an unmistakable voice. He walked toward me and stopped less than two inches from my face. All the while, Antonio still held me.

"I promised you less than twenty-four hours ago that you would suffer. I always keep my promises. Especially to reeking bitches like you who try to kill me in my own home." He slapped me across the face.

Remaining stoic, I looked back up at him with a sneer of contempt. If I had had the ability to kill him right then and there, I would have. The opportunity had presented itself when I sat face-to-face with him at his house, but regrettably, I'd waited too long.

"I was going to kill you anyway," he continued. "But when you stupidly told me everything you had done to fuck up my business, all you did was make your own death that much worse." His voice rose as he drew closer, his nose almost touching mine. "You think your husband suffered when he burned to death? That's nothing, compared to what you're going to go through tonight, lady!"

With no other recourse, I spit in Salvatore Iaccona's face. He wiped the wetness from his cheek before backhanding me, striking my already throbbing nose, which caused it to bleed again. As a last resort, I used the only leverage I had been desperately holding on to.

"You can't kill me! Don't you get it, Sal? I have videotapes and audiotapes that have each one of you talking about everything from Michael's murder to Niccolo's to Frank Trapini's. It's in the mail, on its way to the FBI. You see, they'll know it was you that killed me! You're already done!" I laughed. "If you're smart, you'll let me go, and leave the country. I estimate that you have less than twelve hours before the FBI gets the files. You'll get the death penalty! Let me go."

Sal stood quietly for a few seconds before a grin spread slowly across his face. Justin and Antonio smiled as well.

"What difference does it make? If what you're saying is true, then the FBI will already know we've killed before, including that greasy piece of shit Joey Filaci—your lover—so what's one more?" He paused. "And not that you'll care, because you'll be dead by then, but after we take care of you, we *are* leaving the country."

I was about to declare that I was a law enforcement officer. But I quickly realized they were already facing the death of a federal agent, and I silently reminded myself that I was no longer a cop. With nothing left to say, no more pleas to make, no more attempts to get them to rethink their actions, I stayed silent. Salvatore, on the other hand, began to sing. He began snapping his fingers and humming, before belting out the words to a tune that sounded vaguely familiar.

"In the mornin', in the evenin', ain't we got fun!" he sang.

So much for leverage. Struggling and screaming again, I fought hard as they dragged me to the stairwell from which Singin' Sal had emerged, and down the steps. He was whistling while Justin and Antonio threw me through the double doors that led to the preparation room. As I began to stand, Antonio grabbed me again and dragged me over to one of the steel tables that occupied the room, a table that had a cooler full of ice and Donovan Esposito next to it. Steven Snyder stood horrified against the farthest wall. I played to his expression of weakness and fear.

"Steven!" I screamed as Antonio lifted me onto the table. "Steven! Help me! You don't know what you're doing! You could get the death penalty for this! Do you want to die, Steven?" I pleaded to no avail.

Steven Snyder evaded my stares and turned a deaf ear to my screams. Petey Iaccona, William Petrosini, and two other men I didn't recognize entered the room just then.

"You sniveling, wormy little shit!" I shouted at Steven Snyder. "Take a good look around you, Steven! You'll be here soon after me when you die by lethal injection!" Steven, no longer able to take my screams and threats, straightened his jacket and started to walk out of the room. I prayed he had come to his senses and was going to call the police.

"Get the fuck back here!" Justin grabbed Steven and slammed him against a wall. "Where the fuck do you think you're going?"

Steven stuttered. "I—I just . . . I don't think . . . I don't think this is a good idea, Paulie. We—we're gonna get caught!"

"You stay right here. If you move, you're getting buried with her."

I began to sob. "They didn't tell you, did they, Steven? They didn't tell you they were leaving the country! They're gonna leave you behind, aren't they?"

Steven Snyder looked like he was near a breakdown, but he didn't move.

"Don't listen to her!" Sal barked at Steven. "Get her tied down, Tony! We don't have all fuckin' night, for Christ's sake! Put some tape over her mouth, too. The only thing I want to hear out of her are bona fide screams of pain."

Antonio walked over to a large table to find tape, while Justin and the other two men fastened the restraints on my arms and legs. Watching Donovan Esposito put on rubber gloves gave me a brief opportunity to rattle him also.

"Doctor! Did you hear me? Do you want to die, too? Oh, by the way," I began to laugh, my voice sounding on the verge of insanity. "Not only are the files of your murders on the way to the FBI, but the pictures of you and the blonde coming out of the hotel room are also on the way to your wife!"

He started at me, a look of pure abhorrence on his face.

"You fucking whore . . ." he began.

"Not now, Donnie!" Sal ordered. "We don't have time for this shit right now! You said you couldn't stand the bitch anyway, so what difference does it make? Get yourself prepped and ready to go. Let's do this!"

"With pleasure," Donovan said, turning back to his table.

When he was finished doing whatever it was he needed to do, he walked toward me, pulling a mobile cart that had several steel instruments on top of it—instruments that gravely concerned me. All of the men surrounded the table as I lay strapped down, with no mobility at all. Antonio held my head straight, so I was unable to turn it side to side, only able to look above at the fluorescent lights.

My heart raced at such a speed I thought I might die of a heart attack. Luck didn't appear to be on my side. I was still coherent when Donovan Esposito picked up an instrument that resembled scissors, but instead of being straight, the blades were curved. They almost resembled wire cutters, but on a much larger scale. The space in the middle of the blades wasn't very large—too large for a wire but just right for something else, something the size of a finger.

When Petey Iaccona grabbed my left hand and pulled it forward, separating my fingers, I began to scream, while the men laughed. Struggling again, I found that the last of my strength had been expended. With images of my children flashing before my eyes, I looked at the lights and succumbed to my fate.

Only then did I begin to pray. I prayed for a swift and painless death, a death that was unlikely. I prayed that soon Michael would come and take me to spend eternity with him. I prayed that my children would know I died fighting and protecting them. I prayed they would grow up not feeling the void of their dead mother, but knowing they would see me again. I prayed for Sean and I prayed for my parents. My endless prayers were interrupted by Sal's booming voice.

"This is it, Mrs. Gallagher, or Hagerman," he said with sarcastic joy. "You wanted to see your husband again. Here, you get your wish. Now comes your suffering, and along with your suffering comes a souvenir. A remembrance, of a sort, of the union you shared between yourself and that fuckin' asshole FBI agent!"

The men began to laugh, and my confusion about his words didn't last long. When Donovan Esposito put the instrument around my ring finger, I knew exactly what Sal meant. There wasn't time to brace myself for the unimaginable pain I was about to endure. The diamond ring, which symbolized my lifetime commitment to Michael, was pushed forward, to make room for the bone cutter. There wasn't even time to close my eyes before the doctor clamped the instrument together, severing my finger completely. Sal held out the bloody finger, waving it in front of my face, as I screamed in pain like never before.

"Finger lickin' good, eh, Detective?" he chided.

The pain was too much and I began vomiting. With Antonio still holding my head in his viselike hands, I wasn't able to turn. Because there was nowhere for the bile to go, I began to aspirate it. All of the liquid was sucked back down into my lungs. I could suffocate to death. This was it. *Please God, let this be it. Let me die like this, quickly,* I begged silently as I gagged and struggled for air. Sal wouldn't have it.

"Turn her fuckin' head over, Tony! Jesus Christ, if she dies like that I'm gonna be pissed. I'm not done yet!" he screamed.

As ordered, Antonio turned my head sharply to

the left, allowing me to regurgitate quickly and avoid death. A shame really—death would have been much better. I was ultimately able to catch my breath as Donovan took my finger and placed it in the cooler that sat next to the table.

"That's all they're gonna get, honey. Just yer finger! Trust me when I tell you that no one will ever find your body. You'll be like the female Jimmy Hoffa. You should be honored! Your finger, with the ring of course, will be in the mail to the FBI at the same time we're on our plane out of here." He leaned over and grabbed my chin, forcing me to look at him. "But in case you think that's the end of it, think again. Your finger is only the beginning, darlin'."

Dizziness and disorientation were starting to take over. I tried my best to focus on Sal's face but couldn't.

Donovan grabbed the next instrument and turned it on, a very small version of a buzz saw, the blade approximately the size of a silver dollar. Hearing the grinding, buzzing sound of the instrument was enough to make me convulse on the table, causing all of the men to hold me down harder. That was the last feeling I had.

Thinking maybe I had aspirated a little too much, it dawned on me that now I was dying. The pain from my finger was gone; I couldn't feel it. In fact, I couldn't feel anything. My body, as it died, started to slowly lose feeling from my toes on up. There was no sense of time or place, no sense of pain or feeling at all. When the hands of death reached my head, the lights in the room started to dim, and the sounds could no longer be heard. The men disappeared and everything became dark—everything except a small light in the far corner of the room that started to brighten.

Patiently, I watched as the light grew. Smiling, I was able to sit up and hold my hand out as Michael emerged, wearing the tuxedo he'd worn the day we were married. I felt at peace. Music drifted into the room, as if off in the distance, but loud enough that we could hear it. Taking my hand, he smiled as I stood up and embraced him, slowly rocking back and forth to the music. We would be together forever. We would be to—

"Wake up, sweetheart!"

I focused back on the lights above. The sounds of the vibrating, grinding saw told me the nightmare wasn't over yet. Although I had a brief reprieve of unconsciousness, these men would make good on their word: they were going to make me suffer. I felt better about it somehow, calmer. Michael was waiting for me, waiting to dance and take me away with him. And that was okay.

My preempted reunion with Michael had seemed to last hours, but Donovan was in the same spot he was when I'd blacked out. Justin and Petey pulled my gold tank top up, exposing my stomach and the area where my liver was.

Donovan Esposito began to reach toward my abdomen, holding the instrument. This time, I was able to close my eyes. I can't remember which came first, the blast, or the feeling of the blade against my skin. Regardless, the next few seconds threw me into utter madness.

Just as Donovan began to cut my skin, a blast, loud enough to deafen my ears, exploded through the double doors. Smoke enveloped the room and a barrage of gunfire seemed to come from all sides. I opened my eyes in time to see Petey Iaccona thrown against the wall, a spray of bullets penetrating his entire torso. He slumped to the ground, leaving a wide smear of blood against the sterile white walls.

There was a lot of yelling and screaming. Justin Brown crouched down along the table to give himself time to grab his pistol. When he came up to fire it, he took a shot directly in his forehead. I'll never forget the look on his face as he was catapulted backward.

So engrossed in the chaos, I wasn't aware that one of the men, dressed in black and wearing a dark helmet and dark face shield—a SWAT team member, I thought—was frantically pulling at my restraints in an attempt to free them. He resorted to pulling a switchblade out of his pants and cut the restraints off. Overcome by smoke from the blast and gunfire, I was coughing and trying to breathe as the SWAT officer lifted me off the table and ran with me in his arms through the double doors. Yells of surrender and orders of "Don't move" spread throughout the room. The last time I saw Salvatore Iaccona, he was facedown on the floor being handcuffed.

Feeling the fresh air wash over my face, I knew a miracle had occurred and my prayers had been answered. I was going to live. How or why was irrelevant at that point. The only thing relevant was that I was saved and had once again escaped the hands of death. However, this time, I had come entirely too close.

The SWAT officer who carried me headed toward a waiting ambulance. The flashing lights of the numerous police and emergency vehicles blinded me. As I was bounced and jarred around in his arms, my pain resurfaced in my hand, my stomach, and my face. For once, the pain was welcomed. The pain told me I was still alive and kicking. The pain told me I would see my children again. If I'd had the strength, I would've screamed in celebration.

When the officer jumped over a curb, I cried out from the jolt. Stopping, he gently set me down on the pavement, cradling my head in his arms.

"Bring that ambulance over here, now!" he yelled.

Hearing his voice made my heart stop. I bolted upright and looked at my own reflection in the shiny black shield that he wore, a shield that covered his face. My pain became a distant memory. It was then that he reached to me, ever so tenderly, brushing the hair away from my face, a signature gesture I had received hundreds of times before. *It can't be!* my head screamed.

Almost violently, I reached toward the officer with my good hand and began pulling at the shield to rip it off. Grabbing my wrist, he prevented this, and backed away before reaching up to his face. He slowly began pulling the shield up himself.

As I looked at the face staring back at me, I began shaking my head back and forth in disbelief. It wasn't possible. It couldn't be.

"Yes, CeeCee," he said, reading my thoughts. "It's me . . . Michael."

CHAPTER FIFTEEN

Maybe this was another dream, similar to the one I'd had inside the funeral home. But remembering the dance Michael and I had shared brought forth several differences between then and now. The first was that now I felt excruciating pain. The second was that as my eyes were locked on Michael's, I saw he was breathing hard and sweating, unlike the perfection of our earlier reunion. Still, this wasn't enough to convince me that I was currently facing my dead husband. My mind scrambled for the explanation.

"Who are you?" I asked breathlessly, backing away from him. "Why would you do this to me? Is this a sick joke?"

He pulled his helmet completely off, exposing his thick brown hair. Then he put his hand out and slowly took a step toward me.

"It's me, Cee. This isn't a joke." He spoke slow and soft. "I know you're scared right now, but please, listen to me. This was set up to protect you and the kids, and I will tell you everything, but we need to get you to a hospital." He nodded at my left hand, minus a digit and still bleeding heavily.

My missing finger was the furthest thing from my

mind right now. On my knees, I moved forward to be closer to him, enough that I could reach my good hand out and barely touch his face. His skin was real—it had stubble on it, for crying out loud. His hair felt the same as I remembered. When I pulled his left glove off and saw the wedding ring I thought had been buried with his body, that was the moment I finally believed. It was the moment that I knew my prayers had been answered. Michael was alive, and standing right in front of me.

"Michael?" My voice quivered, before the sobs came. "Michael!"

My legs felt weak, even kneeling, but I managed to lean forward and grab ahold of him, planting my face in the front of his shirt and screaming. Screaming and sobbing so hard into his shirt, I began to feel light-headed again, but I didn't let go. He knelt down with me and held me tighter than I did him. Feeling his chest hiccup against my face let me know that he too was sobbing. All of the past several months came flooding back. The feelings of despair, heartache, loneliness, and sorrow all brought me to this point. It brought Michael back to me.

Oh, how I screamed and sobbed, and screamed. The front of Michael's shirt was soaked, and we had drawn an audience of police officers and FBI agents. The whole damn city could've been standing there watching us, but as far as I was concerned, it was just me and my Michael.

After what seemed an eternity, but not yet long enough, Michael tenderly pulled away and put his finger under my chin, raising my face to his. His eyes, red and swollen from his own sea of emotions, looked into mine.

"I missed you so much I thought I would die, but we'll get to all of that." He soothingly caressed my cheek. "I'm going to try to help you into the ambulance. You have to go to the hospital now."

My chest convulsed in an attempt to get air. My eyes felt swollen and watery. I did my best to let Michael help me, but I never took my eyes off him for a second. Everything seemed so foggy and blurry, I feared that if I shut my eyes, he would be gone when I opened them.

Three EMTs who stood by the back door of the ambulance helped me get inside and onto the gurney. They immediately began taking my vital signs while bandaging my left hand in a massive amount of white gauze. My eyes were still on Michael as he stood at the ambulance door, and his were on mine.

"Ma'am?" the EMT taking my vitals said, his face showing lines of deep concern. "Your heart rate is a little too high for my taste right now. I need you to do me a favor and take a deep breath and hold it for twenty seconds. Can you do that for me?"

Listening to the beeps slow down as I held my breath, I saw the man begin to relax. Maybe I was closer to a heart attack than I thought, but it appeared they had it under control.

"I think we've got her stabilized. Lou, shut the door so we can get going," the EMT who'd bandaged my hand said to the man who was taking my vitals.

They started to shut the rear doors of the ambulance when I sat up in a panic. Before I could say anything, Michael had already addressed my fear.

"Hold up, guys!" He put his hand in between the doors to prevent them from closing, and opened them back up as he stepped inside. "You're not taking her anywhere without me." He gave me a wink and sat down on a padded bench.

Feeling relieved, I lay back down, turning my head toward him. There was another knock at the back doors just as we began to pull away. Stopping the ambulance, an EMT opened the doors to one of the SWAT members, who was holding a small red cooler—the cooler that held my finger.

"Sorry, but you might want this." The officer shoved the cooler forward.

"What the hell is it?" The EMT looked irritated.

"It's her finger." He nodded at me, and my stomach churned.

As the EMT took the cooler, I saw two more familiar faces approaching the ambulance, Naomi and Coop.

"Wait!" I ordered, before he closed the doors again.

Propping myself up on my elbows, I did my best to smile at them. Naomi was crying, and Coop looked as if he was in shock.

"Hey there, strangers."

"God, CeeCee, please tell me you're okay," Naomi whispered, poking her head in.

"I'm gonna be. Now that I have him back, I'll be just fine, Naomi." I nodded at Michael.

Coop was still staring at Michael, as if dumbfounded. Apparently, the other officers had just filled them in on Michael, and on Justin Brown.

"Man oh man, Michael." Coop shook his head. "I wouldn't have believed it until I saw it with my own eyes. It's good to have you back, buddy." He stretched out his hand, which Michael shook lightly. "And Justin. Who would've thought—"

"Not right now, Coop," Naomi intervened. "All in

good time. Right now, CeeCee needs to get to the hospital. CeeCee, I've called your father and Eric. The sheriff is on his way here. I'll fill him in."

Nodding at her as the doors closed, I breathed a sigh of relief. It was finally over. On the short drive to the hospital, Michael held my right hand the entire way and kept asking me which parts of my body hurt. Since the list was lengthy, I kept telling him I'd be fine.

As soon as we arrived at the hospital, I was taken to an operating room. The EMT told me the sooner they reattached my finger, the better off I'd be. As I was prepped for the surgery, I heard Michael, in the hallway, talking louder than usual. Smiling to myself, I knew what was happening. Michael was telling the doctor that he would be in the operating room during the surgery, whether the doctor liked it or not. When Michael came through the doors a short time later wearing surgical scrubs, I knew he had won the argument.

Once all of the X-rays taken earlier returned, the doctor was ready to start. Surprisingly, my nose wasn't broken, and the only attention my abdomen needed was a butterfly Band-Aid. Donovan Esposito hadn't cut me before the blast, but the force from it threw him forward, scraping the blade of the saw across my stomach. It was nothing more than a deep scratch. Right before the surgery began, I told the doctor that my lungs needed to be looked at because I thought I had slightly aspirated.

"You probably choked on your vomit, CeeCee, but I guarantee you didn't aspirate it. If that were the case, we'd have you on a ventilator right now, or you probably would have died. Aspirating vomit destroys lung tissue immediately, so consider yourself lucky."

He couldn't possibly comprehend just how lucky I felt. People dream about having their loved ones brought back from the dead. Only I had experienced such a miracle.

The surgery went smoothly, and less than three hours later I was lying in the recovery room with Michael still at my side. I tried to remember what day it was or the last time I had slept, but it was no use. As hard as I fought the exhaustion that overcame me, it was a battle I quickly lost. I closed my eyes and fell into a sleep that lasted for almost seventeen hours.

Since I had an IV of continuous pain medication, I actually felt decent when I woke up. Expecting my body to ache and scream out in pain at every small movement, I was pleasantly surprised to sit up pain free and see Michael sitting in the same chair, as I remembered. He hadn't moved. He was still wearing his SWAT uniform, and his head rested on his shoulder as he slept.

Smiling, I had to pinch myself as a reminder that he was real. I stared at him for several minutes before rousing him awake.

"Michael," I called out to him.

He sat upright, rubbing his eyes. "What? You okay, baby?"

"I'm perfect. What time is it?"

He looked at his watch. "It's about one in the morning. Let me get the nurse." He stood up.

"No, I'm fine, really. Come over here."

He sat on my bed, and I rested my head on his shoulder. Euphoria didn't come close to describing what I felt.

"The doctor was in earlier. He said your hand looks good, and you should regain full use of your finger in the next couple of months. Other than feeling some numbness in the tip, you'll be as good as new," he said softly, stroking my hair.

Lifting the white gauze mitten that engulfed my hand, I was truly grateful to the doctor, and to the SWAT member who'd recovered the cooler with my finger in it. Michael raised an issue that hadn't even crossed my mind yet. Everything had happened so quickly, it was difficult to put things into perspective.

"Naomi was in, too. She called Eric and told him not to bring the girls in. You're going to have to sit them down and explain the circumstances to them . . . like me, for instance. If he brought them in now, and they saw me, they'd go into shock." He rubbed his eyes again. "I'm going to have to get used to people looking at me like I'm a ghost. The sheriff, your father, and some of the officers about fell over when they saw me. Your dad's coming back, but I had to give him some type of an explanation."

I brought my head up from his shoulder. "I'm certainly waiting to hear an explanation too, as you can imagine. I'm ready, Michael. I have to know."

He nodded but suggested we have our talk at home. The doctor said I could have been discharged much earlier, but Michael had allowed me to sleep. Within an hour, Michael and I were on our way home together, something that hadn't occurred in several months. Pulling into the driveway, he commented on the front window, the one that had been blown out during the explosion.

"I see you got it fixed." His voice was flat.

"Cost a pretty penny. Not to mention, I was blown against the wall when it happened."

He turned to me, an intense look on his face. "It wasn't supposed to happen like that. I . . . Let's go inside, and I'll explain."

We were both quiet, walking through the front door. Both of us had known there was a high probability that we would never see our home again. It was a wonderful sight. Michael closed his eyes and inhaled deeply. I could only imagine what he was feeling.

"I would dream about this day, the day I could finally come home." He shook his head and looked around.

He walked in and out of every room while I lit a fire. Ironic, since we were sitting in this same room, with a fire in the fireplace, the last time I'd seen him. I was patient as Michael changed out of his SWAT uniform and into something more comfortable. His clothes were just as he had left them; I'd never touched a thing. When he joined me on the couch, he looked amazing.

"Are you sure you want to do this now? It's almost four in the morning." He snuggled up as close as possible without sitting on my lap.

"I've slept for almost an entire day. Start at the very beginning."

Michael began to tell me of the elaborate plot devised by the FBI to fake his own death. It was the only way, in his mind, to save my life and the lives of our children.

CHAPTER SIXTEEN

Michael took a long, deep breath. "You know I was investigating both families," he began. I nodded. "We were receiving information daily about LifeTech Industries' connection to the mob, only we weren't sure which family it was, or what they were involved in. About a month before things got really heated, I followed one of the trucks to the Iaccona warehouse in Youngstown. It was then I figured out what was going on, but I couldn't prove it. These guys were carrying medical coolers out, and it didn't take a genius to know that it wasn't a skin graft inside, but something else. We started pulling their financial accounts, records, licenses, and everything we could think of, but they were clean as a whistle."

"But you had tape recordings of—"

He held his hand up. "We'll get to that. Keep in mind, LifeTech Industries is a legitimate tissue-donor corporation, but also a front for organ trade." I stayed quiet while he continued. "Only when I heard, by chance, of a homeless man missing a liver in Detroit did I start to understand the depth of what they were doing. But we had hit a brick wall. Until Niccolo Filaci came to see me." Michael had a blank stare directed at the fire, as if remembering it all. "I knew he was pissed off because they wouldn't let him in, but he was willing to talk, so why would I care? He gave me a lot of information, including where Sal's secret office was." He loudly sighed. "It was shortly after I first met with Niccolo that he began to tell me about threats toward me from the Iacconas. Niccolo even gave up his own family, but I could never figure out how either family knew who I was. Until now."

"Justin Brown." I already knew.

"That's right. He knew enough about you, that your husband was an FBI agent in Cleveland. The family knew there was heat on them. He followed me one night to the warehouse. He was taking a wild guess that I was the agent in charge of the investigation. Of course, I didn't know about it until later, but obviously, when he saw me park in front of the warehouse, it was confirmed. I was the agent trying to destroy everything. That's when the real threats began."

"He killed them, you know."

"Who?"

"The homeless murders. It was Justin. He confessed on the way to the funeral home."

"I figured that out while you were sleeping in the hospital."

"How long does it take for someone to die when they're getting a major organ cut from their body?" An image of the funeral home, specifically the image of Donovan Esposito cutting out my liver, flashed through my head. I got immediate chills.

"A liver or both kidneys would cause death, but only one kidney wouldn't. That's why some of your victims were strangled and some tortured. Your first victim must've made them angry, angry enough they cut off his hand."

"I know the feeling." Half giggling out of sheer nervousness, I raised the white glove that covered my own hand.

"It was easy for them. They would find some poor homeless person and tell them they could make big money. They'd arrange a meeting somewhere, and that's where Justin would kill them."

"But isn't there some type of time element to getting these organs into the recipients?"

"Absolutely. For the most part, they would get the organ, courtesy of Dr. Esposito, throw them in the cooler, and leave on a chartered jet from the Mansfield airport. They'd switch planes in Chicago or Atlanta, and head mainly to the Philippines. They would have only about a day to get the organ there. In the Philippines, the doctors would be literally waiting with the recipient on the table when Frank Trapini would bring the cooler in."

I had a thought. "I had a victim, a female. Her last name was Cross. Michael, she wasn't homeless!"

"They were getting desperate, Cee. We think their boss in the Philipines upped the orders. Troy Cross was up to his ass in LifeTech Industries stock."

"I knew it!"

"He owed them a lot of money and wasn't paying, so they took his wife. We found out that Troy Cross told this to a detective at Richland Metro, but I couldn't figure out why they didn't do anything about it, until I realized he had told Justin."

"He lied to me," I thought aloud. "He told me Troy Cross wouldn't give anything up."

"Justin didn't know where you were when you

had that conversation. He knew you had left Florida by then, but didn't know where you'd gone. He needed to be careful."

I had another epiphany. "Oh my God! This entire time I couldn't figure out how the Iacconas knew I'd gone to Cleveland. Now I know." I began shaking my head. "The day I had the conversation with Justin about Troy Cross, I was in Cleveland but told him I was still in Florida. I remember they announced the score to the Cleveland Browns game as I stood right in front of the stadium. He must've heard it."

"I'd say that's a pretty safe assumption. We couldn't figure that part out, either."

"Why would they move the operation down here, to Mansfield, when they knew I worked here and was married to you?"

"Again, because of Justin. He was the insider we could never identify. After Niccolo told me that the Iacconas were making threats, I broke into Sal's office and planted the bugs. Nothing was admissible, Cee, because the bugs were put in there illegally. At that point, I wasn't worried about criminal charges. I was worried about the safety of my family, so I had to know everything."

"Michael," I said, my eyes brimming with tears, "why didn't you ever tell me any of this before?"

"I didn't want to worry you. I wanted to feel like I had it completely under control. Which I did, until Niccolo was murdered and the murders began here in Mansfield."

"I don't understand."

"Niccolo was telling me he thought they were going to take him out, but I told him he was being paranoid. He had already put one of the bugs in his father's office for me, so he said I owed him some protection. I laughed at him . . ." He was quiet for a few moments. "When I saw his murder on the news, I felt like shit, but also, I knew these people weren't fucking around. Your name began to come up more and more in their conversations. The insider—Justin— was telling them you were getting too close. That's when they made the decision to have me, and possibly you, killed. Even more shocking, Leon Filaci ordered the same. You heard the tapes. Things began to boil, there were more homeless victims, more threats toward us, and there was nothing we, the FBI, could do, since we had no hard evidence. It was Alan Keane who suggested we fake my death."

"But, why, for Christ's sake? There *had* to have been another way!" I was beginning to feel a lot of anger toward Alan Keane.

He looked at me. "Cee, there wasn't! Don't you understand? We were backed into a corner! If they thought I was dead, they'd think the heat was off, so they'd go about their business and forget about you! We knew it would at the very least buy us some time, time to gather the evidence we needed to bring them all down."

It was hard to absorb everything Michael was telling me. As scary as it had been for him at the time, I couldn't help but think they were wrong for faking his death.

I was shaking my head. "All right, so things were bad. Tell me about the night of the explosion."

"God, I almost backed out a thousand times. After we made love that night, I called Alan and told him I couldn't do it. I couldn't bear to go months and possibly forever without seeing you. Remember? I tried to get you and the kids to go on vacation. If you had agreed, I would've told Alan the deal was off. I only needed a couple of weeks. And more than any of that, I couldn't bear to see you go through the heartache of thinking you lost me."

"What did he say?" I asked, regretting my decision to blow off Michael's suggested vacation.

"He said, and I quote, 'Okay, Michael. But how will you bear it if they kill her? How will she bear it if you really are dead?' He was right." Michael's eyes began to water. "Never, ever in my life has anything been as hard as the night I walked out that door, knowing what was coming. I kept thinking it was wrong, so wrong." He paused. "And when the blast . . . when the blast blew through the window, they had to hold me back. They weren't supposed to use that many explosives. I was terrified that you had gotten hurt."

"What I want to know is, who the hell was inside of the car?"

"A cadaver, courtesy of the University of Kentucky's medical school."

"Another part I don't understand: Salvatore and Justin admitted to me that *they* killed you!"

"Did they actually say they did it, Cee? Salvatore thought the Filacis got to me first, but he wanted to take the credit anyway."

It was all making sense. "So that's why the FBI got here so quick and took over the crime scene. That's why the hush-hush funeral. Alan said it was because he wanted the mob to think you were still alive, but in reality, he did it because it would be easier to bring you back if only a few people knew."

Michael nodded. "They had to have three guys

put me in the car that night, I was so worried about you."

"Where did you go?"

"At first, I went back to Washington, DC, for a large number of meetings with the FBI's top supervisors. After that, I was put up in a safe house in Erie, Pennsylvania. That's when it became pure hell for me." He tilted his head back. "Those nights of lying there, staring at the ceiling, aching for you, were some of the worst in my life—"

"Don't even talk to me about long nights and aching!" I interrupted. "Do you have any idea at all what I went through, Michael? My life literally stopped! Eric took custody of the girls, I quit my job, and basically quit living!" I began choking up. "I know it was hard for you, but at least you knew I was alive!"

I began to sob, and Michael pulled me close and held me tight. Remembering those nights not so long ago was an extremely difficult task.

He rocked me back and forth. "I know, I know . . . I'm so sorry. I knew what you were going through, believe me." He pulled away and looked at me. "The house was wired, Cee—by the FBI and by the Iacconas."

I was shocked and looked around. "What? Are the wires still here?"

"No, no. They were taken out when you left for Florida. I'm just telling you that so you'll know I was kept informed of everything, down to the times you stayed in bed and cried for days. There was video, video of you crying, sobbing, drinking, and screaming. I thought I would go out of my mind! Every time Alan sent one to me, I began to get scared to watch it. We also had agents watching you."

"The guy in the park! The day I was there with the girls!" I exclaimed, remembering. "You also had one pretending to be a vending-machine guy. I saw him in the department parking lot one day."

He nodded. "And the hang-up phone calls. I needed to hear your voice or I wouldn't have made it."

"Those were you?" A part of me felt incredibly naive—not that anyone on earth would've thought their dead husband was crank-calling.

He caressed my cheek. "There was one night when I couldn't take it anymore, and I snuck back here."

"You did? When?"

He looked at me for a long time. It was then I knew the exact night he had returned, and how I regretted it.

"I had been watching how you were progressively getting worse, and that night . . . that night I found you on the kitchen floor with the gun in your hand, and I knew, I knew what you were thinking about." His face looked slightly angry. "How could you even think about doing something like that, CeeCee? What about Selina and Isabelle? What about you?"

I stood up, on the defensive. "Wait just one minute! Don't you dare put yourself in my shoes, because you have no fucking idea what I went through! None! I had been drinking a lot, and things . . . they just caught up with me. But as you can see, I'm fine!"

"I'm sorry. Please, sit down." He patted the couch. "I took the bullets out of the gun that night. I don't know if you ever realized it."

"You touched me, didn't you?" I asked, vividly remembering the dream I'd had, where he caressed my face.

"Barely, but you started to wake up, so I had to go."

"Next, please."

"It was Alan that gambled on you. I had no idea he was hoping you would go out on your own and get the evidence. He never let me in on it until you left for Florida. They didn't know about the tapes I had until you found them. Salvatore knew you found them the same time we did. That's when I got more worried. When Alan told me what he was counting on, I told him the entire thing was off and that I was going home. As far as I was concerned, he was putting you in more danger than I'd ever imagined."

"But he didn't, Michael. I'm the one who decided to risk it all. It wasn't like he put the idea in my head or anything."

"I know, but I didn't like it just the same. When you resigned, he deemed it a stroke of brilliance on your part. I came unglued. And when they lost track of you in Florida, I finally grew a pair of balls and told him it was over. I flew into Cleveland that night on the verge of a breakdown, because I thought Tommy Miglia had gotten to you."

The mention of Tommy's name made my hair stand up on end. I braced myself, waiting for Michael to bring up the murder, but he never did.

"When I found out you were still alive, I was thrilled. Until Alan told me you had hooked up with Joseph Filaci." Michael's eyes locked on mine.

I felt a twinge of guilt, but also a bout of sadness, when I thought of him.

"Michael, before you ask, you need to know something. Joseph saved my life, literally. And no, nothing, and I repeat, nothing, happened between us. He helped me. I couldn't have done it all without him. Joseph died trying to help me."

Michael's eyes shifted away for a brief second. "I know. But, as you can imagine, I couldn't help but wonder . . ." He looked away. "Not that I could blame you, but it terrified me that you would find someone before this was all cleared up. It was a possibility that I had to seriously consider."

"If you think I could jump into bed with someone so soon after your death, then all I can say is, you don't give me much credit, or respect." I didn't want to be angry, but I wanted Michael to know the truth.

He leaned forward, putting his hand on my shoulder. "No, CeeCee, that's not what I meant. It's just that people do different things when they're grieving. I've never seen you grieve before, so I didn't know how you'd handle it. That's all I was trying to say!"

Running my good fingers through his hair, I realized it didn't matter. All that mattered was that he was sitting here with me right now.

"I'm sorry. I didn't mean to get defensive. I will tell you, honestly, I cared for Joseph as a friend, a good friend. I'm sure your previous dealings with him weren't the greatest, but he truly was a good person! He didn't deserve to die." My tears emerged once again.

Michael had an unusual look on his face, like he wanted to tell me something, but he relaxed and continued with the events that had led up to tonight.

"Let's just leave it for now and get back to the important stuff."

I nodded.

"If you only knew the times I was so close to you I could've reached out and touched you, you'd be shocked. We were always five minutes behind, just missing you. When I knew you had survived the explosion at the warehouse, we found you, finally, in Cleveland and followed you to the nightclub where you met Joseph. We had every intention of taking you into protective custody."

"You did? They were shooting at me there! Why the hell didn't anyone help me? Or Joseph?" I couldn't believe it.

"We tried, CeeCee. When you guys walked out and Antonio fired the first shot, the shot that hit Joseph, we started shooting back. A lot of the shots you heard came from us."

I thought back and merely shook my head. If only I could've known.

"As soon as Antonio and Petey began chasing you down the alley, I was right behind them. They realized I was after them, and they cut out in the opposite direction. I lost you soon after that."

The thought that entered my head at that moment made me close my eyes and groan. I hoped I was wrong.

"You didn't happen to run down the dock along the river, in the flats, did you? The one that ran in front of the strip bar?" I didn't want the answer but I asked anyway.

"Yeah. Why?"

I began shaking my head. "Because I was underneath the goddamn dock in the freezing water, hiding. I thought you guys were Antonio and Petey!"

It was unbelievable, really. To think that as I floated, on the verge of hypothermia, in the water underneath the dock, my husband—my "dead" husband—ran precisely six inches above me. And I never knew it. I thought it was the bad guys.

"You were under the dock?" Michael looked dumb-founded.

"Yup. That's when I ran into the strip bar and called Justin. I tried Naomi and Coop first, but they didn't answer. After that, you know the rest." I had a thought. "How did you find me at the funeral home?"

"I'm assuming you and Justin had a fight in the truck?"

"Yeah, how did you know?"

"A lot of people called in a domestic to the highway patrol. We were monitoring all of the police channels and heard it come across. When the plate returned to Justin, we put it all together."

"But how did you figure out the funeral home?"

"Because of you, Cee. Remember, right before I left? You had investigated the doctors and thought they had something to do with it. It didn't take long, but I had a hunch, and had Richland Metro check for cars in the lot of Quinn-Herstin. They ran the plates. There were two cars there, one registered to Dono-van Esposito, the other to William Petrosini. That's when I knew Justin was headed there, and I quickly organized the SWAT team."

"You got there just in time." I shuddered, remem-bering how close to dying I had come.

"Thank God. There's a lot of loose ends that need to be tied up, but for now, it's over. Justin and Petey are dead, and the rest are in custody, except for William Petrosino and Henry Mastragna. William somehow managed to get out a side door before we entered, but don't worry, we'll find him. Henry is in the Philippines."

"I remember Justin's face when he died." I paused. "It's something I'll never forget."

"You can thank yours truly for taking care of him."
Michael gave a sly smile.

"You shot Justin?"

"Honey, he drew his pistol on me right when I
came in the door. It wasn't like I had a choice or anything. After what he did to you, I think he went out
way too easy." He was right.

We sat for a long time in silence, absorbing everything that had been revealed. The sun had come up a
short time ago, but we were oblivious. I think I speak
for both of us when I say that still things felt like a
dream. I know we were both exhausted mentally
and physically, but we had both been through major
trauma. A post-traumatic-stress type of ordeal. I
mean, come on, my husband was dead and then re-
appears. It would make any human being feel slightly
off. Michael broke our silence with a question that
unnerved me.

"CeeCee, I have to ask you something."

"Go ahead. Ask anything, Michael."

He took a deep breath. "Did you break into Salvatore Iaccona's house and confront him?"

It was a long time before I answered him. But it was
apparent that I would have to answer several questions about my actions in the upcoming months.

"Yes, Michael. I did. And if you want the truth, I
had every intention of killing him that night, but
Petey came home. I barely got out the window." I
sighed. "I guess I should tell you this now, so there
are no surprises. I did a lot of things in the last couple
of weeks that could be construed as unethical, if not
downright illegal. As a matter of fact, there are several things I could probably go to prison for—for a
long, long time."

He squeezed my hand. "I can promise you right now that you are not going to prison, okay? Now, as much as I hate to bring this up right now, I have to. Do you have the files and tapes you acquired during your investigation?"

"They should be at the FBI office as we speak, all sent anonymously, of course. I had initially sent them to a friend in Atlanta, but I called her before I left Youngstown and told her to mail them overnight to the FBI in Cleveland. There is enough information to bring down every member of the Iaccona family."

"Thank God, it's finally over," he whispered.

He surprised me by forcing me down on the couch. Before I realized what his intentions were, we had our clothes off and were making love—over and over and over.

It was late afternoon before we eventually settled down and got some sleep. I took a brief opportunity between our lovemaking to call the girls and talk to them. They couldn't wait to see me. To think I would be able to tell them that Michael was alive was a miracle in itself. Michael missed Sean horribly. We talked about our reunion with all of the children and how it would transpire. We talked about everything. We both slept all night, clinging to each for dear life.

Michael had several phone calls to make the next day. The case was far from being closed, so he was in his office for a while and even had to leave for several hours—despite my protests. I found him later in the day sitting in our bedroom, staring at the ceiling.

"Honey? What's wrong?" I was concerned.

He sat up and swung his legs over the side of the bed, patting the area next to him for me to sit on. He put his arm around me as I sat down.

"What is it?" I asked again.

"Oh, I think you'll consider it good news. Alan received the files, and he told us to 'hold on to our asses.' They've gotten other information, and he told me this whole thing is going to explode very soon, no pun intended." He smiled. I did not. "Something else . . . I was going to tell you last night, but I wanted to know all of the details for sure first."

"Tell me what?"

"It's about Joseph, CeeCee. Joseph Filaci is alive."

CHAPTER SEVENTEEN

"Say that again." My heart skipped.

"Joseph is alive. He survived the shooting."

Jumping onto my feet off the bed, I stared at him, a smile widening on my face. In the last forty-eight hours, two men that I cared about had risen from the dead. I'd never play another lottery ticket for the rest of my life. The luck I was experiencing couldn't possibly get any better.

"Where is he? I want to see him! Is he okay?" I felt exhilarated.

"CeeCee, just calm down for a minute, and *sit down*!

The bullet that hit Joseph in the chest barely missed all of his major organs. An FBI agent was with him within minutes, calling for an ambulance. He was taken to an 'undisclosed hospital,' where he was rushed into surgery. Needless to say, he came out of it perfectly.

"I have to be honest with you, Cee, I thought he was dead, too. I ran right by him and he didn't look good. Alan called and told me the night we were at the hospital, but he didn't know any specifics yet. Joseph was still in surgery."

"But he's okay?"

"Yes, he'll be fine. He looked fine when I saw him this morning."

"You saw him!" I stood up again.

Michael raised his eyebrows and nodded at the bed, signaling me to sit down before he would even consider telling me the rest. I sat, anxious to hear it.

"That's why I left this morning, to see him. Alan called and told me he was okay. He also was there when Joseph woke up early this morning. He said the first thing out of Joseph's mouth was his asking if *you* were okay."

"Michael, please, you can go with me, but can we please go see him?"

He sighed. "CeeCee, listen to me. It's a little more complicated than that—"

"But you said he was okay!" I interrupted, but then had a horrifying thought. "You guys arrested him, didn't you?" I was furious. "That's why I can't see him, because he was taken into custody, right? This is bullshit, Michael!"

"God damn it, CeeCee, will you just listen for a minute?" His voice rose angrily before he smiled and began to laugh. "How could I possibly forget what a persistent cop you are?" He shook his head, still smiling. "No, honey, he has not been arrested. I wouldn't have allowed it after what he did for you."

I smiled. I had underestimated my Michael.

"There were two agents posted outside of his door for his *own* safety. I went to see Joseph, to thank him for helping you. As you might guess, he was shocked to see me alive and was a little on the defensive. Joseph has some serious feelings for you, Cee. It was obvious."

"I'm aware of it. Move on." We'd get into that later.

"Okay." He took the hint. "So I thanked him, and he was less than gracious. I understood why. He looked at me like I had failed his brother, which I had, and I told him as much. After I admitted I had fucked up, he started to come around. He told me I had an amazing wife and that I was very lucky."

"And . . . ?"

"And at that point, we started talking. He told me how you opened his eyes to the life he's been living, and he didn't want it anymore. He said he envied me. I had everything that he wished for. I think that meant you, but . . ."

Waving my hand and shaking my head, I wanted Michael to stay on track. Something that was seemingly hard to do.

"Yeah, right." He focused again. "He, uh . . . Where was I? Oh, he was saying how he wanted a normal life and such. That's when I came up with an idea. I pitched it to him, and believe it or not, he loved it. I made a series of phone calls, and it's getting arranged as we speak." Michael smiled.

"Well? What's the arrangement?"

"Joseph Filaci is going into the witness-protection program."

My jaw dropped. "He is? He agreed to that?"

Michael nodded. "Yes, he did. It couldn't have worked out better, actually. You see, no one but the FBI knows that he survived the shooting that night. Alan signed him into the hospital under an alias anyway, so it was perfect. Some of the details were sticky, but we managed to come to an agreement."

"His father?"

"That was one of them. Joseph wanted his father to know he was still alive, and he wanted us to leave his family alone. I told him I couldn't do it unless we got a little more from him."

"He saved my life, Michael. What more do you—?"

It was Michael's turn to interrupt. "I understand that, but the FBI would never approve anything based on that fact alone."

"I guess I understand. So what did he say?"

"Joseph is going to give up everybody. And I mean *every*body, everybody but his own family, of course."

I was stunned. "He *is*?"

Michael nodded. "They're going to do the interview later this evening and start as early as tomorrow to get him processed for the program. CeeCee, the information he's giving up is going to take down just about every organized-crime family in the country. He even agreed to give us Vincent Vicari."

Giving up one of New York's most powerful crime families, the granddaddy of them all, was serious— and dangerous.

"Please tell me you guys are going to really protect him, Michael."

"Of course we will, but keep in mind, Joseph Filaci was killed in a shoot-out in Cleveland with the Iacconas."

"You agreed to leave his family alone?"

"Reluctantly. There wasn't much we could do, since you gave him all of the files."

Remaining silent, I looked at the ground. I didn't know that Michael knew the Filaci files had been turned over to Joseph. But in retrospect, if my act of kindness toward Joseph kept him alive or out of prison, then I'd do it again in a heartbeat. Michael,

understanding my silence as a confession, mercifully moved on.

"He did have one last stipulation before he agreed
to the deal. He wanted to see you, Cee."

"I'm assuming you told him that would be fine."

"Yes, and I also told him how worried you were
about him. He seemed happy about that," Michael
grumbled.

"Great!" I smiled. "So when do I get to see him?"

"It's going to take a few days to get everything together. For now, they're putting him in a safe house
in Fairport Harbor with twenty-four-hour protection, until he goes permanently. We're both going to
meet him up there in the next week or so."

"Where's he going after that?"

"Frankly, they didn't tell me, and I didn't ask," he
said matter-of-factly.

It appeared we had passed the point where my
enthusiasm for Joseph's resurrection was becoming
taxing for Michael. Therefore, I let the rest of my
questions lie and made a sincere attempt to conceal
my joy, for Michael's sake.

Only when I reflect back on everything do the
weeks following the night in the funeral home seem
like a blur. Alan Keane wasn't joking when he told us
to hold on to our asses. The aftermath of it all was
monstrous, to put it lightly.

Within one week, the indictments came down. After Joseph's information and the information they
had taken from informants, pilots, messengers, and
others, the FBI conducted the largest takedown of
organized crime in history.

They conducted multiple raids in Ohio, Pennsylvania, New York, California, and Florida. All of the

New York crime families were hit: the Bonazzos, the Rigatis, the Colicellas, and most importantly, the Vicaris. The indictments for the families ranged from murder to racketeering, and most were tried under the National Organ Transplant Act. The New York Police Department had been tracking their own homeless murders for years and was now able to tie them to the families. There were indictments for numerous doctors (including Esposito's partner, Dr. Neal Schmidt), nurses, businessmen, politicians, community leaders, pro-football-team owners, college-football coaches, racetrack owners, and unfortunately, several police officers who were on the payroll of the crime families.

It was after the feds had searched Salvatore Iaccona's home and offices that one of the most shocking indictments was issued. Ohio, one of the hardest-hit states, was still reeling from the arrests when the news was made public that the governor, Graham Myre, had been arrested along with four members of his staff.

Governor Myre boisterously announced that he was guilty of nothing but having stock in LifeTech Industries, a business he had thought was legitimate. Unfortunately for Myre, Salvatore had secretly taped several of their meetings together in which they discussed the governor's cut of the money from the Philippines. Salvatore had kept them for future blackmailing purposes against Myre.

Alan Keane called daily, keeping us abreast of the raids and arrests. When the raids first started, William Petrosini's house was second on the list. According to Alan, the SWAT team had just rammed the front door of William's house when they heard a single gunshot come from upstairs. They found William with a self-inflicted fatal gunshot wound to his head. He was sitting on his bathroom floor.

The FBI's investigation took them overseas to places like the Philippines, Vietnam, Indonesia, and the Middle East. In the Philippines, they found the hospital that was receiving the organs from the Iacconas. Alan said it was an enormous operation.

Henry Mastragna was finally located. He had paid a Filipino family five dollars to hide him in a back room of their seedy market. Henry stupidly reached for a pistol when the FBI entered. He died right there of multiple gunshots.

As the dust began to settle on the operation, news of the need for organ donors started to make headlines. Impressively, the media got it right, and for once, Michael and I weren't mentioned. The FBI thought it was best for obvious safety reasons.

The media conducted interviews, taped specials, and put out documentaries on why the need to be an organ donor is so great. Most people didn't know the horror stories of what went on in the black market. Not to mention, since most of the organs on the black market aren't tested for blood type, disease, and such, a lot of people die when they receive them. Telling someone every time they renew their driver's license and decline to be an organ donor that one more person will be killed or mutilated for their organs as a result is a message that tends to hit home.

Organ donation in the United States went up thirteen percent the following year, but it still wasn't enough to make a dent. Michael said that ninety percent of the population would have to be organ donors to wipe out the illegal trade, and that wouldn't happen any time soon. Unfortunately, wiping out the larger organ traders merely made it easier for the smaller ones to rise up and take over. The Body Mafias would, it seemed, continue to exist forever. The raids and the arrests caused the prices of the organs on the black market to skyrocket, since they were harder to obtain, and now more people wanted a piece of it.

When I took the time to think about it, my head spun. It seemed that the only good the investigation did was to make the organ trade business more profitable. Michael told me not to look at it that way.

Several days after Michael told me Joseph was still alive, and the raids were just beginning, I told the girls Michael was alive. He had desperately wanted to see them and Sean. It was difficult to explain. They didn't understand, and telling them "It's complicated" didn't quite make it any easier. Michael left so that I could sit and tell Selina and Isabelle the truth. Selina looked at me like I was crazy. I knew she had been paying attention the last several months as I went deeper into insanity.

"Mom," she said slowly and loudly, as if I were deaf, "I know you think Michael is still alive, but . . . have you talked to Daddy about this? Maybe you should see a doctor!"

Laughing, I put my arm around her. "Honey, Daddy knows. If you don't believe me, then call him, or you can see Michael with your own eyes."

Isabelle, who up to this point had been more interested in my finger getting cut off than Michael, answered for her sister.

"I want to see Michael!"

Selina rolled her eyes at me and repeated Isabelle's request.

Michael had his cell phone with him so I could call when it was time to make his appearance. I told him Selina thought I was crazy, but he was excited. He must've only been at the end of the street, because he was home within minutes of my call.

Selina looked at me curiously when she heard the front door open, and she almost fainted when Michael walked into the room.

"Still think I'm crazy?"

Selina ignored me as her eyes opened to the size of teacups and she howled loudly. Isabelle, screaming just as loud, raced her sister to tackle him in the doorway. Me, I stood there and bawled.

Michael's own eyes were tearing like faucets as he caught both girls, spilling backward in a barrage of hugs and sloppy kisses. The girls spent the rest of the night catching Michael up on the last several months of their busy social lives and sports conquests.

"This is gonna be the best Christmas ever!" Isabelle announced. "When do we get to see Sean? I miss him!"

It now dawned on me that Christmas was less than three weeks away. The house hadn't been decorated, no tree had been put up, and I hadn't shopped at all. Then there was the dreaded phone call I still needed to make to Vanessa.

"I'm going to call Sean's mommy tonight and see if he can't stay this weekend. If so, we'll all decorate the house together. I'm still waiting on Christmas lists from the both of you!"

Putting it off as long as I could, I eventually found

my way into Michael's office to call Vanessa. He followed. Michael didn't want to shock her right off by calling himself. As predicted, she was a complete pain in the ass about my news. At one point, she referred to me as a liquored-up, crazy-skank whore who needed to be locked up in a mental institution. That was when I handed the phone to Michael. Vanessa and I had never gotten along, so it was best that she hear it from him. As soon as he said hello, I could hear her screaming into the phone. Rolling my eyes, I left the office so Michael could finish talking to her.

He joined me soon after. "She said she's sorry about the 'crazy skank' comment." He was smiling.

"Sorry if I don't accept. So what's the deal with Sean?"

"She's going to sit him down right now and tell him. He's been having a really hard time—poor little guy. She'll call me as soon as they're done so he can talk to me on the phone, and then he'll be down this weekend."

"Wonderful!" I clapped my hands. "I miss him, too. She wouldn't let me see him anymore after . . . Well, you know."

He nodded. "I'll see what I can do to prevent that from ever happening again should I really drop dead."

"That's not funny, Michael."

The following weekend was the best time any of us had had in months. None of us thought a reunion like this was possible. Michael almost fell apart when he saw Sean, and held him for a long time. As planned, we decorated the house, put up the tree, and made Christmas cookies. Once in a while, I'd have to shake the thought that I was dreaming out of my head. It all seemed so surreal.

Naomi and Coop made frequent appearances, wanting us to spend New Year's Eve with them in Cancún, but we declined. We had both traveled enough and wanted nothing more than to bring in the new year together at home.

For Christmas, Michael gave me a new diamond ring the size of a small country. My wedding ring had been damaged badly when my finger was severed. Speaking of my finger, the bandages had come off and the stitches were out. It was healing nicely.

Our meeting with Joseph had been postponed. The raids were taking longer than expected, so the processing wouldn't get done until after New Year's. The week between Christmas and New Year's, I received a phone call from Alan Keane. He said he wanted to meet with me, but wouldn't say why on the phone. He also strongly suggested that I not tell Michael right away about our meeting. We agreed to meet the following afternoon at a small park near downtown that had a large pond, Freedom Park.

I have to admit, curiosity about the purpose of the meeting was getting the best of me. I didn't sleep well the night before and found myself nervous most of the day. My thoughts shifted back and forth in an attempt to figure out why he wanted to see me. Arriving half an hour early, I was startled to see that Alan was already there. He was sitting on a bench along the pond, throwing food to the ducks.

"Alan?" I walked up behind him and stood.

"CeeCee, it's good to see you." He stood up and turned around to shake my hand. "Here, there's plenty of room for the both of us."

Taking my place on the bench, I remained stoic. "What is it that you wanted, Alan?"

"First, let me say how glad I am that you're okay. I can't imagine what you went through and, well, I'm sorry." His eyes looked down.

"I'm sure that's not the reason you called me here . . . to tell me you're sorry?"

"Believe it or not, that's part of it." He reached into the paper bag holding the duck food and threw some out to the waiting birds. "I know Michael explained everything, but yes, it was my idea. He never wanted to go along with it, CeeCee."

"I know that now, and, apology accepted. What's the rest of it?"

"You were amazing, you know, everything you did. Even I underestimated your intelligence, but I knew you'd pull through. I was doing some research, and it looks like you've helped the FBI out quite a bit over the years. You're a rare find, CeeCee."

I sighed. "What do you want, Alan?"

"I want you to come and work for me—for the FBI. It's all been approved. We're just waiting on your answer." He was staring at me with a kind and gentle look on his face.

If someone had hit me in the back of the head with a ball bat right then, I wouldn't have been more surprised. The FBI wanted *me*?

"I don't understand, Alan. Why me?"

"The biggest bust-up in the history of organized crime has *you* to thank, that's why. None of it would have ever happened without you. Please say yes, CeeCee. We need someone like you."

My head was spinning, a familiar event these days. "What did Michael say about this?"

"I haven't told him yet. I thought it would be best if you discussed it with him first. If you want time to think about it, take it. Talk to Michael. But please, I hope you give the offer serious consideration."

Knowing I already had an answer, I didn't feel right about stringing him along, so I told him.

"Alan, as flattering as your offer is, the answer is no. Being a federal agent is not me, nor will it ever be. I hope you can understand that." I lightly shook my head. "I don't know what I'm going to do right now. This whole thing has shown me how precious and short life can be. Right now, I just want to spend time with Michael and the kids. If I *do* go back to work, it'll be as a cop, a city cop. That's what—and who—I am."

He nodded, and remained silent for a short while. Reaching inside his overcoat, he pulled out a medium-size manila envelope and handed it to me.

"I understand, CeeCee. Here, take this."

"What is it?" I took the envelope from him and began to open it.

When I pulled out the stack of photographs and saw the one on top, I stood up. Pulse racing and breathing heavily, I looked around, then back at the pictures. They were photographs taken of me the night I'd killed Tommy Miglia. They were photographs of me *actually killing* Tommy Miglia and dumping him into the bay.

"What is this, Alan? Is this a setup? Are you arresting me?" I braced myself, waiting for the other agents to swoop in and place me under arrest.

He shook his head. "No, CeeCee, it's not a setup, you're not being arrested, and what you hold there in your hand are the only copies. They're yours to do with what you want."

"But how? Why?"

"We had agents watching you in Florida. We had gotten information that Salvatore ordered the hit on you there. The agents took the photographs. It's over, CeeCee. The authorities in Florida have closed the case. There's no evidence, no witnesses. It'll forever remain unsolved. As far as they're concerned, it's just another unknown Mafia hit. We know it was self-defense."

I was incredulous. "I don't give a shit whether the case is solved or not! What I do give a shit about is the fact that I was almost beheaded by Tommy Miglia and his wire, and there were two agents that stood there doing nothing to help me! I could've died, Alan!"

"CeeCee, they were running over to help you when you stabbed him. They knew you had killed him and that you were okay. They called me immediately and asked me what to do." He pleaded with me. "Don't you understand, CeeCee? If we'd intervened then, the entire operation would've been compromised! Your life would've been in more danger! You would've had to live the rest of your life out in witness protection. Is that what you would've wanted?"

Shaking my head, feeling the tears burn my eyes, I knew he was right. It didn't seem to me they had been in *that* big of a hurry to help me, if they took the time to take pictures.

Alan continued. He had calmed down considerably and lowered his voice. "Look, CeeCee, I'm sorry. I told them to leave you alone. I knew you'd be able to handle it. Once you destroy those pictures, the incident is forever washed clean."

My voice shaking, I knew I owed Alan a substantial amount of gratitude.

"Thank you, Alan." I already knew the answer, but I asked my last question. "Michael doesn't know, does he?"

He shook his head. "No, and he never will, unless you tell him. I'm fairly sure he'd understand, considering the circumstances." He smiled. "He loves you more than life itself, you know."

"I know. Believe me, I know."

"Take care of yourself, CeeCee, and be well."

Alan walked away, leaving me to stand by the bench holding an envelope that contained evidence of one of my darkest hours. After he left, I walked over to a metal garbage barrel that sat next to a picnic table. Taking my cigarette lighter out of my pocket, I lit a corner of the envelope and held it as it burned, dropping it into the barrel just before the flames reached my hand. Taking no chances, I made sure it burned completely before I took a small twig and stirred the ashes around inside.

Michael was in the kitchen starting dinner when I got home. Taking my coat off, I took a seat at the table.

"Where were you, hon?" He was putting spaghetti into a large pot of boiling water.

"I was with Alan Keane. He called yesterday and wanted to meet with me."

Ignoring the spaghetti, Michael walked around the counter and sat down in the chair next to mine. He looked distraught—and surprised.

"What? Why? Why didn't you tell me? What did he want?"

"He offered me a job." I smiled at the look of shock on Michael's face. "He said the FBI could use a gal like me."

"What did you say?" His eyes narrowed to mere slits.

"No, of course."

"And that was it?"

I hesitated. "That was it. The spaghetti smells good."

Deciding at that moment that it was not in Michael's best interest to hear about Tommy Miglia, I changed the subject. Maybe one day I'd tell him, but now wasn't the time. It would upset him, and quite frankly, I didn't want to talk about it.

Two days after my meeting with Alan, Sheriff Stephens paid me a visit. To be blunt, I was a little hurt that he'd waited this long to see me, which he addressed immediately.

"I wanted to give you time to settle in, CeeCee, before I came over, but I couldn't take it anymore and just had to see you!" Walking through the door, he embraced me while slapping me gently on the back.

"It's good to see you, too. I was beginning to think you had enough of my antics over the years and finally wrote me off!" I laughed. We sat in my living room.

"Don't be ridiculous. How are you doing? You look wonderful!"

We spent the better part of an hour catching up. Michael made a brief appearance before sequestering himself back in his office. He was on a paid furlough of sorts from the FBI. Essentially, they told him to come back to work when he damn well pleased, a subject the sheriff eventually got to in respect to my own situation.

"I want you back, CeeCee. Now I don't mean tomorrow, or next week, but when you're ready, your job is waiting for you."

Sighing, I leaned back against the couch. "I don't know, Sheriff. Honestly, I haven't thought about it much. Everything that's happened has allowed me to put some things into perspective about what's important and what's not. I just don't know if the job is *as* important to me anymore."

He grinned. "Oh, I think it is. Have you truly thought about what you have done? All of the lives you have saved because of the Mafia bust? You did it because *that* is who you are. You are a cop, and one of the best I've ever known." He leaned forward, his eyes intense. "It's in your blood, CeeCee. Three months from now when the dust has settled and your life is back together, you'll be thinking. You'll be thinking about how much you miss the job. I guarantee it."

He was probably right, but I couldn't bring myself to admit it to him. I noticed Michael had returned. He stood in the entryway, listening to what the sheriff said. He was smiling, and without his speaking a word, I knew he agreed.

"Sheriff, I doubt it. I mean, I don't think I can go back to that life again. Please understand."

He looked crushed, and Michael's smile faded. As the sheriff nodded and slowly stood up to leave, I knew at that moment I would never have another chance.

He was right: it was in my blood. If nothing else, knowing that I had saved the lives of possibly hundreds of people sunk in. Who knew? If I went back, maybe I'd save more. Regardless, it was about the victims, the victims whose killer would never be caught or whose crime would go unpunished. People deserved better, and if it meant that by my returning to work, they got better, then I had my answer. Funny, I felt a slight flip of excitement when I made my split-second decision.

As Michael was opening the door for the sheriff, I giggled quietly to myself while I walked toward the both of them.

"Sheriff, wait. There's been a slight change of plans . . ."

CHAPTER EIGHTEEN

The day finally came when it was time to meet Joseph. Four days after New Year's, to be exact. Today was also the day he would be leaving for his unknown destination.

So, excited about our meeting, I was up at sunrise, walking around the house, rehearsing what I wanted to say to him so that I wouldn't forget. The ride to Fairport Harbor seemed to take forever. A small town east of Cleveland, it's situated on Lake Erie. We would be meeting Joseph near the pier of the public-beach area. I'd been to Fairport Harbor before and was familiar with the place. It always reminded me of what Coney Island would look like if shrunken to the size of a pinhead. There were a couple of rides, carousels, and games situated along the beachfront. Since it was January, the area was completely desolate.

When we pulled into the parking lot, I saw a black SUV with two men in it parked in front of the pier. FBI agents, undoubtedly. The pier, which stretched approximately three hundred feet over the waters of Lake Erie, had three small benches at the end of it, one of which had Joseph Filaci sitting on it. Michael barely had the car stopped before I was opening the door.

"Is it okay to go?"

"Go on. I'll wait here." He smiled.

Walking toward the pier, I saw Joseph look in my direction and stand up. Not wanting to appear too eager, I maintained my quick pace toward him. Only when I was about thirty feet away did I say, "Fuck it," and break into a run. Joseph's smile was as wide as my own as I threw myself at him, hugged him tightly, and began to cry.

"Oh, Joseph, I thought you were dead!" I sobbed. "It scared the shit out of me!"

He broke our embrace to wipe the tears from my cheeks and smile at me. He led me to one of the benches, where we both sat down, and began to talk.

"I'm okay, CeeCee, really." He breathed deeply. "If you only knew how good it is to see you. God, I couldn't wait for this day to come. I was awake all last night because I was so excited."

"Me, too." I had calmed down.

"I was terrified they had gotten you after the club. When I woke up in the hospital, all I could think about was if you got away. None of the agents there knew anything at the time, so it was difficult for me. When Agent Keane told me that you were okay, I was so relieved."

"I know the feeling."

Joseph turned his head toward the parking lot and nodded before he looked at me again.

"You've got to be beside yourself with happiness, knowing Michael is alive."

"You can imagine, it was a bit of a shock. He was one of the SWAT officers that rescued me at the funeral home. He took his mask off, and voilà! My dead husband was back." I stared out over the lake, remembering.

"Agent Keane told me what you went through." He took my hand. "I'm sorry, CeeCee, I feel responsible. I should've been able to protect you better."

I was stunned. "Joseph! It wasn't your fault you got shot, for God's sake! How could you think such a thing? I ought to slap you for saying that."

"Go ahead . . . that's how I feel." He smirked.

"It's utterly ridiculous." I playfully punched his shoulder. "Now, I'm assuming you were updated on everything. How about those raids?"

"They were certainly something, weren't they?" His smile faded.

"You don't seem too happy about it."

"A lot of people that I have known for many years went down that day, CeeCee. A lot of them went down because of me. I still don't know how I feel about it, but like I told your husband, I just want to start over. And if giving everybody up allows me to do that, then so be it. Let the chips fall."

"Joseph, are you sure this is what you want? I have to tell you that, knowing you, I was a little surprised when Michael told me you agreed to all of this." The concern showed on my face. "What about your father?"

"I was allowed to explain everything to him, and he took it quite well, considering. Of course, he didn't know that I gave everybody up. I told him how I helped you, how you gave us the files and protected our family, and how with your help Niccolo's killers were brought down. I told him I had no choice but to go into the witness-protection program. I wanted out."

"What did he say?"

"Shockingly, to me anyways, he understood. He said he didn't want to lose both of his sons. He even played the grieving father quite well at my funeral, according to the agents. I'll be able to meet with him several times a year, so we can still see each other. My mother passed away years ago, so I'm all he has left." He paused. "He also wanted me to tell you, thank you."

"And again, you're sure this is what you want?"

"I'm sure. I've never been as sure about anything in my life." His smile returned. "It was because of you."

"What did I do?"

"You compromised everything to see that those men got what they deserved. Me? I would have probably just had everybody killed, but you, you put your own life on the line just so they could be tried through the legal system, the right way. Amazing." He shook his head. "And all for the love of your husband." He paused. "I never thought a love like that could exist, until I fell in love with *you*, CeeCee."

My eyes felt the tears that began to surface out of nothing but pity. I can only imagine what it is like to love someone when the feeling isn't reciprocated. He didn't allow me to respond to his confession.

"I *needed* to tell you. I know that when I leave today, I'll probably never see you again. I know you love your husband more than life, but for some foolish reason, I needed you to know. That's all."

I nodded and felt compelled to reply. "I care for you, and I'll always wish you well, Joseph. If things were different, who knows? If it weren't for Michael, we wouldn't have met in the first place. Start your new life, be happy, and never forget our friendship."

He looked at the ground. "He's lucky, your husband. I told him that, too. I could have lied and told him something happened between us when he asked, but I would never compromise your happiness."

"He asked you if something happened between us?" Michael had failed to relay that part of the conversation.

He nodded. "You can't blame him. If you were my wife, and the circumstances that we were in arose, I'd be worried, too. Michael told me he will always owe me for helping you, and said thank you. Losing *you* would have to be one of the worst things in the world. I know, because my nights ahead will be dreams full of *you*. You'll be forever in my heart, CeeCee Gallagher."

"You'll be in mine as well, Joseph."

With nothing left to say, we strode down the pier hand in hand toward the awaiting agents for Joseph to begin his new life. I noticed I couldn't see Michael anywhere. After one last embrace, I stood and watched as Joseph entered the waiting vehicle. Michael reappeared then, walking up from behind, encircling me in his arms. We both watched as they pulled away, Joseph giving a slight wave from the backseat. Then Joseph was gone. I wiped the last tear from my eye before I turned to Michael.

"Where were you just now?"

"Had to find a restroom—you guys took longer than I thought. How did it go?"

"It went well, but very sad. I hope things work out

for him. He deserves it," I said in a voice that was almost inaudible. "That bothered you, didn't it?" I referred to the hugs Joseph and I had shared.

He looked up at the sky and back at me, smiling. "Yes, it bothered me. Sorry."

"Don't be. I understand, even though, you know, you are the only man I will ever love in my life." I grinned widely.

"He was deeply in love with you, you know," Michael said, just as quietly.

"How did you know that?"

"He told me, Cee."

Evidently, Joseph had forgotten to relay his part of the conversation, just as Michael had left out a bit of his own. I had a feeling I would never know exactly what had been said between the two of them. I nodded as Michael and I, remaining silent and arms interlocked, walked out to the end of the pier. While looking out over the lake, Michael patted his coat and reached for something.

"What are you doing?"

"Close your eyes and hold out your hands."

"C'mon, Michael, just—"

"Do it."

Holding out my hands as ordered, I knew what Michael was putting into them. When he told me I could open my eyes, I felt a significant amount of delight in seeing my detective sergeant's badge in one hand and department-issued weapon in the other.

"The sheriff thought you might need those when you go back to work." He grinned.

"They're good to see." I wasn't lying.

Since it was the right moment, I told Michael to do

the same. I had brought the item with me today, anticipating we would have time alone.

"It's your turn. Close your eyes and hold out your hand."

He smiled and looked at me skeptically, before he did as directed. As I placed the item in his hand, I told him he could open his eyes. When he looked down at it, his smile faded, replaced by a look of unreserved shock.

"This isn't . . . Is this what I think it is?" He looked at me, breathing hard.

"Yes, Michael." My own smile widened. "It's what you think it is: a pregnancy test. As you can see, it's positive. *We* are going to have a baby."

Picking me off the ground and yelling aloud, Michael was thrilled. It was then, on that day, at that moment, that my life . . . began again.

Colleen Thompson

TOUCH OF EVIL

Tight

The noose cuts off all air, leaving its victim struggling hopelessly against death. One by one, the members of a small town zydeco band are being murdered by a macabre killer.

Tight

Sheriff Justine Wofford is boxed in on all sides, investigating a series of gruesome hangings everyone else considers suicide. Hospitalized by a severe blow to the head, unable to remember the details of the attack, under fire from her own department, she reaches out to the man she's sworn to avoid at any cost.

Tight

Their affair was a close-kept secret, their bodies coming together with explosive heat even as she tried to maintain emotional distance. But now Justine can't stay away from Ross. Somehow, he's mixed up in this case and his hold on her is only getting tighter.

ISBN 13: 978-0-8439-6244-4

STACY

DITTRICH

Detective CeeCee Gallagher is no stranger to high-pressure cases. But this one could easily cost her career...and her life. A macabre serial killer is on the loose, leaving the bodies of his young victims made up to resemble dolls. With only a Bible passage sent by the killer to guide her, CeeCee will have to sacrifice everything to find him and end his reign of terror before another child is murdered.

THE
DEVIL'S
CLOSET

A CeeCee Gallagher Thriller

ISBN 13: 978-0-8439-6159-1

A CEECEE GALLAGHER THRILLER

STACY DITTRICH

AUTHOR OF *THE DEVIL'S CLOSET*

According to legend, Mary Jane was hanged as a witch and still haunts her grave. But when a teenage girl is found brutally murdered there, Detective CeeCee Gallagher knows no ghost is responsible. It's up to her to hunt down the very real killer before he strikes again. Her investigation will take her across the country and land her deep in the middle of a secret so shocking the locals have kept it hidden for a hundred years. With her career—and her life—on the line, CeeCee will have to face her darkest fears if she wants to uncover the truth about…

MARY JANE'S GRAVE

ISBN 13: 978-0-8439-6160-7